The night in Mike's bed had been wonderful

But Molly was appalled that she'd slept with him.

In the past she'd experienced little difficulty identifying unsuitable men and keeping them at arm's distance. But Mike Randall had slipped past her defenses. She sighed and thought of his cobalt-blue eyes, his cheerful smile. She thought of the way he looked at her, as if no one else existed. And he was marvelous in bed. She hated herself for knowing how wonderful and sexy he looked without clothing, for knowing the taste of his kisses and the feel of his skilled hands.

The guilty truth was that she, who despised injustice, was treating someone unfairly. Not just any someone, but a wonderful man who deserved better. Worse, she couldn't explain why she was behaving so contrarily and so uncharacteristically.

Where and when had she lost control of the situation?

ABOUT THE AUTHOR

For Margaret St. George, writing fills a
creative need, one she has been satisfying
since she was sixteen years old. This is her
tenth novel, though most of her books have
been historical romances. A full-time
writer, Margaret enjoys gardening and
traveling in her spare hours. She lives with
her husband and family in the mountains of
Colorado.

Books by Margaret St. George

HARLEQUIN AMERICAN ROMANCE
142—WINTER MAGIC
159—CASTLES AND FAIRY TALES

Don't miss any of our special offers. Write to us at the
following address for information on our newest releases.

Harlequin Reader Service
901 Fuhrmann Blvd., P.O. Box 1397, Buffalo, NY 14240
Canadian address: P.O. Box 603,
Fort Erie, Ont. L2A 5X3

The Heart
Club
Margaret St. George

Harlequin Books

TORONTO • NEW YORK • LONDON
AMSTERDAM • PARIS • SYDNEY • HAMBURG
STOCKHOLM • ATHENS • TOKYO • MILAN

Published June 1987

First printing April 1987

ISBN 0-373-16203-0

Chapter One

If there was one thing Molly McPherson hated—besides broccoli, being poor and things that were supposed to work but didn't—it was injustice. Any kind of injustice. The injustice could be as small as not getting your soft drink after putting your money in the soft-drink machine, or the injustice could be as large and awful as what had happened to Gran and her friends. Whatever the example, when life turned unfair it made Molly's Irish blood boil.

In the past she had accepted injustice as most people did. When the soft-drink machine snapped up her money, she groaned, muttered darkly, then fed more coins into the machine. If she was standing in line and someone cut in front of her, she fumed but did nothing. When her new dress shrank in the dryer to Barbie-doll size, she had ground her teeth and railed against the unfairness of it all.

What could a person do? Not much. Or so it had seemed.

Then, two years ago, she had returned to her apartment after a party celebrating the opening of her art gallery and had discovered her home had been burglarized. Talk about injustice. Her privacy had been invaded and her nice things taken. The white fox coat she'd had on layaway for half of her life was gone. And the two good paintings she had paid for bit by painful bit. And the Lenox dinnerware her mother had collected over the years for Molly's college graduation gift—all gone.

The injustice of the burglary had stunned her. Yes, eventually she could replace the items, but they wouldn't be the *same* items. No sentimental value would attach to a set of dinnerware she bought herself. And there was no chance she could confront the burglar and personally wring his neck. It wasn't fair.

The burglary was also the last straw. A determined glint had fired her dark eyes and a battle flag had fluttered up a mental pole. She was through rolling over and playing dead. There was nothing to be done about the burglary, but there were things to be done about other forms of injustice.

Now when the wretched soft-drink machine swallowed her money without producing a soft drink, Molly requested the manager and politely but firmly demanded her money back. When someone passed a bad check at her gallery, she hired a tough-guy collection agency and told them not to come back until they had her money or the return of the painting. If her new dress came out of the dryer two sizes smaller, she marched it back to the store where she'd purchased it and didn't budge until the wrong had been righted.

Granted, her war against injustice had been a small war, but she had enjoyed a few victories and a lot of satisfaction. Until this business with Gran.

What had happened to Lucille Pratt, Molly's grandmother, was an injustice of mammoth proportion. Whenever Molly thought about it, her cheeks burned with anger. Something had to be done, that's all there was to it; an injustice of this magnitude simply could not be allowed to pass unchallenged.

That was why Molly McPherson had closed her gallery and driven across the Potomac to the United States Patent and Trademark offices in Crystal City. She didn't know if she could help Gran, but she knew she had to try.

There were nine buildings in the complex and naturally she tried the wrong one first. A frazzled-looking secretary directed her to another building, which was also not the one she sought. Bending her head against a frosty wind, she sidestepped a patch of ice then entered a third building. As she approached the desk, Molly reminded herself that being a crusader for justice was not easy. Frustrations and obstacles were strewn across the path.

"Can I help you?" a receptionist asked, hanging up the telephone. Immediately it rang again.

"I hope so. I'm trying to locate Mr. Mike Randall." Molly glanced at the waiting area, noting that every chair was occupied. Calling on Mr. Randall was not as simple as she had imagined. But then, few things ever were.

"Mike Randall, let's see." The receptionist flipped open one of the ledgers stacked on the corner of her desk and ran a crimson fingernail down a page. "Oh, yes, here it is. Ten o'clock. He's expecting you."

"He is?"

Molly didn't recall setting an appointment, but neither was she one to question a bit of luck when it came her way. Maybe this was an omen indicating Gran's situation wasn't as hopeless as it appeared.

The receptionist dialed the phone. "Mr. Randall? Your ten o'clock is here...." She smiled at Molly and pointed toward one of the corridors. "Take the elevator to the third floor then turn left. You're looking for Novelties, Gadgets and Games."

That much Molly had already discovered. She'd spent most of yesterday morning on the phone being routed from one patent department to another. At some point between gnashing her teeth and yanking out her hair, she'd narrowed the possibilities to Novelties, Gadgets and Games. Once connected to that department, she'd wrested Mike Randall's name from a female voice at the other end.

When the elevator rattled to a shaky halt, she stepped forward and turned left. The corridor was thick with traffic. Large metal carts piled high with files and index manuals attempted to maneuver around wheeled canvas bins stuffed with letters, manila envelopes and odd-shaped boxes. Every few feet someone had tacked a banner to the wall: "Eighteen by '88." If any organization existed amid the chaos, it wasn't readily discernible.

Pausing before the door to Novelties, Gadgets and Games, Molly drew a breath and smoothed the slim skirt of her cream-colored wool suit. She folded her coat over her arm and patted an errant curl of springy auburn hair. This was it. She was about to confirm her darkest suspicions or lay them to rest.

Stepping inside, she entered another small reception area. A half-dozen office doors faced a secretary or receptionist's desk. Molly recognized another bureaucratic maze when she saw one. Smothering a sigh, she decided normal people lacked the patience for this sort of thing. Pretending not to see the woman who half rose behind her desk to wave a form of some kind, Molly strode directly to a door bearing Mike Randall's stenciled name.

She rapped quickly then opened the door a crack. "Are you Mike Randall?" she said to a dark head bent over a desk.

The man frowning down at an awesomely cluttered desk wore a blue-and-red striped tie and a blue button-down shirt rolled up to his elbows. Overhead lights struck red glints from his brown hair and cast the shadow of his lashes across his cheeks.

Then he looked up and smiled, and Molly's heart stopped midbeat. There are moments in everyone's life when a mental neon explodes in the back of the brain and starts flashing brightly colored arrows and exclamation points and a message that says, "This is a special moment, pay attention. This means you, Molly McPherson."

She was definitely paying attention. Mike Randall was simply the most gorgeous man Molly had ever seen. Tousled dark hair around a tanned forehead. Strong dark eyebrows above eyes so blue Paul Newman would have wept with envy. Jawline strong, mouth firm and generous. He had shoulders as broad as a house.

Molly felt as if she'd been struck by a thunderbolt. She had no idea where she was or why she was even there. Except it was meant to be. Whoever arranged such things as Romeo and Juliet, as Héloïse and Abelard, had arranged for her to be here with Michael C. Randall, who was staring at her with the same dazed expression that she had.

Something had happened, instantly, spontaneously. As such a startling event had never before happened to Molly, she didn't know what it was, but a tremble had appeared in her fingertips and a rush of heat spread from her breast to the roots of her hair.

"Come in," Mike Randall said.

Because she had to say something, and because she desperately wanted to place this strange situation in some sort of perspective, Molly cleared her throat and said, "Edmund Hillary must have felt like this when he finally reached the top of Everest. I thought I'd never find you."

He laughed and stood behind his desk. "It is overwhelming, isn't it? Just a minute, I'll clear a place for you to sit."

His voice was arresting, one of those deep voices that DJ's cultivated, a voice that could speak with authority or

sink to an intimate whisper. It was a voice that poured dark
honey and made Molly feel fluttery inside.

Watching as he removed a stack of papers from the chair
facing his desk, Molly guessed Mike Randall was about six
feet tall. Despite the fact that she was only five foot three in
her stocking feet, Molly liked tall men. It was probably a
throwback to caveman times. Tall men made short women
feel safe. Not that she needed a man's protection; she was
doing fine on her own, thank you. Still...

Aware that he was watching her as she was watching him,
Molly decided he was twenty-eight or nine, a few years older
than she was. A lean athletic build indicated he probably
played tennis or golf; he had an easy smile that made her feel
as if someone had kindled a fire in the pit of her stomach.

Lord. Why wasn't she meeting Mike Randall on the deck
of a cruise ship or in the back of a stretch limo? There was
no justice.

"Sorry about the mess." Still staring at her, he spread his
hands, indicating tiers of manuals and stacks of files piled
against the walls. A row of boxes climbed toward the ceiling. "We're perpetually behind. If you applied for a patent
today, it would take about twenty-three months before it was
granted. We're hoping to cut the backlog to eighteen months
by next year."

"Eighteen in '88," Molly said, recalling the banners
strung along the corridor walls. She was having difficulty
focusing her thoughts on the conversation. When Mike
Randall looked at her with those blue, blue eyes, her mind
went as soft as new paint and her nerves surged to the surface of her skin.

"Right." His admiring gaze skimmed her auburn curls,
her pearl earrings and green silk blouse. For a long moment they looked at each other, then he cleared his throat
and asked, "Did you fill out the form?"

"No," Molly said, her thoughts coming back to earth. "No, I didn't." She should have guessed. You couldn't ask a government employee if he was single or married without first filling out a form.

"No problem. I have one here." After rummaging through the files covering his desk, he produced a yellow folder and removed the pencil from behind his ear. "Name?"

"Molly McPherson."

"Address?"

"I'm staying with my grandmother while my apartment is being painted." She gave him Gran's address and shifted in her chair. This was the damnedest thing. She had never thought of an office as an intimate place. But Mike Randall's office felt like an intimate hideaway. She was acutely conscious of being alone with him. And when he looked up at her, which was frequently, those blue eyes did things to Molly that she didn't really want done.

"Telephone? Marital status?"

"Single." He gave her a long look and her pulse accelerated in her ears. This was getting entirely out of hand, Molly thought, wetting her lips with the tip of her tongue. She was seriously in danger of forgetting everything that was important.

Mike Randall's gaze dropped to her crossed legs and a flicker of appreciation warmed his eyes before he moved the pencil to the next section on the form. "Are you currently employed? And what is your reason for seeking a change?"

"Am I...?" Suddenly the questions made sense and Molly smiled. "Mr. Randall..."

"Mike."

"Mike, I'm afraid there's been a mistake. I'm not seeking employment."

"You're not? Karen said you were my ten o'clock interview."

"I'm sorry, but I'm here concerning another matter."

A rueful smile curved his mouth. "I'm sorry too." His eyes lingered on the soft light touching the curve of her cheek. "We're desperate for additional examiners."

While Molly sat here with this great-looking man, some poor soul was cooling her heels in a cramped waiting room. Assuming the poor soul had found the correct building. Molly struggled with her conscience for about two seconds then decided against yielding her time to the unfortunate ten o'clock.

"Can we start over?" she asked.

"You're certain I can't persuade you to...?" When she smiled and shook her curls, he pushed away the form, released an exaggerated sigh then gave her a dazzling smile. "All right, Miss McPherson, how can I help you?"

He could help her by sweeping her into his arms and carrying her away to some storybook land of happily ever after. The thought was so uncharacteristic that Molly blinked and shook her head. What on earth was wrong with her today? She was here on serious business. Besides, Mike Randall was a patent officer. Forcibly she reminded herself that she had her sights set higher than a patent officer.

"I'm not sure how to explain this," she said finally. "And, by the way, it's Molly, not Miss McPherson."

"Start at the beginning," he said as if they had all the time in the world. As if his desk were not stacked with a dozen files marked urgent.

"The beginning dates back at least forty years."

"Really?" When he smiled the corners of his eyes crinkled. "I could have sworn you were about twenty-five or six."

"Twenty-six." Good grief, she was flirting with him. Probably because her skin felt as if it were on fire and every time he looked at her, she felt breathless. Silently she commanded herself to focus on the problem. "I'm here on behalf of my grandmother, Lucille Pratt. Forty years ago Gran and three of her friends formed a Friday afternoon bridge group which they named the Heart Club."

"The name sounds familiar."

"As the years passed, two of the Heart Club members developed arthritis in their hands which made handling cards difficult. So the group purchased an automatic shuffler. Later, Gran and Gladys Price also developed arthritis. By now the first two had it worse than before. So the group improvised by using tile racks from a Scrabble game to hold the cards. But dealing remained a serious problem."

"Fascinating," Mike Randall said, gazing at her.

She looked at him, momentarily distracted, then continued, feeling the familiar anger build as she concentrated on telling Gran's story. "About three years ago the Heart Club invented a dealing device that attached to the automatic shuffler. It's rather simple, really. But it solved the problem of dealing four bridge hands."

"Something like the Croupier?"

"No, Mr. Randall—Mike—not 'something like' the Croupier. It *is* the Croupier."

His eyebrow lifted. "I approved and granted the patent for the Croupier. I believe the patent was issued in a company name, but I don't think the company was called the Heart Club. Of course I'd have to check our records to be certain."

Molly leaned forward. "That's why I'm here. To discover who obtained the patent on the Croupier. Because the Croupier is the Heart Club's invention. It was stolen from them."

He looked into her flashing eyes and his expression sobered. "That's a serious allegation. Can you prove what you're saying?"

Molly didn't know if she had acceptable legal proof, but she knew damned well the idea had been stolen.

"Two years ago, Gran and the other Heart Club members decided other people like themselves might benefit from the dealing device they had invented. Through a friend of a friend of a friend—that kind of thing—they learned of a man named Harry Blackman." The name left a brackish taste in her mouth. "Mr. Blackman has apparently been successful manufacturing and marketing novelty type items."

She paused for a moment. Mike was a good listener. He watched her with an intent expression, never taking his eyes from her face.

"Alice Harper, the member who came up with Mr. Blackman's name, made an appointment with him. She explained the dealing device and asked what it would cost to manufacture and market the item."

"I'd imagine Blackman would have to examine the device before making an estimate."

"That's what happened. Mr. Blackman requested a sample device and Alice Harper took one to his office."

"And?"

Anger deepened the color of Molly's eyes to a smoldering chocolate. "When Alice returned, Mr. Blackman gave her a cost breakdown. The production costs were enormous. For older women of limited means the sum was simply impossible. Unthinkable."

"All the Heart Club members are your grandmother's age?" When Molly confirmed the women were all approaching seventy, Randall nodded. "Let me guess—Harry Blackman didn't return the dealing device."

"That's right. Blackman told Alice he would wait for their decision as to whether or not they wished to proceed with manufacturing. Alice Harper wrote to inform Mr. Blackman the production costs were prohibitive. Far beyond their financial means. But Blackman didn't return the device. It didn't seem important at the time, and they forgot about it until—"

"Until November." Mike Randall nodded and ran a hand through his hair.

Molly's fists clenched in her lap and a pink flush rose from her throat. "Two months ago—in time for Christmas sales—the Croupier turned up everywhere. You couldn't walk into a store without falling over a display of Croupiers. The Croupier was this season's hottest gift item." She stared at Mike. "I want to know if Harry Blackman's name is on the Croupier patent. Because if it is, then he stole the Heart Club's device. And, from the look of it, he profited hundreds of thousands of dollars."

"Miss McPherson—Molly—"

"This whole thing is so unfair! None of the Heart Club members are financially secure. The money Harry Blackman stole from them—I'm talking about his profits on the Croupier—would have meant a comfortable old age. It makes me furious!"

She exhaled slowly, not speaking again until her voice was under control. "It breaks my heart to see Gran reading the travel section of the newspaper. She'd love to get out of this cold weather and visit her brother in Florida. But she can't afford an extended trip. None of the Heart Club can."

Mike pushed his fingers down his pencil, turned it over and tapped the eraser against the desk top. Molly noticed he had large strong hands before she turned her eyes away. "Did Alice Harper retain a copy of any correspondence with Blackman?"

"There probably wasn't much correspondence. And I doubt she'd have thought to make a copy. Plus, most of this happened a couple of years ago. The Croupier probably would have been marketed earlier if it wasn't for the patent delay you mentioned."

"Another thing—did the Heart Club or any of its members secure a patent prior to Blackman's application? Assuming, of course, that Blackman does hold the patent."

Molly's brows rose. "Wouldn't you have a record of that?"

Mike Randall sighed. "I wish I could say yes. Unfortunately, patent searches are still conducted by hand. It doesn't happen often, but occasionally a prior patent can be overlooked."

Molly's look deepened to a stare. "By hand? You're kidding. I assumed all patents were recorded on computers."

"They will be soon. We've been given the funding to computerize, but it'll take several years to program all this data. You see, the U.S. Patent and Trademark division receives twelve thousand pieces of mail every single day. We have twenty-six million documents in our files, of which three hundred thousand are circulating through our buildings at any one time." He shrugged and rubbed an impatient hand across his jaw. "Occasionally a document gets buried in a pile like the one behind you and it doesn't surface for weeks. Mistakes can be made."

Molly glanced at the stacks of papers and files. "I'd go crazy if I worked here." She couldn't believe what she was hearing.

His laugh was rich and deep, the sort of laugh that conveyed warmth and intimacy. "Where *do* you work?"

"I own a small art gallery across the river." The river, of course, was the Potomac. Although Molly lived in Virginia, her gallery was within easy walking distance from the White House. "I specialize in art restoration."

"An interesting field. I'd like to know more about it."

They regarded each other across the desk, and Molly was aware the conversation had veered toward the personal. There were a hundred questions she wanted to ask. Where had he grown up? What kinds of books and movies did he like? Was he an opera buff? Did he know that when he looked at her the way he was doing now, he made her feel sixteen and shaky inside?

As if realizing he was staring, Mike rose suddenly behind his desk and cleared his throat. "Well. The first step in discovering who holds the patent is the Search Room. Would you like to come along, or would you prefer I phoned you after I've located the documentation?"

His movement stirred the scent of the after-shave he wore. Inhaling, Molly tried to identify the brand. It made her think of romantic locales and whispered intimacies. She found herself saying, "If you don't object, I'd like to tag along."

The Search Room was larger than a football field and had the hushed genteel ambience of a library. Long tables ran the length of the room on two sides. The pegged oak furniture was of antique vintage.

"This is where we store those millions of documents I told you about," Mike explained. "Behind these doors twists a honeycomb of narrow aisles stacked floor to ceiling with shoes."

"Shoes?"

"Shoes are the wooden file boxes that hold the documents. Thomas Jefferson originated the expression when he was a patent commissioner. Whenever Jefferson had an idea for an invention—and he was a prolific inventor—he scribbled the idea on paper then saved it in a shoebox. Hence—shoes."

Molly smiled and studied him thoughtfully. "You know, I have an idea you're one of those people who like to know how things work. You probably have an intimate acquaintance with the inside of your washing machine."

He laughed and a few heads looked up from the tables. "You're right." He grinned down at her. "Mechanics fascinate me. And statistics." For an instant, his gaze dropped to her breasts and hips.

A rush of color heightened the pink in Molly's cheeks. The admiration she read in his incredibly blue eyes pleased her. A dismaying thought. Shifting her coat to the other arm, she gazed about the immense room while she willed her pulse to a more normal rate. "This is overwhelming."

"Ah, but you have an expert guide." Taking her arm, Mike led her to the classification manual and its index. Together they weighed fifteen pounds. "Just thought you'd like to know," he said, smiling.

Molly could only nod. To her astonishment his touch was electrifying. Wildly, she wondered if she should consult a doctor when she left here. It wasn't like her to respond so quickly or so violently to a man's attentions. Maybe her hormones were running amuck. She'd been drinking a lot of coffee lately, maybe...

"First we locate the class—in this case, games. Then the subclass, which should be cards. If I could remember which week the Croupier was patented, we could locate it quickly in the *Official Gazette*. The O.G. lists all the patents granted each Tuesday. About fifteen hundred of them."

"Per week?" She parroted back the words, but she wasn't exactly sure what she was asking.

"Uh-huh." He was leafing through the classification manual.

Desperate to focus her thoughts on something other than his baritone voice and eyes that sent warm shivers shooting toward her toes, Molly selected a random OG and flipped through the pages. Two weeks ago patents had been issued for an improved portable pottie for campers, a toy space station and, among the many, many others, patents for a peanut butter that spread easily, an airplane component, and a mouse trap.

"I can't believe this." She looked up at him. He was bent over the manual, his pencil between his teeth. "People are still inventing mouse traps?"

"Mmm. We have over three thousand mouse trap patents."

"Amazing."

"Here we are—here's the shoe number. I'll be back in a minute with the documents. Don't go away."

When he returned, carrying a white file folder, Molly watched him cross the room, helplessly feeling her skin tighten. His rolled up sleeves, the tousled hair, the smile that illuminated his features when he saw her—they made her heart do flip-flops in her chest. Why, oh why couldn't Mike Randall have been a millionaire?

Swallowing hard, she slid her eyes toward the file and forced herself to think about business. "Is Harry Blackman the patent holder?"

Mike sat beside her at the table, near enough that his after-shave filled her head with unbusinesslike thoughts.

He opened the file and spread the papers in front of her. "First, no error was made. There was no patent previous to this one." Removing a drawing, he indicated the name typed at the top. "The Croupier's patent was issued to the F.B.C. Company." His gaze met Molly's. "But here's the kicker— all correspondence with the F.B.C. Company was received from and directed to Mr. Harry Blackman."

"I knew it!" Dark fire flashed from Molly's eyes and her mouth pressed into a furious line.

Mike placed the drawing in front of her. "Is this the device your grandmother and friends invented?"

Leaning forward, Molly carefully studied the drawing. "Not exactly," she finally admitted. The Croupier was shaped like a plastic fan with the folds of the fan curving down. When in operation, the cards would drop from the four slots in the fan ends and stack onto the table. That much was identical.

"What differences do you see?" he asked, gazing at her bent head.

"The design has been streamlined. It doesn't look as homemade as the Heart Club's device," she reluctantly conceded. "If I'm interpreting this drawing correctly, the shuffler has been incorporated into the device instead of remaining an outside attachment."

"Yes, that's indicated here." Mike leaned forward and his shoulder brushed Molly's. An electric tingle poured down her arm like warm liquid and she blinked rapidly. "The design melds the shuffler and dealer into one unit."

One unit. It sounded sexy. Molly bit her lip and rubbed furiously at the tingle in her arm. No doubt about it: she was seriously ill, as tense as drawn wire. Hot and cold. Her mind had turned to mush.

She stared at the drawing until it refocused in her thoughts. "Also," she said, amazed that her voice sounded so normal, "The number of cards dealt can be adjusted for various games. On the Heart Club's model, there were no switch settings. It dealt only a bridge hand."

Mike Randall dropped back in his chair and looked at her with a concerned expression. "I'm sorry, Molly," he said gently. "But I don't think the Heart Club has much of a case. From what you've said, it doesn't seem likely they have anything in writing, plus the design isn't precisely what they invented."

This, she heard. The craziness dropped from her mind and her thoughts sharpened and cooled. "But it was the Heart Club's idea! Without them, this item wouldn't exist. The Croupier may look more finished and be somewhat improved, but it's still the device Gran and her friends invented!"

"But the Heart Club didn't protect their invention with a patent. Harry Blackman did."

"Damn!" Molly pushed to her feet and glared at him. "Harry Blackman stole this invention. That's illegal."

"Unethical, certainly. But applying for a patent is not illegal. You'd have to prove everything you've said plus establish intent to defraud. Intent is almost impossible to prove. The bottom line is: Harry Blackman patented the idea first. Regardless where the idea originated, it's his now."

"We'll see about that." Angry heat pulsed in Molly's cheeks, her hands tightened at her sides. "I have an appointment tomorrow with an attorney."

Although she had suspected Blackman's involvement, it shocked her to discover the truth. She couldn't believe anyone was so unscrupulous as to victimize four elderly women. Secretly, she had hoped to discover she was wrong about Blackman, that someone unconnected to the Heart Club had patented the Croupier. Such a discovery would have been surprising, but she could have accepted it.

"This is reprehensible," she stated flatly. "It isn't fair."

"I agree."

"Harry Blackman can't be allowed to get away with this."

"There's nothing to be done. Blackman holds the patent, Molly. He's on solid legal ground."

"He's a crook!" She stared into Mike's steady gaze and thought hard. "How long does a patent last?"

"Seventeen years. And it can't be renewed. After seventeen years, the invention passes into the public domain."

A sigh parted her lips. "The Heart Club can't wait seventeen years for justice." She gripped the strap of her purse and squared her shoulders. "Harry Blackman stole thousands of dollars from the Heart Club. There has to be some kind of recourse. I'll find it."

Mike Randall followed her to the door of the Search Room. "I hope you're right, but I don't think—"

"The law protects the innocent," Molly said. A scattering of freckles stood out on her white face. "And Harry Blackman is not innocent. He cheated four nice old ladies out of what is rightfully theirs. He has to be punished. At the very least he has to give back what he stole!"

Mike lifted his hands in a gesture of surrender. "I'm on your side, remember?"

"*You* issued the fraudulent patent!" Molly stared at him, then bit her lips in embarrassment. "I'm sorry, Mike. This isn't your fault. I'm just upset. If you knew Gran and her friends, you'd know what I mean. They're—" she spread her hands, "—they're all so nice. They don't deserve to be victimized."

Sympathy softened his eyes. "I'm genuinely sorry. I wish there was something I could do."

"Well…" She managed a smile as she thrust out her hand and shook it. "Thank you, Mike. I appreciate your help." Heat shot from their clasped hands and spread clear through to her stomach.

"I wish I could have done more. Molly… I'd like to call you." His gaze traveled along the curve of her lips. "To learn how all this comes out."

Her small hand had vanished in his, enclosed by a warmth that was doing strange things to her nervous system. "I'd like that," she said in a whisper. "I'm staying at Gran's." She wet her lips.

"Lucille Pratt, wasn't it?"

"Yes." Hastily, she disengaged her fingers then looked away from Mike Randall's intent blue eyes and turned into the corridor with a feeling of relief.

The sooner she got away from Mike Randall the better. There was something about that man that made her feel as if she'd been felled by a tropical fever. And that wasn't good. Already she regretted telling him to phone.

For the first time in years Molly had forgotten her plan so totally it might not have existed. She'd experienced some strange form of romantic amnesia that had blotted the future, the grand plan, from her mind.

Standing in front of the elevators, resisting the urge to look back to see if he was watching, Molly straightened her spine. She knew what she wanted, she had always known. And she didn't intend to compromise by falling for the wrong man.

Chapter Two

Mike Randall leaned against the doorway to the Search Room and watched her go. She had a damned sexy walk. She didn't swing her hips or sway on her high heels or do anything overtly sexual. But she had a grace and energy he found provocative. She walked like a woman who knew where she was going, and he liked that. Her step was confident and determined. He liked everything about Molly McPherson: her concern for her grandmother, the curve of her smile, her small terrific figure, the sprinkle of freckles dusting her nose.

Something had happened the moment he saw her. An hour ago, if someone had asked, he would have said he didn't believe in love at first sight. Now, as crazy as it sounded, he wasn't as certain.

Smiling at such uncharacteristic thoughts, he returned to his office—cubicle was more the word—and he leaned backward in his chair, pencil clamped between his teeth. He thought about the Croupier, the Heart Club and Harry Blackman.

There were cases of spontaneous invention, incidences where two people working independently of each other made the same discovery at the same time. An astonishing coincidence, but it happened. The discovery of DNA sprang immediately to mind.

However, this didn't seem likely in the case of the Croupier. On the face of it, it certainly appeared Harry Blackman had stolen the Heart Club's idea, had made a few minor improvements and had reaped a fortune. Launching the Croupier just before Christmas suggested Blackman was no novice at profiting from novelties. Perhaps he was no novice at stealing ideas either, but proving it was another matter altogether. Reluctantly, Mike reached the same conclusion he'd arrived at before. Molly and her grandmother didn't have a case.

He tapped the pencil against his teeth, wishing he could do something to help. He also wished he knew what Molly McPherson was thinking. She was angry on behalf of the Heart Club. And she didn't strike him as the type of person to shrug off an injustice. The determined glint in her lovely eyes had made him uneasy. Especially when she'd said, "Harry Blackman can't be allowed to get away with this."

That glint and those words were worrisome. They indicated she wasn't willing to accept what had happened. But as far as he could see, there was nothing she could do. The thought of Molly McPherson fighting a man like Blackman impressed Mike as about as logical as sending Doris Day to defeat Godzilla.

Aside from her red hair, that's who she reminded him of, he realized suddenly—a young Doris Day. Freckled, great-looking and projecting a wholesome sexuality that brought out the protectiveness in him. The last thought made him smile. Considering her determined walk, he doubted Molly McPherson was the type of woman to welcome a man's protection. He had an idea she would be challengingly stubborn about her opinions, determinedly self-sufficient. The kind of woman he most admired.

Still smiling, he bent over a drawing of a computer gadget that was supposed to capture an intruder in one's living room, shoot the intruder in the foot, dial the police and then administer first aid to the injured intruder. Unfortunately the model Mike had requested had shot a dozen Band-Aids at his secretary, hadn't dialed anyone and had then sprayed fake bullets around his office before going inoperative. He wrote the inventor and detailed the gadget's flaws, then opened another file.

"Hey, boss, it's quitting time." Carla poked her head in his door later that afternoon. "Are you going to the Five O'Clock for the Friday night it's-over-for-another-week celebration?"

He glanced at his watch. "Not this week. I'm due at my folk's house for dinner."

Carla made a face. "Too bad. I wanted to hear about your ten o'clock. Karen said she was a knockout. Did you hire her?"

"No such luck. There was a mix-up. The ten o'clock applicant didn't show. The gorgeous lady you saw wanted a patent search."

Carla rolled her eyes and sighed elaborately. "*Everyone* wants a patent search. The whole world. And they want it yesterday." She pushed her arms into her coat. "See you Monday."

"Pray for computers." It was the standard greeting and farewell.

Mike's thoughts returned to Molly McPherson as he drove toward his parent's home. The more he considered Harry Blackman, the angrier he became. As an inventor himself, Mike Randall understood the hopes and dreams invested in every invention. Few of those hopes were ever realized, as very few inventions actually became a commercial success. The majority of the millions of documents stored in the shoes represented someone's broken dreams. When an invention did become a rousing success, it was a triumph for inventors everywhere. But in the case of the Croupier, Blackman had apparently stolen the triumph.

"You seem distracted tonight, Michael," his mother said when she'd removed the dinner dishes and had served coffee. "Does this have anything to do with a girl?"

Mike smiled at his mother with affection. Clara Randall made no secret of the fact that she wanted grandchildren.

"As a matter of fact, I was thinking about someone I met today."

His father winked. "That's how it starts." William Randall was part of the Washington platoon that administered the postal service. Aside from a thicket of white hair and his widening girth, he looked like an older version of his son. Leaning back in an upholstered chair, he lit his after-dinner pipe and waited expectantly. "Tell us about her, or your mother isn't going to give us a moment's peace."

When Mike finished telling them about Molly and the Heart Club, his mother frowned thoughtfully. "You know, this sounds a bit familiar. I wonder if this could be the same Heart Club your great-aunt Jane belongs to? I think they've been meeting for about forty years, since they were all young women. And Jane has arthritis . . ."

Mike sat up straighter. "I knew I'd heard the name before. Aunt Jane mentioned a Heart Club when she was here for Christmas dinner."

The other facts fit too. Jane Carter was approaching seventy and her financial situation was perilous at best. She lived on social security and a small pension from the school where she had taught before retiring. Mike suspected his father contributed something to Jane's support but it would be in the form of birthday and Christmas gifts. Jane's pride wouldn't have permitted anything more overt.

"Mike," his mother said, placing her hand on his wrist, "would you call Jane? I'll feel better if I know this isn't her club."

"I will, too." He found her number and dialed the kitchen phone. After exchanging pleasantries, he told Jane why he'd called.

"Damn," she said softly, her voice as vigorous as a woman half her age. "We'd hoped no one would learn how foolish we were."

So it was the same Heart Club. "Aunt Jane, why didn't you bring the Croupier to me?"

"To tell you the truth, Michael, none of us thought about a patent. And if we had, I think we'd have guessed the manufacturer took care of that sort of thing. In retrospect we were just plain dumb."

Mike stared at the wallpaper as a rush of anger tightened his lips. The swindle had suddenly become very personal. Blackman had conned someone in Mike's family. And Mike had issued the patent that made the swindle possible. Hell, he was responsible.

"Aunt Jane," he said. She was a prickly spinster on the outside, as soft as a marshmallow inside. She and the Heart Club had been easy pickings for a bastard like Blackman. "I wish there was something I could do."

"Well, there isn't," she said quickly. "Don't worry, Michael. I'm confident justice will out."

"And the good guys will triumph in the end?" He covered his eyes. In real life it didn't happen that way. In real life crooks like Blackman victimized elderly women and walked away rich.

"Indeed yes," she said crisply. "Everything comes full circle. One gets from life what one puts into it. I swan, I sound just like Alice, speaking in clichés."

"If the clichés were true, Aunt Jane, the Heart Club would be receiving the profits from the Croupier."

"What's done is done." Abruptly, she changed the subject. "What did you think of Lucille's granddaughter? Isn't Molly a lovely girl?"

"I'm surrounded by matchmakers," he said, smiling.

"It's time you settled down and started making babies instead of gadgets, dear. It's what young people do."

When he returned to the living room, his mother looked up expectantly. "Was it Jane's Heart Club?" At Mike's nod, she continued, "Oh dear, that's terrible. A little extra money would have made such a difference to Jane."

"We'll hire a lawyer and—"

Mike shook his head and told his parents what he'd told Molly. "There isn't a case, Dad. Blackman has the patent; he owns the Croupier."

They looked at him with crestfallen expressions. Then his mother sighed. "It isn't fair. Jane's worked hard all her life. She deserved a little good luck."

Mike agreed. At the back of his mind, he'd been wondering if he was interested in the plight of the Heart Club because he was interested in Molly McPherson. Now there was more to it than that.

Mike Randall was a man whose loyalties ran deep. And Harry Blackman had victimized a member of his family. He agreed with Molly McPherson that Blackman couldn't be allowed to get away with this.

MOLLY WASN'T IN A GOOD MOOD. The bad guys seemed to be winning these days. She'd gotten another bad check at the gallery, a beefy woman had cut in front of her at the checkout stand, someone had left a dent in her fender and no note of apology or an offer to pay for the damage. Arms full of groceries, she stepped out of her car and nudged the door shut.

"Here. Let me give you a hand."

"Mike Randall?" Immediately her mood improved as she blinked at him in surprise and wondered if she'd chewed off her lipstick and what her hair looked like. As she surrendered the sacks of groceries their hands brushed and a tingle of warmth sped up her arm. She hadn't imagined him. He was as handsome today as he'd been yesterday and just as nerve-racking. She rubbed the tingle in her arm and wondered if she had some chemical imbalance that reacted to Mike Randall and made her go strange inside. "This is service above and beyond."

He smiled over a stalk of celery. "Did you see an attorney today?"

"Yes." She held open Gran's front door as Mike carried the groceries inside. "The kitchen is through the living room. Gran? I'm home."

The living room was crowded with furniture as plumply upholstered as Gran herself. Family photographs crowded the table tops, a giant fern filled the bay window. It was a small room, almost Victorian, but comfortable.

Mike placed the grocery sacks on a polished tile counter and glanced around the kitchen. "It smells like nutmeg and ginger. Makes me think of my aunt Jane's kitchen."

"Would you like a cup of coffee? Gran's coffee is the best you ever tasted."

Looking at Mike over the rim of her cup, Molly decided she'd been crazy to hope he wouldn't call. Mike Randall was one terrific-looking man. Today he wore brown cords and a cream-colored sweater under a herringbone jacket. In the afternoon light his tousled hair gleamed with red highlights and his eyes were a marvelous cobalt blue. Beneath the taole, his knee was a few inches from her own and she could feel his warmth.

"If you don't mind telling me, what did the lawyer say?"

"I spent a hundred dollars for nothing," Molly said, sighing. She stirred her coffee. "The lawyer said the same thing you did. What Harry Blackman did was rotten, but not illegal. There's no recourse."

"Dammit. I was afraid of that."

Molly looked up at him and tilted an eyebrow. But before she could question the emotion in his voice, Gran bustled into the kitchen and Molly made introductions.

Lucille Pratt beamed over the rims of the glasses she wore on the tip of her nose. "We've met before. You're Jane Carter's great-nephew, aren't you? You drove Jane here once when she missed her bus." She patted Mike's shoulder. Gran was a patter.

"Why didn't you tell me your aunt Jane is a member of the Heart Club?" Molly asked.

"I didn't know it myself until last night."

Small world. No wonder Mike Randall had appeared on her doorstep, Molly thought. Now she recognized the difference she'd been trying to identify. Yesterday she'd read sympathy in his blue eyes, today she saw anger.

As Gran and Mike renewed a brief acquaintance, Molly smiled affectionately at her grandmother, seeing her as Mike must. Gran had a pillowy figure Molly considered exactly the right size for comfortable hugging. She might be approaching seventy, but Lucille Pratt hadn't given in to the vagaries of age. Behind her bifocals her eyes were bright and curious, her step was firm and youthful. She wore her hair short and curly white and added a touch of pink lipstick and a splash of lemony cologne. She loved mysteries and crossword puzzles and if there was such a thing as a generation gap, Gran didn't know about it. She was a delightful blend of modern thinking and the wisdom of experience.

"Molly, you didn't offer Mike any cookies." Gran gave her a wink that said the way to a man's heart was through his stomach. Molly smiled. Gran and her friends knew and lived by all the old sayings. "Do you like ginger cookies?"

"I love ginger cookies."

After placing enough cookies to feed India in front of Mike, Lucille Pratt joined them at the table. "I like to watch a man eat. It makes cooking worthwhile." Her voice was cheerful as she watched Mike sample the ginger cookies, but Molly knew Gran was thinking about Corwin Pratt, Grandpa, who had died five years before. "Well then," Gran said. "I didn't realize you two knew each other."

"We didn't until yesterday." Molly explained how she'd met Mike at the patent offices.

"You went to the patent office?" A line of concern appeared between Gran's eyes.

"Mike discovered the Croupier is patented in a company name, but the principal is Harry Blackman."

Mike's eyes hardened. "I agree with Molly. Something should be done about this."

"Now, children." Lucille Pratt removed her glasses and cleaned them against her apron hem. "There's nothing that can be done. There's no reason to get involved in this. I think Jane would say the same thing." When they protested, she waved the glasses in front of her ample bosom. "I know. And I appreciate your concern. But what's done is done. It's best to let sleeping dogs lie."

"Gran, how can you say that? Harry Blackman cheated you and the others out of thousands of dollars!" Molly said hotly. "Aren't you furious?"

"Of course I am." A determined glint flashed in Gran's eyes or perhaps it was sunlight sparkling across the glasses she had resettled on the end of her nose. "It's infuriating to be the proof of the saying 'There's no fool like an old fool.'"

"Honest people are easy targets, Mrs. Pratt. It's not a matter of being foolish; it's a matter of trust and expectations. Unfortunately not all people are worthy of trust."

"So it seems," Lucille Pratt said softly. "Well, let's speak of more pleasant things. The snow is melting, and it's going to be nice out today, don't you think?"

Later, Molly followed Mike outside onto the small porch. "Thanks for stopping by. I appreciate your concern."

"I like your grandmother, Molly. She's a nice lady."

"So is your Aunt Jane. They all are."

Mike watched the winter sun teasing sparks from her auburn curls. "What are we going to do about this?"

"I don't know. I'm so frustrated I could scream." She met his eyes. "I know I'm not willing to forget about it. Any ideas?"

"Not at the moment." They were silent. "You think about it and so will I," Mike offered finally. "Maybe we'll come up with something." His fingers brushed the sleeve of her sweater as he tried to identify the perfume she wore. "Would you be interested in dinner tomorrow night? To exchange ideas?"

Having dinner with Mike Randall would be playing with fire, Molly knew that. On the other hand, he was willing to help Gran and the Heart Club. If Mike came up with a solution to Gran's problem, Molly was obligated to hear it. She told herself she was doing this for Gran as she accepted Mike's invitation.

"I'll pick you up at seven."

Hoping she hadn't made a mistake, Molly watched him walk toward a late-model Chrysler and smiled when he waved before pulling from the curb.

"The plan," she said aloud. "Remember the plan."

Her plan didn't include Mike Randall.

MIKE TOOK HER to one of the older quieter restaurants where they could talk without shouting to be heard. One of the terrific things about the D.C. area was the multitude of great restaurants. Molly was glad she'd chosen her green silk dinner suit with the fur collar. Glancing at Mike across the snowy table linen, she noticed he'd devoted extra care also. The slightly disheveled look she'd thought so appealing was gone. Tonight the part in his thick hair was razor sharp. He wore a maroon silk tie and a charcoal-gray three-piece suit.

"So, any ideas?" Molly asked when they'd been served drinks.

"Nothing legal," he answered with a smile. "How about you?"

"Nothing. I can't get past the anger," Molly admitted. "Everytime I think about the Croupier, I get so furious I can't think clearly." Gran had been looking at Florida brochures again. Molly could hardly bear to think about it.

Mike frowned at his drink. "I feel responsible for this."

"It isn't your fault. You didn't know your aunt had an interest in the Croupier." Tiny flames flickered in his eyes, reflecting the candlelight, and Molly noticed several women glancing their way, studying Mike from the corners of predatory eyes.

"I know. But still... Aunt Jane really should find another apartment. Her neighborhood isn't what it once was. But rents are high and she won't accept financial assistance."

"Gran's the same. She won't let me have her house painted, won't even discuss it. And she won't allow me to mention to Mom and Dad that she could use a little help."

"You aren't a local girl?"

"I grew up in Vail, Colorado."

Mike's brow tilted curiously. "How did a Colorado girl end in Washington D.C.?"

Molly shrugged, hoping to slide past the question. But Mike continued to watch her, waiting. He was a good listener, the type of person who focused his entire attention on the speaker as if there were no other people in the room. The problem with good listeners, Molly thought, was that someone had to talk. In this case, her. And good listeners usually saw through a conversational dodge. She thought about that for a moment.

First, there was no point in lying to herself and denying that she was attracted to Mike Randall. Being near him did strange exotic things to her nervous system. Second, she knew Mike Randall couldn't possibly offer the future she wanted. That was crystal clear. Third, unless she did something, and quickly, to establish a distance between them, she might easily make a foolish mistake that would ruin her life plan.

Reluctantly she concluded the best course—the only course, really—was to tell him the truth. Unless she missed her guess, learning about her plan would send Mike Randall running. Biting her lip, Molly glanced at the candlelight darting light patterns across his smile. She'd never done this before, bluntly and deliberately run off an interesting man. But she'd never been this drawn to a man so obviously wrong for her.

A hint of defensiveness steadied her chin as she drew a long breath. "The truth is, I moved to Washington D.C. because the men outnumber the women here. And because the number of millionaires per capita is the highest in the United States. I want to marry money. The best chance of that happening is here." It sounded cold as hell, but that's how it was.

Surprise then disappointment flickered across Mike's expression. For a long moment he didn't say anything, then he spoke quietly. "I didn't figure you for a gold digger, Molly."

Color flamed in her cheeks. She'd wanted to nip this attraction before it blossomed, but she hadn't expected him to be as blunt as she had been.

"I guess that's what I am, a gold digger." It was the first time she'd said it aloud. It sounded awful. Arranging a smile on her lips, she said lightly, "But, like Gran always says, it's just as easy to fall in love with a rich man as a poor man."

The sudden coolness in his gaze irritated her and made her feel uncomfortable. All right, she'd told him to back off, a patent officer wasn't good enough for Molly McPherson. But dammit, she wanted more out of life than a patent officer could offer. She didn't like it, she wasn't proud of it, but a patent officer *wasn't* good enough. She wanted more. She didn't want a generic life, she wanted a brand name future.

Even so, she suddenly felt small and lessened by the admission. Maybe the truth hadn't been such a great idea. Her intent had been to place a more realistic perspective between herself and Mike. She'd meant to put the skids to the chemistry crackling between them; she had not meant to insult him.

Of course, that was what she'd done. "Look, Mike, I hope you understand there's nothing personal in this." She bit her lip, watching him. "I grew up without money in an area where money is the be-all and end-all. I always told myself that someday I'd have that kind of life."

He shifted in his chair and glanced out over the restaurant. It was the first time he had looked away from her all evening. "You don't have to justify your feelings, Molly."

"I'm not justifying, I'm explaining." This wasn't going well. For reasons Molly couldn't comprehend, she hated the fact that she'd damaged his opinion of her, even though that had been the purpose for revealing her plan. "My father owns a bookstore and my mother is a librarian. We had a comfortable life growing up. Or rather, it would have been comfortable just about anywhere else. But in Vail my sisters and I were the poor kids. It's tough to be the poor kids, Mike."

The McPhersons had been a long way from destitute; they'd been poor only in a relative sense. Molly's mother and father owned a rambling log home that snuggled against the slope of the mountains, they owned two cars, had a modestly comfortable bank account and had sent all their daughters to college. Molly hadn't realized she was missing anything until she was a teenager. Until then she'd enjoyed an almost perfect childhood. The McPherson home was filled with laughter, good books, an abundance of love.

But shortly after turning thirteen, Molly had experienced a taste of a new and magical world she had previously only glimpsed. It began with Sue Cush, whose father was heir to the Cush distilling fortune. Every year the Cush family skiied Vail before they departed for the south of France. Molly met Sue on the ski slopes and a brief holiday friendship ensued. It was either the best or the worst thing that had happened to her. Either way, the encounter radically changed Molly's outlook.

For the first time she saw the inside of one of the lavish penthouse condominiums. The sumptuousness staggered her. Until that moment she hadn't suspected such luxury existed or that anyone could take it for granted. And there was Sue herself, as exotic to Molly as a creature from a Hollywood stage set.

Sue Cush didn't ski in faded Levi's; she wore stylish ensembles in silky rainbow colors. Her equipment was the best money could buy, nothing like Molly's battered hand-me-down skis. Sue Cush wore Joy perfume and bought her lipstick at the Chanel counter. Her mother's hairdresser, who traveled with the family, did Sue's hair every morning. Sue Cush had never wanted anything she couldn't have. Sue Cush had never curled her own hair or made her own bed or picked up her clothes or washed a dish. She didn't expect to ever do any of those things. Other people performed those services.

Molly had seen herself through Sue's eyes as one of the "other people," and she didn't like it. She didn't like the new awareness of wonderful things she could never have. And she told herself that someday...

"You don't know what it's like," Molly said slowly remembering, "to be surrounded by beautiful things and not be able to have them. Every summer while I was growing up, I worked at one of the big hotels waiting tables. The guests would come in wearing fabulous clothes, real jewelry, carrying the best sports equipment money could buy. Everything in Vail was the best that money could buy."

Vail was filled with shops that catered to the carriage trade, shops far beyond the means of most of the townies. When Molly's family shopped, they drove down to Denver to Penneys and Sears. But every day through the impressionable years Molly had walked past the Vail shop windows, passed display cases crammed with artwork, furs, sculpture, expensive clothing, beautiful things she couldn't possibly afford.

She tried to explain this to Mike, how she had watched the guests flying out of Vail to other exotic-sounding places, how she had longed to go and do, too. Eventually her voice trailed. "Anyway, I wasn't born to money and there's no possibility of inheriting any..."

"So you plan to marry it."

The flat quality of his voice caused her chin to stiffen. "That's right," she said defensively. "That's the plan."

"Well." He signaled the waiter for their check. "Good luck. I hope you find your millionaire." A polite smile, impersonal, touched his lips. "Would you like more coffee, or...?"

"No. I'm ready to go." She didn't recall eating her steak. She felt defensive and frustrated, as if, given enough time, she might have been able to make him understand. "We didn't talk about Gran and your aunt Jane."

"Maybe some other time."

But his voice told her there wouldn't be another time. Silently, Molly accepted his help as he held out her coat, and she tried to ignore the warm strength of his fingers as they brushed her shoulders. Damn.

Throughout the silent ride back to Gran's house, she attempted to grasp why she was upset. She'd accomplished what she had wanted—Mike Randall had withdrawn. The long penetrating looks had stopped, and the accidental touches. So why did she feel tense and irritated?

Standing on Gran's porch, they faced each other, the moment awkward and uncomfortable. Despite everything, and to her great annoyance, Molly discovered she was looking at Mike's generous mouth and wondering if his kiss would be as sensual an experience as she suspected. She knew she wasn't going to find out. "Thank you for dinner," she said, clasping her gloves in front of her coat.

"It's been an interesting evening." Pushing back his sleeve, Mike made a point of glancing at his watch, then he turned down the steps toward his car. "Good night."

Frowning, Molly watched him go. Then she quietly let herself inside, went directly to her room and sat on the edge of the bed. She'd done the right thing, the only thing. Tilting her head backward, she stared at the ceiling.

It wasn't fair. Mike Randall should have been a millionaire.

AFTER A FEW BLOCKS Mike pulled the car to the curb and sat in the darkness listening to the engine idle as he tried to sort through what he was feeling. Uppermost was the sting of rejection. Molly had made it clear she wasn't interested in a low-paid patent officer with no prospects. The bluntness of it had surprised him. The biggest surprise, however, had been to discover how wrong he'd been about her.

Generally he considered himself a good judge of character. But he hadn't seen this one coming. His impression of Molly McPherson had been one of a caring straightforward woman. Someone he liked, someone he could possibly care deeply about. He hadn't glimpsed the calculating side of her nature or the mercenary aspects.

Eventually he guided the car from the curb and eased into traffic. "Count yourself lucky, son," he said aloud. "That girl isn't for you."

At least he'd found out in time, before he'd mentioned any of his inventions. And he might have. He was proud of how well Shield was succeeding. He'd invented a window-washing liquid for car windshields that could be used in subzero weather without streaking or icing. The product was a hot item in the cold northern states. It was being used in thousands of gas stations. And everytime a station bought a carton of Shield, Mike Randall made money. Shield was his most commercially successful invention to date, but there were others. And there would be more. The patent officer he was trying to hire was a replacement for himself.

He'd already given notice and planned to devote himself full time to his inventions.

If Molly had known about Shield, maybe she wouldn't have written him off so quickly. He thought about that. Eventually he concluded he was glad he hadn't mentioned his inventions. He didn't want a woman to care about him because of his bank account.

Money didn't mean much to him, it never had. For the last few years he had lived comfortably on his salary from the patent office and the royalties from his inventions went directly to his investment broker. Four times a year, like it or not, Roger Bradley insisted that Mike sit down for an accounting. Rog reviewed his portfolio, telling him what new real estate he owned, what stocks and debentures, advised whether Mike should buy this or divest that. It was dull stuff. Dull enough that he was always a little surprised when something reminded him that money made the world go around for a lot of people.

This thought brought him back to Molly McPherson.

By the time he turned the Chrysler into his driveway, he'd conquered the element of pride that objected to being dismissed as unsuitable and he was able to view the evening more objectively. At least she had been up front and honest. He'd give her that. She knew what she wanted and she wasn't shy about going after it.

That should have been the end of Molly McPherson as far as he was concerned. He wasn't interested in a woman who was for sale to the highest bidder. But there was still the Heart Club. On that point he and Molly were firmly of the same opinion. Something had to be done.

After thinking about it during the next day, Mike decided it was wrong to place personal considerations above helping Jane and her friends. And, if help was possible, it would have to come from Molly and him. After a brief hesitation, he telephoned her at the gallery.

"Molly? It's Mike Randall. I think I owe you an apology. I behaved badly last night."

"No, you didn't. It was me. I think I offended you and I didn't mean to."

"Pride goeth before whatever," he said lightly. "At least we know where we stand. The reason I'm calling is to ask if you still want to discuss Harry Blackman."

"Yes, I do."

"Fine." He suggested they meet after work at a coffee shop not far from Molly's gallery. Grogan's was busy, brightly lit, and served the best coffee in town. It was a long way from silver and linen and chateaubriand.

After hanging up, Mike leaned back in his chair and chewed on his pencil. Okay, the relationship would be impersonal, strictly business. She had drawn a line and made it clear he wasn't to step over. Fine. He'd resist the temptation to show her how wrong she'd been about him.

If he dazzled her with talk about Shield, what would he gain in the end? Maybe she'd fall for him, but he'd never know if it was Mike Randall or his bank account that had tipped the scales.

No, this woman was not for him. He cared about people; she cared about expensive things. How that squared with her obvious commitment to the Heart Club, he couldn't figure. But apparently it did.

It was too bad, because she was special. And he'd never wanted a woman as much as he wanted Molly McPherson.

WHEN SHE WALKED into the coffee shop and saw Mike waiting, Molly paused and asked herself why she'd agreed to meet him. Yes, she hoped they could find a solution to the Heart Club's problem, but in her heart she suspected there really wasn't an answer. Meeting Mike was only wasting her time and his and wasn't fair to either of them.

Besides, she still felt awkward about last night. But if she'd worried that seeing him again would be uncomfortable—and she had—the anxiety had been unnecessary.

His smile was warm and cheerful when he stood to pull back her chair. "You look terrific," he commented, running a quick look over her dark wool suit. "Are you hungry? Would you like some pie with your coffee?"

Immediately Molly felt better. She'd done the right thing telling him about her plan. Now he didn't have to offer dinner or do the macho number. They could be honest with each other. And she didn't have to feel guilty about straining his budget.

"Look, before we discuss the Heart Club..." She wasn't sure how to say this. "Can we...Mike, I'd like us to be friends. I like you and I think you like me, and our families are interwoven. Gran and your aunt have been friends for over forty years and I just...I'd like us to be friends," she finished lamely. "You might not believe this, but there's more to me than just being a gold digger." The word continued to stick in her throat.

"Friends it is." Leaning back in his chair, he smiled at her. "I like honesty in friends. Frankly I don't have many friends honest enough to admit they're more interested in a man's wallet than in the man himself."

She stared at him. "God, that sounds awful." Standing abruptly, Molly fumbled for her coat and purse. "Look, this probably wasn't a good idea."

"Molly, wait. I'm sorry." The smile vanished from his lips. "I don't know why I said that, but I was out of line. I apologize. Really, I'd like us to be friends."

Undecided, she glanced toward the coffee shop door then at Mike. As he continued speaking, she slowly sat down.

"You and I don't think alike about money, Molly. To me it isn't very important. To you it is. I'm not saying you're wrong. I'm just saying we see the subject differently. Okay?"

Every man she'd ever met who didn't have money tried to tell her money wasn't important. Molly had an idea that people who had money thought it was plenty important. Like fish thought water was important.

"Okay," she said finally. "Friends?"

"Friends."

"All right." She eased off her coat and cradled her coffee between her hands. It was time to change the subject. "What are we going to do about Gran and your aunt Jane? Do you think it would help to speak to Harry Blackman? Maybe threaten him with a lawsuit or something?"

"We could. But do you think that would do any good?"

"Probably not." She sighed. And she wished Mike wouldn't look at her so intently. Molly knew they had no future, but her body hadn't gotten the message. Tiny nervous impulses raced along the surface of her skin whenever he looked at her mouth. "Blackman probably knows we don't have a legal leg to stand on."

"Let's begin by you telling me everything you know about Harry Blackman."

"There isn't much." Knowing he was watching her lips made her mouth feel wooden and stiff. "Blackman's been successful manufacturing and marketing novelty-type items. He has an office in D.C., a home in Georgetown. And he swindled the Heart Club. That's all I know."

Mike pushed a hand through his hair and his brows came together in a frown. "What kind of bastard would victimize four nice old ladies?"

"I can't imagine. I picture him as a cold-eyed thug. The kind of stinko that pulls wings off butterflies." Molly gazed around the coffee shop, her glance skimming the customers. "I really would like to meet Blackman face to face. Just to see him. For all we know, he could be sitting over there at the next table."

"You think we should spy on him?" Mike's smile teased her.

She hadn't thought of it before. "Maybe I do," Molly said slowly, testing the idea. She tapped a finger against her chin. "Yes, that's exactly what I'm suggesting. How would you feel about that? Checking Blackman out. I'd like to see what the bastard looks like."

Mike's smile widened to a grin. "Are you serious, Miss Moneypenny?"

"I think so, Mr. Bond. Yes."

"Do you think that's wise, Molly? Seriously, Blackman could be dangerous. We don't know much about him, but we do know he's not nice people."

"But that's my point—we don't know anything about him." She leaned forward, letting the idea take hold of her imagination. "Look, Mike, I admit there doesn't seem to be much we can do to help the Heart Club. But I'm too angry to just walk away. At least I'd like to see the man who swindled my grandmother."

"Why do I have this idea that you're going to spy on Blackman with or without me?" Determination glowed on her face. Radiant, she looked ready to march forth and do battle. Mike suppressed a sigh. There was something wildly seductive about a woman whose dark eyes snapped with vitality and purpose.

"Mike, would you agree that what Blackman did is wrong?"

"Absolutely." He wondered if her mouth was as soft and yielding as it looked.

"And would you further agree that four elderly women are helpless to do anything about it?"

"Granted." Molly McPherson had a figure that should be outlawed. And why was he thinking these things?

"Finally, would you agree that if anything is going to be done, it has to be done by me?" She spread her hands and looked at him. "That is, by us—if you're willing."

This time he didn't suppress the sigh. He looked into her beautiful freckled Doris Day face and admitted to a rampant streak of old-fashioned romanticism. Women in distress reduced him to putty. Common sense departed and he wanted to rush to the rescue. He thought about the four women in the Heart Club then looked into Molly McPherson's chocolate-brown eyes.

"I'm in," he said. He'd probably regret this, he already did. But he couldn't let Molly spy on Blackman alone. "We'll have a look at him."

Her smile was pleased. "Okay, 007. We've made a start."

"I hate to throw a wet blanket over the party, but spying on Blackman isn't going to change anything."

"Maybe seeing him will help us think of some way to make him do the right thing. He should give back the money."

Suddenly Mike laughed, the sound warm and rich and genuinely amused. "This is crazy. We're two sensible mature people and we're talking about spying on someone."

Molly's smile matched his. "That's the penalty people pay for living in D.C. Such nuttiness seems logical."

She had a smile that lit the room, Mike thought. "All right, we need to make some plans. Can you get some time off next week?"

"I have a part-time girl who helps at the gallery. I can put her on full time for a few days. And I'm not involved in a restoration project right now." Although it was startling to think they were actually going to do this, there was something satisfying about knowing she would see what Blackman looked like. It was better than doing nothing.

She raised her coffee cup in a toast: "To justice!"

Mike touched his cup to hers. "To our spying career. May it be brief and productive."

Molly looked into blue eyes twinkling with amusement and experienced a tiny pang of regret. It would have been so nice if Mike Randall had been filthy rich. So perfect.

Well, it was an imperfect world. Soft-drink machines went on the fritz, people ran their cars into other people's cars, nice old ladies got themselves swindled by cold-hearted thugs, the interesting men were either married or broke. So it went.

She turned her gaze to the window and looked out at D.C. Somewhere out there her millionaire was waiting. Usually the thought cheered her.

Chapter Three

A year before Molly wouldn't have believed it, but the old Washington cliché was correct: If you'd been to one embassy party, you'd been to them all. They weren't even parties, not really, they were more like business meetings in fancy dress.

After tasting her champagne, she let her gaze drift across the elegantly furnished room. Louis XIV furniture, polished cherrywood paneling, a Chopin sonata floating from the balcony. Most of the men had gathered before a marble tiled fireplace to argue politics and cut deals or whatever else politicians did at parties. The women had collected in smaller groups to discuss fashion designers and servants and the party they had attended last night and the party they would attend tomorrow.

It was boring. Utterly and stupefyingly boring.

The realization surprised Molly and she straightened abruptly, trying to push the thought out of her mind.

"Are we keeping you awake?" Greg Livingston, her friend and date for the evening, smiled down at her. "I know these things are deadly, but you're not supposed to give it away by falling asleep on your feet. You're supposed to pretend you're having a great time."

"Sorry." She accepted the fresh flute of champagne he'd brought her. "Did you corner Senator Roberts?"

He nodded. "Business concluded, thank you. Now, let's talk about you. You look sensational, by the way." Approval warmed the gaze he skimmed over her black floor-length gown, slit to the knee and draped low in back. "Have you noticed the short man standing in the doorway? The one staring at you like you're a bonbon?"

"The balding guy with the funny-colored mustache?" Molly made a face.

"Stavros Polopas. He owns a fleet of Greek tankers, Molly darling. *Very* wealthy. He recently shed wife number four and the grapevine has it that he's looking for wife number five, preferably a wholesome American girl, much like your sweet self."

Molly studied the Greek gazillionaire, then released an elaborate sigh. "Forget it, Greg. He's too old, too much married, too ugly and too bald."

Taking her arm, Greg edged her toward the velvet draperies and a better view of Stavros Polopas. "Molly, darling, do I have to tell you again that you're going about this wrong? You can't think about things like age and hair. You must think about the money. Polopas has *mucho* money."

"Come on, Greg. I happen to like hair. The guy is as bald as a bell. And he's old enough to be my grandfather." It was depressing. "What I'm looking for is someone like you." She gave him a wistful smile. "You're the right age, great looking, embarrassingly rich and fun to be with."

He grinned down at her. "And gay."

"And gay. Well, you can't have everything. It wouldn't be fair." He laughed and Molly pressed his arm affectionately. She'd met Greg shortly after arriving in Washington, D.C., and had liked him immediately. When he needed a date for a government function, she occasionally went along, and he was continually on the lookout for eligible millionaires for her. It was a pleasant arrangement, except she hadn't yet met Mr. Right.

"Not true," Greg disagreed. "I've introduced you to a dozen Mr. Rights." Tilting his head, he gave her a shrewd look. "Do you know what your problem is?"

"I have an idea you're going to tell me."

"You want it all. You want to love the guy with the money."

"What's wrong with that?" Molly asked.

Cupping her shoulders, Greg turned her to face the doorway and the Greek tanker magnate. "It's an unfortunate fact that most men who are old enough to have amassed a fortune are not going to threaten TV's latest heart throb. Take Mr. Polopas."

"You take him."

"No one's going to fall madly in love with Mr. Polopas at first sight. He's short, fat and lamentably lacking in the hair department. He's wearing most of his dinner on his coat and he has a mustache that resembles a Brillo pad. But if you're looking to marry money, Molly darling, you have to overlook these small imperfections. You aren't going to find a bigger bankroll than Stavros Polopas. What you need to remember is: first the money, then the love."

Molly narrowed her eyes and tried to conjure a lovable fellow beneath Polopas's shiny head and strange mustache. "If you're suggesting I'd fall in love with him later, I don't think so. There's got to be something better," she muttered.

Greg raised an amused eyebrow and ticked off names on his fingertips. "Like Randy Aldercamp? Of the Aldercamp industrial fortune? Let's see, I believe he's the one you sent packing when you discovered all he did was play. For some strange reason, you thought he should have a grander job than spending his father's money. Then there was Walter Missen. Remember Walter? You gave him his walking papers because you thought it was weird and wasteful to own two houses in Palm Beach. You believed one mansion in one town was enough. And then we had Sonny Von Bunman—he was the one who gave you a sable coat after your second dinner date. But you said you couldn't accept that kind of gift and insulted him by sending it back. Need I go on?"

Molly grinned weakly. "Okay, so I've met a few with hair who are in the right age bracket. But none of them were right somehow."

"Darling, they were *all* Mr. Right." He tilted her face up to him. "The problem is you, Molly darling," he said gently.

"That doesn't make sense," she snapped, suddenly irritated. "It just hasn't worked out. But it will. I know what I want."

"And I know what I want. Which, right now, is a nightcap in some posh place so lavish it will take your mind off Mr. Polopas. Who seems besotted with you, by the way. Are you absolutely certain you don't want to be Mrs. Polopas number five? The darling of the Greek Isles set?" His eyes twinkled. Molly laughed. "Not for a million dollars. Not even for two or three million." She refused his offer of a nightcap with genuine regret. "I'm sorry, Greg, but I need to make this a short evening so I can get an early start tomorrow. I want to finish a painting I'm cleaning. I need to tie up a few loose ends so I'll have a few days to work on Gran's problem."

But Greg wasn't interested in Gran's problem, not really, so she didn't elaborate. When the chauffeur had whisked them across the river, Greg walked her to Gran's front porch and kissed her forehead. "Not to worry, Molly darling. The right man is out there somewhere. We'll find him for you."

It was no doubt accidental, Molly thought, that Greg was facing in the direction of the United States Patent and Trademark offices when he said it.

THE MCPHERSON ART GALLERY was a modest success, but it couldn't be said that Molly's gallery had taken D.C. by storm. After borrowing an enormous sum from her brother-in-law, Molly had opened it a year and a half ago. Bill Porterfield wasn't pressing her to repay the loan, thank God, as it appeared her success wasn't going to be the overnight variety. These things took time.

Standing near the window that fronted the street, she gazed outside, taking pleasure in the sight of the White House seen through the branches of winter-bared trees. The location was bound to help.

Turning, she scanned the main gallery, pleased by the good light and attractive groupings. Some paintings she bought outright, others she accepted on consignment. Last week she'd had a successful showing for three local artists. She'd made money, the artists had made money, everyone was happy.

Today, she'd had only three customers. It was feast or famine. Who could figure it? If it hadn't been for her restoration work, she'd have had to close the doors and call it quits.

Shaking her auburn curls, Molly crossed to her workroom at the back of the gallery and lifted her smock from a peg.

"I've got one more cleanup for Mrs. Patten," she said to Ruth. "Will you take care of the front if anyone comes in?"

"Sure." Ruth held a frame to the light and inspected it for scratches. "Thanks for the extra hours on Thursday and

Friday. I appreciate it.'' Ruth was an art student at George Washington University, working her way through.

"I need the time off for—" How could she explain a spying mission? "For a special project. Are you sure it won't interfere with your classes?"

"My Thursday classes are in the evening, and Friday is a free day. There's a scratch on this frame, in the lower right-hand corner."

"Put it on the repair pile. I'll get to it when I can."

The bell tinkled on the front door and Ruth tossed back a long blond ponytail. "Maybe it's a live one," she said with a wink. She smoothed her plaid skirt and hurried into the gallery.

Molly listened a moment and decided Ruth was right—the customer sounded as if he knew what he wanted and, even better, the McPherson Gallery had what he wanted. Confident in Ruth's abilities, Molly returned her attention to Mrs. Patten's painting.

It was an early Picasso. Nice, but not to Molly's taste. At the moment it was a mess. The Patten's den had caught fire and several of their paintings had suffered smoke damage. Molly had already cleaned the others and had them delivered to the Patten's. This was the last, then she could hopefully move on to something more challenging.

While it gave her a comfortable sense of satisfaction to rescue paintings like Mrs. Patten's, what she enjoyed most was a total reclamation project. One where she not only had to clean the painting, but touch up the paint as well. This could be a thought-provoking challenge depending upon the age of the painting involved. Often it meant mixing paints by methods not used for centuries, striving to match the artist's original tints now faded by time.

Thankfully Molly was fortunate enough to be on the Smithsonian's overflow list, and occasionally they assigned her something wonderful to work on. Before Christmas she'd restored a Rubens. And had coasted on the glory of it for weeks. Mr. Bostwick at the Smithsonian had promised that sometime soon, she'd have a chance to work on a small Monet.

After removing Mrs. Patten's Picasso from the frame, Molly assembled her cleaning equipment and looked at the painting with a professional eye, wishing she had one-tenth of Picasso's talent. But she didn't.

In fact, Molly was a skilled painter. Not an artist, but a painter. She could copy absolutely anything. Where she fell apart was on original art. She had an eye that could see, truly see, what another artist had done and how he had done it. And she could reproduce his work so accurately that few people could tell the original from the reproduction.

But she could stare all day at a real orange on a real table and still not be able to decide if the shadow on the orange was gold, or gold-brown, or orangy-gold or what the hell.

Something in her brain stubbornly refused to break out the tints and angles until she saw them reproduced on canvas. Then the door to her mind opened and she could see and comprehend. Because of this ability, she was slowly but certainly gaining a reputation for restoration. The Smithsonian had been delighted with her work on the Rubens and had promised her a steady flow of assignments in the future.

That was good news, Molly thought. She genuinely enjoyed rescuing the masters from deterioration and decay. And the restoration work kept the gallery alive.

"What sort of special project are you working on?" Ruth asked, returning to the workroom.

Molly smiled and squeezed paint onto her palette. She would rather have walked naked through the White House lobby than admit she was planning something as crazy as a spying mission. "Nothing important," she said. "Did we make a sale?"

"Sold two Myersons," Ruth said proudly.

"That's terrific! I'll buy lunch." Things were looking up. If the latter part of the week went as well as the first part, Molly thought, Harry Blackman didn't stand a chance. She blinked and caught herself up short. What was she thinking? She and Mike weren't going to do anything except have a look at Blackman. That was all.

"DON'T WORRY if I'm late, Gran," Molly said. She looked through the living-room curtains and tugged on her gloves as she watched Mike Randall's Chrysler pull to the curb.

"That's fine, dear. Mike's a nice young man, I know you're safe with him." Lucille Pratt sounded distracted, and Molly turned to look at her. "The Heart Club is dropping by later," Gran explained. "I was just wondering if I had enough pie on hand."

"I thought the Heart Club met on Fridays. Tomorrow."

"Well, yes, we do. Usually. But..." Gran peered over her glasses, her gaze settling on the TV set. "That's it. There's a program we want to see." Her face brightened. "We thought we'd watch it together."

"That's nice," Molly said automatically, listening to the sound of footsteps crossing the porch. She kissed Gran's cheek and moved toward the door. "Do I look all right?" She was wearing black slacks and a black sweater, a black car coat and a dark stocking cap pulled over her ears.

"You look beautiful, dear. But maybe a touch of color? A bright scarf or something?"

"Too late. Mike's here." Spies didn't wear bright colors. She wiggled her fingers at Gran, blowing her a kiss, then she opened the door to Mike. He too was wearing black slacks and sweater and a dark coat.

They grinned at each other, then, laughing, they ran down the steps to Mike's car. Once inside, he shifted on the seat and smiled. "Aside from feeling ridiculous, I'm raring to go. What's on our agenda?"

"I have it here." She found the notebook in her black purse and flipped it open. "We have two choices. Blackman is probably at his office in D.C. We can go there."

"Or?"

"I have his home address. We can see where and how the bastard lives."

"It appears you have a vocation for spying," he said with admiration.

"Actually, he's listed in the phone book. Anyway, we can drive to his house—it's in Georgetown—and save the office for tomorrow. Or we can go directly to his office."

"I opt for Georgetown. Okay?"

"That's my choice too." She told herself her choice had nothing to do with spending an extra day with Mike Randall. She really did want to know all there was to know about Harry Blackman, thief and scoundrel.

Mike guided the car from the curb. "I can't believe we're actually doing this." Accepting Molly McPherson as a spy was as nutty as trying to visualize himself in that role. In no way was she inconspicuous. Her beautiful face was a pale oval beneath the stocking cap; tendrils of flame escaped from the edges of her cap and seemed to throw off sparks in the winter sunlight slanting through the car window. It was inconceivable that anyone who saw her could possibly forget her. Mike decided it was going to be a long day if he continued with this kind of thinking. Determined to keep the conversation light, he asked, "Do you by any chance have any spying credentials?"

"Sorry, this is my first spying mission." She gave him an impish grin. "I'm not even certain what credentials might be required."

"Hmm. I was afraid of that." A mock frown drew his brows together before he pushed his dark glasses into place. "Well, let's begin with the obvious. Do you have any sneaky qualities that might help us along?"

Molly laughed, enjoying the banter. "Actually, you've raised a point. We could be in trouble here."

"That's occurred to me."

"To tell the truth, I'm not very good at sneaky. You're looking at a retired Girl Scout. Twenty-three badges, all honestly earned. And I was an honor student in college."

"Dean's list?"

"Under the circumstances, I hate to admit it."

Mike smiled. "This isn't looking good for the home team spies. Ever cheat on your income tax? Just a little?"

"Never." This was a crazy conversation and Molly was enjoying it. "And it gets worse. I don't drink much, don't smoke, don't have any revolting habits. At least I don't think I do."

"A woman without vices. The most dangerous kind."

"We'll have to depend on you for sneaky," Molly said. Shifting on the seat, she tucked her legs up under her and smiled at his profile.

"I knew it. We're definitely in trouble. I hate to admit this, but I'm as straight-arrow as you are. Eagle Scout, graduated forth in my class from M.I.T.... I'm racking my brain for some sneaky deed to reassure us both, but I'm coming up blank."

"Uh-huh. We're in big, big trouble, my friend." Although the conversation was light and teasing, Molly had an idea that it was a good thing all they planned to do was have a look at Blackman. They weren't equipped for much else.

Going head-to-head with Harry Blackman would have been like sending the Cub Scouts after the Mafia.

"Well, let's think about this." Skillfully, Mike wove the Chrysler through thickening traffic. "Once I won some money at a horse track that I didn't report to the IRS. That should count for something."

"Shocking." Molly smiled. "But encouraging. Anything else?"

"I pulled strings at the office to get a third cousin hired last spring."

"Pretty sneaky. Now we're getting somewhere." Falling into the game, she furrowed her brow and tried to think of something she'd done that was a little bit rotten. "Let me see . . . I borrowed my sister Sally's best sweater when I was eighteen and never gave it back."

Mike rolled his eyes. "You didn't!"

"And my mother thinks I'm a virgin. Does that count?"

He laughed. "I don't know how your mother feels about it, but I'm fascinated."

A rush of pink colored Molly's cheeks and she turned her eyes to the window. "Do you suppose any of this will help?"

"Seriously, Molly, I doubt there's anything we can do to help. Harry Blackman conned the Heart Club, and there's no legal recourse."

Tilting her head, Molly studied him for a moment. "How about illegal recourse? What if we conned Harry Blackman like he conned the Heart Club?" She was still playing, thinking out loud, not really sure how serious the proposal was.

"Us? The ol' straight arrows?"

Molly didn't blame him for laughing. "You're right," she said, sighing. "I wouldn't have the faintest notion how to swindle someone."

"Actually, it's probably not that difficult. Given two intelligent people with enough motivation and enough information, it could be done. Might even be an interesting challenge." Taking his eyes from the road, Mike winked at her. "But the risks for people like us are unacceptable."

People like us. Molly dropped her eyes and laced her fingers together.

"Would you like a cup of coffee?" Mike asked as they turned onto the Georgetown exit ramp.

"Some spy you are, Randall. We've only been at this for forty mintues and you're ready to stop for coffee?" Relaxing, she smiled. "Or did you bring a thermos?"

"None of the above. I have a coffee maker in the car."

Mike glanced at her from the corner of his eye. Confessing he was an inventor was occasionally uncomfortable. Some people considered inventors a weird breed, right up there with Dr. Frankenstein. Not long ago he had dated a woman who had broken off the relationship because she considered him too eccentric. This had surprised and secretly pleased him as he'd never thought of himself as anything but ordinary.

"You're kidding." Molly stared. "You can brew coffee in your car?"

"It's easier if the passenger does it, but yes."

Molly thought about that a moment. "All right. What do I do?" Now she noticed the inside configuration of Mike Randall's car was subtly different from anything she'd seen before. What she'd mistaken for a large cup-holder was obviously the base for the coffee maker. She leaned forward to peer at the device on the floor between them. "Okay, now what?"

"There's a drawer under your seat. The pot's in there. A two-cupper."

She swung her legs to one side and fumbled for the drawer handle. Inside she found a small pot, a tin of coffee and a tube of Styrofoam cups. She looked at them as if she'd never seen such items before.

"This is amazing." And so sensible. Why didn't all cars use the wasted space under the seat for a drawer? "So far so good. Is there a thermos of water?"

"The spigot is under the dashboard. Beneath the glove box."

"The spigot?" She looked at him with disbelieving eyes, then felt beneath the glove box until she found it. "I can honestly say this is the first time I've ridden in a car that has running water."

"All that's required is a small storage tank."

"What's next?"

He explained how to lift and hook the water storage portion of the brewing mechanism and told her to plug the device into the cigarette lighter. "That's the power source," he said.

Molly listened to the coffee perking then laughed. "Did you invent this or is coffee in the car something Detroit is working on?"

"Well, I did." He glanced at her then back at the road. "I've always been interested in gadgets."

"You're a part-time inventor?" In a way it made sense, Molly decided. If a patent commissioner were an inventor himself, he'd have a better grasp of what he was dealing with at the office.

"Do you think that's eccentric?"

"Not really." Did he look disappointed? "But I'm not into gadgets if you want the truth. They never seem to work. I hate things that don't work as they're supposed to."

"That's the whole point of inventions. To make things work better or to fill a need. Like coffee in the car. How many times have you been stuck in a traffic jam and thought: it would be nice to have a cup of coffee right now.''

"A lot of times," she admitted, smiling. "Are there other innovations in here?"

"Like the refrigerator?"

Molly raised her eyebrows. "Let me guess. You get stuck in a traffic jam and you think: it would be nice to have a sandwich right now. Right? Is it in the glove box?"

He grinned at her. "People don't put gloves in glove boxes anymore. Flat items like maps and car manuals can be stored more easily in a pocket flap."

"May I?" Molly asked, reaching for the glove box/refrigerator handle. Inside was a larger space than she had anticipated. And a bottle of Chablis, two chicken sandwiches, brie and two apples.

"Lunch," Mike explained. "In case we're in the middle of spying and get hungry."

Molly thought about the coffee and the refrigerator then laughed out loud. Mike Randall definitely was interesting. Certainly more interesting than anyone she'd met at an embassy party. The coffee finished perking and she poured two cups, discovering a pull-out tray beneath the casette recorder. "You should market this. Are all your inventions as successful?"

It seemed that he hesitated and that he gave her an odd look before he answered. "Not all of them." The car swept into a wooded lane. "There was the electric ladder, for instance."

"Tell me about it."

"The idea was to create a ladder rather like an escalator. To free a person's hands. Imagine you want to paint your roof or make repairs. Because of the angle of the ladder, you have to hold on leaving only one hand to carry your supplies. If the ladder was automated, you would free both hands and you'd save several trips up and down. Right?''

Molly didn't reply. If her plan worked as she hoped, she would never have to worry about such things as painting or repairing roofs. Such tasks would be hired out or left to servants to organize.

She listened, but gradually her focus of attention shifted away from his words and centered on Mike himself. When he spoke of his inventions, excitement and eagerness lit his features. Intent on explaining the electric ladder, he glanced at her, his eyes direct and absorbed. Mike Randall was a man with a high degree of concentration for the moment. It occurred to Molly that he would be the same when making love. Nothing would exist for Mike but one woman and one moment in time. He would make his woman feel as if no other female existed in the world. Suddenly restless, Molly wet her lips and made herself break the spell by looking away from him. This was dangerous thinking.

"Was it successful?" she asked, reentering the conversation. "Your electric ladder?"

"Hell, no." His laugh made her smile. "The damned platform zoomed up the ladder and threw me on the roof. I rolled off and broke my wrist."

"Back to the drawing board," Molly said, joining his laughter.

"It needs more work." Peering through the windshield, he added, "I think this is the right street. What number are we looking for?"

The houses were stately two-stories set amid mature trees and carefully maintained landscaping. Even with bare branches and a thin coating of snow on the ground, the setting appeared posh and solidly respectable.

"There it is, the white Georgian house," Molly said. "Park across the street."

"Nice area," Mike commented as he eased the car to a halt.

"Somehow I didn't expect his house to look so...so ordinary and respectable."

In silence they studied the neat brick walk running up to a small porch and a carved door. Molly hadn't expected a sign reading Con-man Lives Here, but she hadn't expected an ordinary house either. Without thinking about it, she'd supposed there would be something about Harry Blackman's house that set it apart from the others. But there wasn't.

"Do you think he's in there?"

"Doubtful," Mike answered. "He's probably at his office in the city."

Uneasily, Molly glanced over her shoulder. "I feel as conspicuous as hell."

"You're kidding." Mike grinned at her. "What's conspicuous about two furtive-looking people dressed like Ninjas sitting in a silver Chrysler in a strange neighborhood?"

Molly laughed. "Tell you what. Let's brew up another two-cupper, have our coffee, then call it quits. Suddenly this seems like a bad idea. What if someone looks out their window and calls the police? How would we explain what we're doing here?"

"Elementary, my dear Moneypenny. I'd just tell the police I met this gorgeous redhead and brought her here to get acquainted. Some guys take their dates to expensive restaurants, some guys put on their dancing shoes. I take my dates on spying missions to Georgetown."

"Good, real good. That would work about as well as your electric ladder."

"Ouch." He clapped a hand over his heart. "Low blow."

When the coffee was brewed, Molly cupped the Styrofoam between her palms and leaned against the car door facing him. Now that the car was stopped and they were looking at each other, she was aware of an unavoidable intimacy. Damn those blue eyes of his that seemed to look inside her and melt tissue and bone. She'd never met anyone with eyes like Mike Randall's. They had a language all their own. And right now what those eyes were saying made her squirm in her seat.

"Do people think you're eccentric because you invent things?" she asked, referring to his earlier statement. Talking was easier than the silence that underscored being alone with him.

"Occasionally." Reaching, he casually tucked up a strand of hair that had escaped from her cap. Molly caught a quick breath and held it until his hand dropped to the back of the seat. She tried to pay attention as he told her about someone named Jeanne. "I suppose it was a mismatch from the start. Our levels of curiosity didn't align."

"That's interesting. I've never thought about curiosity as being a relationship breaker."

"Curious people see the world around them. They're interested and interesting. You're a curious person, Molly." He looked into her dark eyes and smiled. "Or we wouldn't be sitting here drinking coffee in front of a stranger's house. Curiosity is a wonderful quality."

She wanted to kiss him. If that was an example of curiosity, then she was quivering with curiosity. It was trembling all through her body. She had wanted to kiss Mike Randall from the moment she stepped into his office and he raised his head to look at her. She wanted to know if his mouth was firm or soft, if his kiss would be gentle or passionate. Did he close his eyes or keep them open? Would the heel of his hand brush her breast or would he just lean forward without touching?

She pressed her fingertips against her temples and squeezed out the unwanted images. Her life was planned; she didn't want any complications. "Let's get out of here. Okay?"

"Is something...?"

Instead of answering, Molly looked up as an old Ford wagon rolled toward them and bumped along the curb in front of Harry Blackman's house.

"Get down," Mike whispered, staring at the car.

Immediately Molly slipped down the seat until her eyes were on a level with the glove box/refrigerator. "What's happening?" She fumbled in the flap pocket and found a newspaper, which she tossed toward Mike.

Hastily he pushed on his dark glasses and lowered the newspaper to his nose. "An older woman is getting out...she's wearing a head scarf, a gray coat, slacks...going around to the back of the wagon."

"Why are we whispering?" Molly whispered.

"I don't know."

"What is she doing now?" Molly asked in a low tone that faded into a whisper. It just seemed better to whisper.

"She's removing a vacuum from the back...and and a bucket. Looks like the bucket is filled with brushes."

"Mike?"

"Yes?"

She lifted an eyebrow and looked up at him. "Why am I down here on the floor? What possible difference could it make if she saw one of us or two of us?"

He blinked then grinned. "None. Come up here and have a look for yourself. Sorry."

Molly raised her head until she could see over the dashboard. The woman was carrying the vacuum and bucket up the brick walkway. She pressed the bell and after a moment the door opened and she vanished inside. Molly pushed up on the seat and stared at Blackman's closed door.

"Just the cleaning lady," Mike said, folding away the newspaper.

Molly bit her lip. She studied the Ford wagon, her heart sinking. She wished she'd gotten a better look at the cleaning lady.

"Molly, I've known you about two weeks. Long enough to know something's troubling you."

"I'm not sure about this, Mike, but that car looks familiar. You're going to think I'm crazy, but one of the Heart Club members does some cleaning to earn extra money."

"Oh, boy." He covered his chin with his fingers. "Tell me you're not saying what I think you're saying."

"I'm not sure what I'm saying. Can you describe the cleaning lady more precisely?"

"She was about five foot five," Mike recalled slowly. "Blond or gray hair, on the plump side. Not young. Does that ring any bells? It's the best I can do."

"That description would fit Alice Harper or Gladys Price. I can't remember which, but one of them cleans houses."

For a moment neither of them spoke. Then Mike removed his cap and pushed a hand through his hair. "Do you realize what you're suggesting?"

"It's an odd coincidence." Leaning forward, Molly examined the Ford wagon. "A very odd coincidence."

They finished their coffee in silence, watching the house. Then they turned to each other at the same moment.

"You know, I think—"

"Maybe we should—"

Mike inclined his head in a bow. "After you."

Molly collected her thoughts and drew a slow breath. "If Alice or Gladys is cleaning Harry Blackman's house it's simply too great a coincidence to be accidental. Would you agree?"

Reluctance knit his expression into a frown. "I agree."

"I feel—I don't know—uneasy about this." Maybe her memory was playing tricks. Maybe the Ford wagon wasn't the same car Molly had seen parked outside Gran's on Friday afternoons. "I really don't think that woman was Alice or Gladys."

"But?"

"But I'd feel a whole lot better if we checked it out."

"Agreed. We'll both feel better." Mike tapped his fingers on the steering wheel. "Here's the plan, okay? We drive to a phone booth and call Alice and Gladys. If they're home, we'll know they aren't cleaning Blackman's house."

"Let's go," Molly said grimly.

They drove to the nearest mall and parked in front of a phone booth located outside a convenience food store. While Molly found Gladys's number in the phone book, Mike tried to decide what they would say if someone answered.

"I don't want to frighten them," he said.

"Pretend to be a salesmen. Salesmen phone all the time."

"Good idea. I'll sell something they can't possibly want. How about solar heating? Do they rent or own their homes?"

"I think they rent," Molly said, trying to remember. "I don't know."

"Okay, let's get this over with." With Molly watching through the Plexiglas booth, he dialed Gladys Price. When a soft voice answered, Mike looked at the sky then assumed a cheery voice. "Good afternoon, ma'am, are you the lady of the house?" Molly rolled her eyes and grinned and he looked away from her. "I'm Mr....ah...Smith. Mr. Smith with the . . ." He threw Molly an urgent look over his shoulder.

"The Gladhand Solar Company," she supplied in a stage whisper.

"With the Gladhand Solar Company. I'll bet you're wishing there was some way to reduce your heating bills now that cold weather has settled over the area. Am I right?" He covered the mouthpiece and stared at Molly. "She isn't hanging up. She said yes." After clearing his throat, he spoke into the mouthpiece. "Well now, I think Gladhand Solar has the answer. But this offer is only for homeowners. Do you own your home, Mrs. Price?"

"Very good," Molly murmured, grinning. "I'll take two of whatever gadget you're selling."

Mike glared. "You do? I see." His glare turned slightly wild-eyed. "Well, ah, there's a second qualification." He frowned at the phone booth wall, trying to think of something. "Do you have a gizzo-gazzo fortified electromagnetic attachment on your roof? You don't think so? Well, Mrs. Price, I'm terribly sorry but I don't think Gladhand can be of service. We have to have the gizzo-gazzo to attach our equipment." From the corner of his eye, he watched Molly cover her laughter and turn aside. "Yes, ma'am. Thank you very much. You have a nice day, too."

"A gizzo-gazzo?" Molly gasped.

"Okay, McPherson." Stepping out of the phone booth, Mike handed her the receiver. "The next one is yours. I hope you hate every minute."

"No can do, Mr. Smith, old friend. Alice Harper either doesn't have a phone, which is unlikely, or her number's unlisted. It isn't in the book." She leaned against the phone booth wall. "Look, Alice can't be the woman we saw. Why would she accept a job from the man who cheated her?"

Mike stood so close that his breath bathed her face in warmth. "Still, there's the Ford wagon, the gray hair and you thought it was her."

"And I have this nagging sense of unease in the pit of my stomach." Which probably had nothing whatever to do with Alice Harper and a whole lot to do with the fact that Mike Randall's mouth was only inches from her own. For a moment she stared at teeth so white she wondered why she hadn't noticed before, then she ducked out from under his arm and pretended to stamp the cold from her feet.

"I don't like this, Molly. We'll both feel better if we know the cleaning lady was not Alice Harper. Let's return to Blackman's and wait for her to come outside."

There really wasn't a choice. They drove back to Harry Blackman's Georgian mansion and parked down the street behind the Ford wagon. While they waited, Mike entertained her with stories of failed inventions. Molly talked about art restoration and how she hoped one day to have her own studio devoted solely to restoration. They discovered a common interest in opera and found they belonged to the same book clubs. They argued the merits of Johnny Carson versus David Letterman.

"Would it be tactless to ask why you stay with the patent office if your true interest is in inventing things?" Molly asked, returning to a previous subject. She bit into a chicken sandwich while Mike poured chilled Chablis into Styrofoam cups.

"At this point nothing could be tactless. I feel like I've known you forever. How many hours have we been sitting here talking?"

"It feels like days."

He was stalling. There was no way to explain that he'd given notice at the office without then explaining how he expected to support himself. And money was a taboo subject. As were most of his inventions. He'd told her about the failed projects; he wanted to tell her about Shield and the inventions that had been successful.

He was spared an answer when Molly gripped his arm and nodded toward the door of Blackman's house. The cleaning lady emerged and walked down the brick path and opened the back of the Ford wagon.

"Is it Alice Harper?"

"I can't tell yet. Did she take something out of the bucket and put it in her pocket? Or did I imagine that?"

"I saw it too."

Molly drew in a sharp breath as the cleaning lady rounded the car. "Oh, Lord. It's Alice," she whispered.

"You're absolutely certain? No possibility of a mistake?"

"I'm certain." Molly stared through the windshield.

The Ford wagon coughed, lurched, then putted around a curve in the lane.

Mike pushed back against the seat and rapped the steering wheel with his fist. "This isn't a game anymore," he said quietly. "Something's going on here."

Molly nodded. She was still gripping his arm. "I'm worried, Mike." She thought about Gran. "I'm worried a lot."

Chapter Four

They drove to a nearby coffee shop and ordered pie and coffee, not speaking until they had been served.

"I don't know what to make of this," Molly said finally. She frowned into her coffee, stirred it with the tip of her finger. "Gran and the others must know Alice is cleaning Harry Blackman's house."

"I wish we knew what she put in her pocket. It looked like film. Did she take a camera inside? Or was the film exposed somewhere else and she just happened to remember it?"

"Good God, Mike." Molly stared at him. "Are you suggesting Alice Harper—Alice Harper, for heaven's sake—is spying on Harry Blackman? With a camera yet?"

"Why is that so surprising? Some of my best friends are spies." The words were light, but he wasn't smiling. "She could easily have hidden a small camera in her bucket."

Molly leaned forward until her clasped hands were almost touching his. "Mike, let's not get crazy here. Alice is almost seventy years old. She's a sweet old lady who's hard of hearing. Sweet old ladies don't go sneaking around other people's houses taking pictures of their belongings."

"This particular sweet old lady has been cheated out of thousands of dollars."

"I know, but Alice Harper? I can't picture it. Mike, it isn't possible." She spread her hands and gave him a helpless shrug. "She can't be spying."

"Until today I would have sworn *I* wouldn't be spying on anyone." His smile faded. "Molly, tell me about Alice."

"Well, let's see. Alice lost her husband to cancer a few years ago; she has arthritis; she wears a hearing aid; she plays bridge with the Heart Club on Fridays. Smiles a lot. I think she's active in her church, plays bingo in the church basement on weekends. That's about it. I'd bet my last dollar that Alice Harper never did a sneaky or dishonest thing in her entire life."

Mike tapped his spoon on the tabletop and looked out the window. "Several questions come to mind."

"You're telling me. Why is Alice doing this? That one is driving me crazy. What's the purpose?"

Mike nodded thoughtfully. "It isn't that she wants a look at Harry Blackman. He's not likely to be home when the cleaning lady is there."

"Plus, Alice has already met him. She's the one who took the Croupier to Blackman's office." Molly pulled off her cap and shook out her hair. A deep sigh lifted her breasts against her sweater. "This isn't good. Something's going on and I wish to hell we knew what it was."

Mike hastily looked up from her breast. "Okay. Would it be fair to say that whatever is going on, the entire Heart Club knows about it?" God, she was beautiful. He wanted to kiss her, to taste her, to run his tongue all over her body.

The look in his eyes startled Molly and for a moment she forgot what they were talking about. Looking away from him, she wet her lips and waited for the moment of light-headedness to pass. "I can't imagine Alice doing anything as significant as cleaning Harry Blackman's house without the others knowing."

He watched her blot her lips, followed the return of the napkin to her lap. "Any suggestions? As to what we do next." The only suggestion he had wouldn't be acceptable to her. And had nothing to do with the problem at hand.

Molly looked into his eyes and wondered helplessly if anyone else had eyes that blue. "Suppose for a moment that the Heart Club really is spying on Harry Blackman, that they want to know more about him..."

"If so, the cleaning lady idea is ingenious." The scent of her perfume had been driving him wild all day. What was it? A blend of carnations and...

"What's worrying me—would they stop with his house? You and I planned to have a look at his office next—"

"Good Lord." Mike straightened abruptly. "You're right." He stared at her. "Do you think...?"

"I think it's worth checking."

"Agreed. We have the name of Blackman's office building. I'll call and ask if they use a janitorial service and if they do, what time the service arrives."

"If they wanted to find out about Harry Blackman, and could get inside, they'd learn more at his office than at his house." She blinked and scrubbed her eyes. "Listen to me. I'm talking like the Heart Club is involved in some kind of conspiracy. Like..."

He wanted to take her hand but he was afraid if he did he wouldn't stop there. He'd pull her into his arms and kiss the frown from between her eyes. "We're getting ahead of ourselves, Molly. Right now we don't know anything except that Alice Harper was at Blackman's house today. There could be a dozen explanations."

"Like what?"

"We'll think of them later. I'll be back in a minute."

She watched him stride toward the row of phones at the rear of the coffee shop then decided she was too nervous to wait. Following him, she watched him feed two dimes and a nickel into the pay phone. After a minute he stared at the receiver and cursed under his breath.

"Out of order." Thrusting his hand into his pocket, he came up with a key ring, selected one and opened the coin box on the bottom of the phone.

Molly's mouth dropped. Dumbfounded, she watched as Mike retrieved his two dimes and the nickel, then he closed the coin box and moved to the next phone. "Wait a minute. How did you get that key?"

"What?" When he understood what she meant, a flush of color spread beneath his tan. "I got tired of having phones steal my quarters. So I made a key. It's quicker and less hassle than asking the operator to mail back a quarter."

The explanation wasn't really necessary. Molly knew all about phones and machines that ripped off quarters and coins. She'd fought that particular injustice for years. And she applauded any and all solutions. Returning to the table, she cupped her hands around her coffee and looked out the window. It was a damned shame to find a man who hated injustice as much as she did, who turned her to jelly with a glance, who liked the same things she did—and he wasn't rich. Fate had played her a nasty trick.

"Blackman's building uses the Ace Janitorial service," Mike said, sliding into the booth next to her. An explosion of heat erupted along Molly's thigh. "The girl wasn't certain but she thought the service arrived after business hours. About five-thirty or six."

THREE HOURS LATER, they were parked across the street from Harry Blackman's office building, a six-story marvel of brick and glass. As they waited, the streetlights flicked on.

"Coffee?" Mike asked.

"One more cup of coffee and I'll gurgle when I walk."

"We're probably borrowing trouble. No doubt there's a reasonable explanation for Alice being at Blackman's."

"When we started this, I thought we were just fooling around. I wanted to have a look at Blackman, that's true. But I thought that would be the end of it. As much as I'd like to see justice done, I know the situation is hopeless. Blackman is going to get away with the swindle." She looked at him in the light of a passing car's headlamps. "Mike, I don't want Alice or Gran or any of the Heart Club involved with a man like Harry Blackman."

Gently, he touched her cheek, his hand light and reassuring. "We don't know what's going on, Molly. It's too soon to worry. Don't you think?"

"We're about to find out," she said as a van cut from the traffic and eased to a halt beneath the streetlight. Ace Janitorial was lettered across the side. Silently, they watched as the driver climbed out and the back doors pushed open from inside. A man and two women climbed out of the back of the van.

Mike swore softly. "Okay. Now it's time to worry." Pointing, he indicated an older woman wearing dark-blue slacks. "That's Aunt Jane."

"Damn." Molly recognized her. "I think we may have seriously underestimated our sweet little old ladies. We can forget that baloney about alternate explanations. The Heart Club is spying on Blackman. Serious spying; no fooling around. They make us look like amateurs."

"We *are* amateurs." Mike shook his head, still watching his aunt. "I can't believe this. I'm seeing it, but I can't believe it. Aunt Jane? Spying?"

"I must be dreaming." Molly pressed her knuckles to her mouth. "Gran thinks a trip to the grocery store is an adventure. Doing the Sunday puzzle is the highlight of her week.'' She turned her stare from the van to Mike. ''What in the hell are they doing?''

''I don't know. But I know this is one tired spy who needs a drink.''

''Make that two. And make them strong.''

After switching on the ignition, Mike looked at her in the glow of the dashboard. ''I don't live far from here. Just across the river. Are you up for a Randall Special? The best martini this side of heaven?''

''Let's go.'' Molly felt dazed. ''I need some time to think about this before I go home and face Gran.''

MIKE RANDALL'S HOUSE sat on a half acre lot at the end of a winding gravel lane. Spreading branches sheltered the low roofline. Though it was dark, Molly had an impression of rust-colored brick and diamond-paned glass. In the spread of light falling from the porch, she saw a ladder leaning against the roof, and a box-shaped article covered with a tarp. The house was larger than she'd expected his salary would permit.

''I apologize for the clutter,'' Mike said as they entered the foyer. The minute he spoke the lights flicked on and he smiled at Molly's startled expression. ''The lights are voice activated.''

''Really? How do you turn them off?''

''By using an item I call a switch.''

She looked up, then laughed. ''Walked into that one, didn't I? Okay, Randall, how about daytime? You don't speak during the day?''

''There are a few flaws in the system,'' he said grandly. ''If you're here during daylight hours, remember to turn the lights off.''

She couldn't imagine why she would ever be here again. And she didn't want to think about it. Glancing into the living room, she decided it was definitely a bachelor's room. The furniture had been chosen more for comfort than for elegance. The facing sofas looked deep and inviting, there were ashes in the hearth indicating the fireplace had been used recently. The colors were a hodgepodge collection, a little of everything.

And the clutter was awesome.

A book-covered coffee table had been pushed to one side and a partially dismantled bicycle stood between the sofas, the screws and chain carefully laid out on a piece of newspaper. Odd mechanical things crowded the mantel above the fireplace and covered most of the table surfaces. Some of the devices ticked, others sort of hiccuped and made strange clicking noises. There were stacks of magazines and books everywhere she looked.

"I know what you're thinking," Mike said, stroking his chin.

"I'm thinking you don't have a prayer of keeping a cleaning lady," Molly said. Hers was an organized nature. Clutter made her crazy.

He grinned. "And I don't want one. This may look like chaos to the untrained mind." He winked when Molly rolled her eyes. "But to a scientist like my esteemed self," he bowed to an imaginary audience, "there is order in this madness. I know exactly where everything is. Should some cleaning lady or other misguided soul—" he gave her a stern cautionary look "—disturb a single nut or bolt, I would be lost. A great and revolutionary invention might be forever denied mankind."

"Ah, but does the world really need an electric ladder?" Molly teased.

"Only time and genius will tell." Smiling he led her into the kitchen. "In the meantime, we spies need a Randall Special."

The kitchen was as cluttered as the living room. To be fair, Molly conceded everything was clean and polished. There wasn't a speck of dust. But she was beginning to understand why the clutter in Mike's office hadn't seemed to bother him. The kitchen counters were strewn with devices, most of which she couldn't identify.

"What *is* all this stuff?" she asked, looking around.

"The future. The world is infatuated with gadgets."

"I'm not convinced that's true," Molly said. "Take for instance that thing in the washing machine that adds softener automatically."

"What about it?"

"It's there, that's what about it. And since it's there, I have to use it or feel guilty. Everytime I open the lid of the washer, there it is, a reminder that, according to TV, life is better and happier if clothes are softer. If you don't add softener you're failing Clothes Washing One-oh-one." She spread her hands. "There's a hint that you're failing as a responsible human being."

"Really?" He looked fascinated. "Now there's a successful invention and a wildly successful marketing approach."

"I guess I can't expect an inventor to understand." Bending, she examined a device that looked like a funnel mounted on a blender. "What's this?"

"I'm glad you asked. That's an omelet machine. It mixes the ingredients for scambled eggs or omelets.

Molly raised an eyebrow. "I can mix scambled eggs in two minutes. Why would I want this device?"

"You're a show-off's dream, Molly. I shall demonstrate the value of enlightenment." After handing her a martini, he opened the refrigerator door.

"Excellent," Molly sighed. "This martini truly is a heavenly invention."

"Now," Mike said, his eyes sparkling. "When you mix scambled eggs, first you have to crack the eggs, right?"

"Right."

"That's messy and takes time. Observe, please." Smiling, he dropped two eggs into the funnel. "The machine cracks the eggs and spits out the shells automatically. You, the average housewife, turn on the scrambler, wait sixty seconds, then add milk and hit the switch, and—voilà—all finished. No muss, no fuss."

Molly leaned her elbows on the counter and looked up at him. "If you say so."

"Watch and prepare to be amazed," he said, reaching for the switch. "The shells will appear in this box."

Something clicked and the machine whirred. Then two eggs shot up out of the funnel with such force they splattered against the ceiling. Bits of egg and shell dripped down onto the counter top.

"You're right," Molly said bending backward to look at the ceiling. "That's amazing."

"I'll be damned." Mike tasted his martini and scowled. "It appears we have a flaw here."

"Could be. Personally, I hate kitchen gadgets." Molly held an icy mouthful of the martini on her tongue. "That's not meant as a criticism, you understand. It's your house. You can fire eggs at the ceiling if you want to."

"Thank you," he said drily.

"I can't help wondering if you've attempted this demonstration before."

"I swear it worked. Except for a bit of sluggishness during the mixing process." Placing his martini glass on the counter, he tipped the machine to look at the bottom. "Would you hand me that screwdriver? It's beside the compost machine."

"You have a compost machine? In the kitchen?" Molly blinked.

"It's the round machine that looks as if it might explode. It won't," he added hastily. "Now, what did I do here? I adjusted this, and..."

"That compost thing looks like it's breathing."

"It isn't. If I tightened the belt..."

"Mike? Shouldn't we clean off the ceiling?" It didn't seem to disturb him that a kitchen appliance had just hurled two eggs at his ceiling, but it was beginning to disturb Molly.

"Here. Use this." He handed her a spray bottle and leaned the omelet machine on its side.

"Mike, number one, I can't reach your ceiling. Number two, even if I could, I don't want to stand near that compost thing. And number three, I didn't come here to clean your house, although I'd like to and someone should. We're here to talk about the Heart Club. Remember? Our little old ladies?"

"Ah, yes. Sorry." He put aside the omelet machine with reluctance and sprayed the ceiling then wiped it clean with a paper towel.

"What is in that bottle?" This time Molly genuinely was amazed. "Did you invent that cleaner?" She peered up at the ceiling. No spot and very little effort.

"I'm still testing it." Taking her arm, he led her into the den. "My company room. Clean and uncluttered."

"Your company is grateful." Sinking into the corner of the sofa, Molly tasted her martini and sighed with pleasure. She eased off her shoes and wiggled her toes. It was that kind of room. A room that invited one to relax and be comfortable.

"Well," Mike said, drawing a finger lightly across her shoulder to get her attention. "Where were we?"

Far, far away. Her mind had drifted toward blue eyes and broad shoulders and thoughts that made her skin feel hot. "Alice Harper," Molly said, applying her mind to the effort. "And should we confront the Heart Club and tell them we know what they're doing?"

Mike's hand dropped to the back of the sofa, almost touching her. "Do we know what they're doing?" He shifted on the sofa to look at her. "I do think we have to talk to the ladies. If they have some crazy idea about getting even with Blackman, we have to put a stop to it."

She looked at his mouth, fascinated by the way his lips seemed to caress the words before they left his mouth. "Do you think that's what they're planning? To get even?"

His finger moved gently back and forth across her shoulder. "There's probably a logical explanation. But I'd like to hear it."

"We can talk to them tomorrow. It's the Friday bridge game." Somehow, they'd moved closer together on the sofa until Molly's thigh was pressed to his. A tiny pulse jumped in her throat.

"We should…" He looked at her mouth and touched her cheek.

"…probably tell them…" Her breath caught and her lips trembled.

"Yes, tell them." His hands smoothed the hair back from her face and his breath joined hers.

She covered his hands with her own and found herself drowning in eyes the color of a stormy sea. "Tell them … yes. Oh, yes."

His mouth covered hers and his kiss was as she had known it would be. Gentle, deliberate, slightly teasing. Then, as her arms stole around his neck, their kiss deepened and became the passionate explosion they had been building toward.

Molly's head arched backward and her eyes closed as he kissed her throat. "Yes, yes," she whispered. Her soft breasts crushed against his chest and his hands were large and warm on her back. "Oh, Mike. Yes."

"Molly." His voice was hoarse against her eyelids. "I've wanted to kiss you from the moment I saw you."

Now she knew what his hair felt like, thick and softer than she had imagined. His jaw was a tiny bit scratchy against her cheek, his lips alternately demanding then gentle. Her hands trembled over his hair, his face, exploring the textures of Mike Randall, the bone and sinew. His shoulders swelled beneath her fingertips and his mouth covered hers, parting her lips with his tongue.

Locked in an embrace, they eased backward until they lay side by side on the deep sofa. Pressed to the warm strength of his body, Molly felt his arousal as strong and as urgent as her own. Wrapping her arms around him, she surrendered to the heated kisses raining over her face, her mouth, her throat. It was as if they had to make up for the hours spent not kissing, not touching.

His large hand moved from her shoulder to her waist to the curve of her hip and pressed her against his body. A soft moan issued from Molly's parted lips as she felt the strength of his need, responded to the mounting passion of her own needs. When he looked into her eyes, the world dropped away and there was nothing left but an island in space, just one man and one woman and a magical melting chemistry that ignited two hearts and bodies.

The phone rang.

And rang and rang with a shrill, insistent tone.

Molly heard it first as if from a vast distance then it grew louder. "Mike?" Her voice was throaty, ragged.

"The telephone is the worst machine ever invented," he murmured against her breast. "Don't go away," he said, his voice hoarse with irritation and desire, as he got to his feet and moved toward the kitchen.

After a moment, Molly swung to a sitting position and touched her fingertips to rosy swollen lips. She straightened her sweater and leaned back on the sofa cushion, waiting for her heart to slow to a normal beat.

If the telephone hadn't rung when it did . . .

She pushed back her hair and covered her eyes. Oh, God, what was she doing? Her life was mapped out, planned. She knew what she wanted and she'd made sacrifices toward that goal. She'd uprooted herself and left family and friends to move to D.C. where the men and the money were. She'd scrimped to buy the right clothes, had cultivated the right friends, everything calculated to move her closer to the life she had chosen for herself.

Was she prepared to throw her dreams away? Could she trade the fantasies of mansions and servants for a cluttered house and gadgets that didn't work? Did she want to spend her life aching for the things she couldn't have? Remembering that once she had had a chance but she'd thrown it all away?

"Wrong number," Mike said, returning to the sofa.

Molly jumped to her feet and stretched in an elaborate yawn. "Will you look at what time it is? I had no idea it was so late." She looked around the room as if searching for her coat and purse though she knew they were in the kitchen. "Well, Mr. Bond," she said brightly, "are you ready to brave the elements and drive this tired spy home?"

He stared at her. "Molly. . ."

"We're agreed then? We'll meet at Gran's about one o'clock and confront the Heart Club with what we know?"

"Molly, what happened while I was gone?"

"There's probably a logical explanation for Alice being at Blackman's and for Jane being—I think I left my things in the kitchen."

He caught her hand and stood beside her. "I'll drive you home if that's what you want," he said slowly, looking into her eyes. "But I thought something wonderful was happening here. I don't want it to end."

"Oh, Mike." She dropped her eyes and pressed her lips together, hiding the tremble. "Don't you see? I'll only end by hurting you."

"I'm a big boy, Molly. Suppose you let me worry about that?"

But the door swung both ways. At the back of her mind was a niggling suspicion that she could be hurt, too. And it could all be avoided, the complications, the possibility for hurt, if she did what she knew was the right thing. The fairest thing for both of them.

"I think I should go home," she said in a low voice. If she stayed, she might never leave. And she would regret it for the rest of her life.

He stood very still. Then he ran his hands up her arms and held her for a moment, gently, quietly. "All right, Molly. Your coat and cap are in the kitchen. I'll warm up the car. And, Molly." He tilted her face up to his. "I'm sorry if I rushed you."

Oh, God. He didn't understand at all.

Chapter Five

Molly was up and out of the house before Gran stirred. Well in advance of the morning traffic, she drove to her gallery and easily found a parking space on the deserted street. There was no reason to be here, she thought, as she unlocked the door and flooded the gallery with light. Ruth would be in all day.

But she knew she couldn't have breakfast with Gran without blurting what she'd learned about the Heart Club's activities. Besides, she felt too restless to take the morning off. Work would take her mind off... things.

But the morning traffic through the gallery was slow and her mind kept returning to last night and Mike Randall. Finally Molly made a sound of disgust and threw on her coat.

"I'll see you Monday," she said to Ruth as she went out the door.

She spent the rest of the morning shopping, window-shopping mostly as she didn't buy anything except a lipstick. But she visited the most exclusive boutiques, shopped the most expensive departments and reminded herself there was more to life than jeans and loafers. There were silks and laces and chiffons as delicate as cobweb. There were silver and china and gleaming brass. She looked at the travel posters pasted across the windows of a travel agency, stroked the dark furs in Lloyds, read the society column in the newspaper over a light lunch.

A glittering wonderful life awaited her. It was all out there. All it took was money, lots and lots of money. And the right man. She couldn't visualize the man in her mind, but she could see her house as clearly as if it rose before her. Stately and serene, polished and smelling of lemon wax. Fresh flowers in Chinese vases. There wouldn't be a speck of dust or clutter; it would look like something out of *House Beautiful* or *Woman's World*. Perfection. She could see Vuitton luggage waiting in a massive foyer, a chauffeur in the Rolls outside and then a flight on a private jet to a penthouse in Monaco.

Molly smiled as she walked back to her car. It was a fantasy courtesy of Hollywood. But it was possible. There were women who lived her dreams, and so could she. All she had to do was marry her millionaire. A man like Randy Aldercamp or Sonny Von Bunman. Or Stavros Polopas. Or the millionaire she hadn't yet met but knew she would. She had it all planned.

Meanwhile, she thought, glancing at her watch, there was the problem with the Heart Club to resolve.

The ladies had assembled when Molly arrived at Gran's house. They were sitting on the sofa, balancing coffee cups on their laps. Gran had set the card table near the bay window and had laid out cards and score pads and the homemade Croupier, but the scene had the look of a stage set and Molly wondered if bridge was actually uppermost in their minds.

Once she had poured herself a cup of Gran's terrific coffee and exchanged greetings, Molly leaned against the kitchen doorway, wondering where Mike was as she studied the ladies with a thoughtful expression.

Beneath springy gray hair they all wore soft grandmotherly colors. Fans of wrinkles crinkled around lightly rouged cheeks and eyes wise with experience. Gladys Price's hands fluttered above an ample breast as she chatted with Alice Harper. Gran and Jane Carter discussed the characters on *Dynasty* with animated gestures, as if the *Dynasty* cast were old friends and badly in need of sage advice.

It was inconceivable that any of these women had ever entertained a thought that was even slightly larcenous.

Molly's gaze lingered on Alice Harper who looked very different today than she had yesterday when dressed in her cleaning lady togs. Today Alice resembled Mrs. Olsen, the kindly older lady who sold coffee on TV. She wore a dove-gray dress with pink collar and cuffs and occasionally reached to fiddle with a hearing aid partially covered by soft white curls.

Jane Carter was the thinnest member of the Heart Club, an upright reed of a woman whom Molly could easily imagine standing sternly erect at the front of a sixth grade class. Unlike the others, Jane had never married, and at first glance her prim carriage suggested the sour disposition associated with spinsters. But Molly knew Jane to be tender-hearted and generous of nature. Her crisp voice and sharp eyes hid a whimsical humor and an incisive intelligence.

Gladys Price, whom Molly considered next, looked enough like Gran to have been Gran's sister. They shared the same pillowy figure and quick laugh; they had both been beauties in their youth and both had married their high school sweethearts. Gladys read as much as Gran but she usually chose romances that reminded her of her salad days and the beaus who had danced around her. She wore a hint of blue shadow on her eyelids and occasionally her teeth clicked when she spoke.

All but Jane had been young wives at the outbreak of World War II and had dutifully tended Victory Gardens and anxiously awaited letters from overseas. Three had raised children and rocked grandchildren on their plump laps. The same three had buried well-loved husbands. All had lived and shared their sorrows and joys and proudly wore their history on softly pleated faces. They had worked for families and churches and charities. They bought cookies from Girl Scouts and dropped their change into the muscular dystrophy box near the grocery checkout stand. They loved Christmas and family holidays.

Molly could no more imagine them involved in a conspiracy than she could imagine the Muppets knocking off Fort Knox. Shaking her head, she looked toward the door as the bell rang, then hastened to admit Mike.

"We have to be wrong," she murmured, closing the door behind him. "Maybe we should forget this."

Then she looked into blue, blue eyes and her breath caught in her throat. For an instant she forgot everything except the thrill of his mouth on her lips and the safety of lying in his arms. An intimate warmth reached out and enfolded her, drawing her toward him like a magnet.

He touched her hair and his fingertips grazed her cheek before he pushed his hands into his pockets. "We didn't imagine anything," he said quietly.

He looked as if he would have said more, but Gran took him by the arm and led him forward, introducing him to Alice and Gladys. Jane beamed proudly when he bent to kiss her on the cheek.

"Where are you going today?" Gran asked cheerfully. She stood beside the card table, straightening the decks of cards.

Mike and Molly exchanged a glance then Mike cleared his throat. "Actually, Molly and I would like to talk to you."

"How nice," Gladys murmured, giving Mike a flirtatious glance. Her teeth clicked slightly as she whispered to Alice, "He reminds me of that fellow—what's his name?—Harrison Ford. So handsome." Gladys lowered one eyelid in a wink that was—well, Molly thought, it was cute.

Suddenly she wanted to take Mike's arm and drag him out of the house before they said something they were certain to regret. This whole idea was ridiculous. They'd made a mistake, that's all there was to it. She gave Mike a nudge with her elbow and inclined her head toward the door. But he wasn't budging.

"Yesterday," Mike began, "Molly and I happened to be in the vicinity of Harry Blackman's house." The ladies looked at each other and their expressions sobered. "We noticed Mrs. Harper entering Blackman's home."

Alice Harper drew a quick breath and covered her lips with arthritic fingers. "Oh, dear," she said, looking at the others.

Molly stepped up beside Mike. There was nothing for it now; they were committed. She exhaled slowly then said, "Later, we happened to be in the vicinity of Blackman's office and we saw Jane. As a member of the Ace Janitorial crew."

Jane looked at Gran. "Rats," she said. Clasping her hands against her skirt, she blinked at Mike and Molly with an expression of a child caught with its hand in the cookie jar.

Then there was silence. A dog barked in the distance. A car passed outside. The wall clock ticked, hesitated, ticked again.

Molly had expected a rush of explanations; she had hoped for an easy solution to the mystery. But no one said anything.

Catching her lower lip between her teeth, she glanced quickly at Mike then spread her hands. "Gran? This can't be a coincidence. Blackman's house and office?"

The members of the Heart Club shifted to gaze at Lucille Pratt, waiting for her to respond. Gran patted Jane's hand absently, then looked at Molly. "Let's see if I understand this. You just happened to be in the vicinity of Harry Blackman's house and later you just happened to be parked outside his office?" The gaze she focused over the glasses perched on the end of her nose indicated that this, too, strained the limits of coincidence.

Gran was nobody's fool, Molly thought with grudging admiration. She knew what Gran was doing, falling back on the old saying: The best defense is a good offense.

"Actually, we didn't just happen to be there," Molly admitted, feeling a rush of color climb her throat. "I wanted to see what Harry Blackman looked like."

Gladys Price bobbed her gray curls in a gesture of understanding. "I'd like to know too. I picture him like those Mafia types on TV. You know, swarthy and all eyebrows and nose, but Alice says he's quite handsome."

Jane sniffed. "Oh, Gladys, you're so man-crazy. You've been man-crazy for fifty years."

"I've had my share of gentlemen callers." Gladys patted her curls and lowered her eyes above a demure smile.

Interested, Alice leaned forward. "Are you still stepping out with Mr. Alderson?"

"Actually I think he's more interested in Lucille than in me." Gladys's soft mouth formed into a pout. "Lucille always did steal my beaus."

Molly's eyebrows soared. Gran hadn't said a word about anyone named Mr. Alderson.

"Poo, Gladys." Gran looked exasperated. She pushed her glasses up her nose with a fluttery gesture. "I play bridge with Mr. Alderson at the senior citizen's center. That's all there is to it.''

"He mentioned having lunch with you at Dickerson's."

"One lunch isn't a romance, for heaven's sake."

"Ladies!" Mike's baritone cut through the room. Stepping backward, he studied them. "I see through this," he said after a moment. They gazed up at him with innocent eyes. Four elderly women daintily balancing cups and saucers on their flowered knees. As harmless as Jell-O pudding. "You're evading an answer."

"You're spying on Harry Blackman, aren't you?" Molly's voice seemed overloud in the sudden silence.

"What did she say?" Alice murmured, pushing her fingers against her hearing aid.

"Spying?" Jane asked in a faint voice. "That's such a strong word."

"Oh my, oh my," Gladys said, looking stricken. Her hands fluttered about her throat like pale birds.

"Hmm. It seems several people were spying on Harry Blackman," Gran said, leveling a shrewd glance at Mike and Molly. But her cushiony breast rose in a deep sigh that told the others the game was up. There was a sudden flurry of hair patting and collar straightening.

"It seems so," Mike agreed. "We've told you why we were at Blackman's. The question is: Why are you ladies cleaning his home and office?"

Jane Carter straightened her spine and clasped her hands in her lap. "Michael, dear. We appreciate your concern, but we'd prefer not to involve you in this." The others nodded vigorous agreement. "It could be dangerous."

It was true then. They were spying on Blackman. Molly bit her tongue. She didn't know whether to laugh aloud or to cover her eyes and shake her head in astonishment. What was equally astonishing was the Heart Club's response to

Jane's statement. They were all bobbing their heads in agreement as if it was perfectly reasonable for a fragile-looking woman approaching her seventieth year to speak seriously of a dangerous undertaking.

"Aunt Jane, what could be dangerous? What are you planning?"

Hastily Gran moved across the room and stood between them, patting them both on the arms. "Now, children. We want you to forget about Harry Blackman. He's our problem and we're taking care of it." Behind her, the Heart Club murmured assent.

Molly caught Gran's patting hand and pressed it. "I'm sorry, Gran," she said gently. "But we can't forget about it." Once beyond the shock of having her worst suspicions confirmed, a line of worry had deepened between Molly's eyebrows. "Please, Gran. We're on your side."

"I know, dear. But Jane's right. Harry Blackman is a scoundrel, and this operation could be dangerous. We'd never forgive ourselves if we involved you two in something perilous."

Mike Randall couldn't believe what he was hearing. He expected talk of grandchildren and church socials from women of this age. He didn't expect words like *operation* and *dangerous*. He pushed a hand through his hair and stared at them.

What he saw was four elderly ladies who had previously passed their days doing nothing more adventuresome than baking cookies and taking care of their homes. He found it difficult to reconcile that image with what he was beginning to suspect was true. The Heart Club had declared war on Harry Blackman.

If Mike had thought sending Molly against Blackman was comparable to sending Doris Day against Godzilla, sending the Heart Club would be like dispatching four elderly chicks straight into a fox's den. Harry Blackman would eat them for lunch. He swore softly and dropped into the nearest chair.

Molly was first to gather her wits. She settled herself firmly on the arm of Mike's chair and crossed her arms over her breast. A stubborn Irish expression firmed her chin.

"Ladies," she said quietly, "we can be as obstinate as you can. We aren't leaving until we know what you're planning." When she read the resistance in the Heart Club's closed expressions, she added, "Mike and I agree you've been cheated. It's unfair and unjust. We know you're angry and that you have no recourse."

"No *legal* recourse," Jane corrected gently.

"Agreed." Molly swept a slow glance along the sofa. "But Gran's statement indicates you haven't given up on the problem. So—" she looked at Mike for confirmation "—we must conclude you're planning something illegal."

A sense of detachment similar to a dreaming state had descended upon Molly's mind. Incredibly, she had just accused Gran and her friends of forming an illegal conspiracy. She could hardly believe she had done such a thing. Worse, she believed it.

"Harry Blackman is a cad and a rat," Gladys said primly. "He cheated us. That isn't right."

"He took advantage of us," Alice added. "For shame!"

Gran nodded. "If the law won't help us," she said, appealing to reason. "We have to help ourselves."

Jane Carter had the last word. "Blackman stole our device and swindled us out of a lot of money. That simply won't do. He has to give back our share of the profits." Her tone of voice indicated this was so obviously logical that no one could refute it.

"Ladies, Harry Blackman is not going to share his profits," Mike said. "He isn't going to give you any of the money."

"We know that, dear." Gran beamed at him as if he'd said something especially clever. "We'll have to steal it from him. Just like he stole the Croupier from us." The others nodded, their expressions earnest.

"Good Lord," Molly whispered. In a stroke the world had spun out of reason. Her grandmother, her own grandmother for heaven's sake, was speaking calmly of stealing. Had the universe gone mad? Or was it something weird in the water?

Whatever it was, it had affected her too. Because at the same time as she was feeling disbelief and astonishment, another part of her was experiencing a surge of admiration. Despite her own dark mutterings, Molly had never once seriously considered stealing the money back. But these four women had managed to override seventy years of conditioning and decided on the unthinkable. This was one injustice they didn't intend to accept.

Feeling as if the breath had left her body in a rush, Molly slumped back against the chair and looked at Mike. "Say something. I'm overwhelmed."

"Ladies..." They were looking at him with polite interest as if this was an ordinary conversation. As if they had not just exploded a bomb at his and Molly's feet. "Ladies, you can't be serious. You don't really intend to steal the money."

"Why not?" Alice inquired. She cast an anxious glance toward Gladys. "Did I miss something? Why can't we steal the money back?"

"Turn up your hearing aid, dear," Gladys advised.

"You didn't miss anything, Alice. Don't worry, we'll steal it back, every cent." Gran reached to pat Alice's knee.

Mike regarded them with an incredulous expression. "You can't. You can't do that!"

Jane tasted her coffee. "Why not, dear?"

"Because..." Mike shot a look at Molly then spread his hands. "Well, because you can't. Stealing is illegal."

"Yes, we discussed that thoroughly. But in this case the law is wrong. So you see, it's all right, dear. Besides, we aren't stealing, not really. We're merely retrieving what is rightfully ours."

"There you are. So you and Molly don't need to worry."

Mike and Molly spoke together. "But you could go to jail!"

"Isn't it exciting?" Gladys laced her fingers together and clasped them under a thrilled smile. "Nothing this exciting has happened to us in years!"

Molly covered her eyes. Mike stared at them in disbelief before he tried again. "Ladies, jail isn't an exciting experience. It's... how can I say this? Jail is not a nice place."

Jane pleated her skirt with her fingers while she considered his point. "I'm not entirely sure I agree, Michael. There's no rent in jail. It's warm there, and the food is wholesome and free. I understand jails have good libraries. And jobs. A person could feel useful."

"And, we'd be together, don't forget that," Alice interrupted. "With jails so overcrowded these days, there would always be people around. We'd never be lonely."

"Of course there aren't any gentlemen," Gladys noted. "But they have classes. We could learn new hobbies, improve our minds."

Alice nodded. "And they have TV. We wouldn't have to miss our stories."

"Good God," Mike said, exhaling slowly. "You make jail sound like a vacation resort."

"Now, Michael, we aren't that naive," Gran said briskly. "We've looked into it and we know there are unpleasant elements. The people one meets in jail aren't really the best sort." Molly made a small sound and toppled against Mike's shoulder. "But we've weighed the risks of being apprehended and the consequences if we are. And we've concluded that going to jail wouldn't be all that intolerable if it comes to that."

"And we haven't forgotten our families," Jane added. "In my case, Michael, there's only your father and mother and you to worry about. But as my last name is not the same as yours, if I'm sent to the slammer no one need know about it or be embarrassed unless you spill the beans."

"Lucille and I only had daughters, who are married now and have different last names," Gladys concurred. "So the same situation applies in our cases. As for Alice, her son lives in Alaska, so we don't think he'll be too inconvenienced if the worst happens."

Molly peered at them through the fingers covering her face. "You've thought this out in detail. You actually intend to go through with it."

"Oh, yes, dear. It's the only fair thing," Gran said. "What Harry Blackman did to us isn't right. We can't just forget about it. To let him sail away without protest would imply that injustice is acceptable."

Molly's hand slid to her lap. She couldn't fight that argument. Not when she'd taken such a strong stand in the past. But Gran? And Jane and Alice and Gladys? Setting out to crook a crook? Molly shook her head helplessly. It was just too impossible. "Isn't there some other way?"

"None we can think of, dear."

Mike looked as stunned as Molly. "Well," he said, shaking his head as if to clear it. "How do you plan to do this?"

Now it was the Heart Club's turn to look shocked. "We can't tell you," Gran said promptly. "That would make you accessories."

"If you knew, then you'd be involved," Jane said, frowning. "We don't want that. The two of you are young. You have your whole lives ahead of you. If we go to jail—well, who cares? We've all had long full lives. But if you two went to jail, that would be a tragic loss."

"There's so much ahead for you," Gladys agreed, looking at Molly sitting on the arm of Mike's chair, leaning against him.

Molly straightened. "We're already involved," she pointed out, trying to keep her voice calm and steady. "We know you're planning to steal the money."

Alice's hands flew to her mouth and her eyes widened. "Are you going to turn us over to the coppers?"

"The coppers?" Mike blinked at her. "No, of course not."

"Thank heavens." Alice fell backward on the sofa and fanned her face with a lace handkerchief.

"But Molly's right. Like it or not, we are involved."

"And neither of us will be able to sleep nights thinking about the four of you risking jail. Please," Molly said. "Please tell us what you're planning."

The Heart Club looked at each other uncertainly.

"I think this requires a discussion," Gran announced finally. "Why don't you children take a little walk around the block? When you return, we'll let you know what we've decided."

Without speaking, Mike and Molly stood from the chair and walked toward the coatrack near the door. Molly pulled on her coat and scarf, then looked back to them from the doorway.

Gran was beaming cheerfully at the others. "More coffee, girls? Is anyone ready for lemon cake?"

Shaking her head incredulously, Molly stepped out onto the porch and drew a deep breath of cold frosty air into her lungs. Then, turning blindly, she walked into Mike's arms.

"I'm worried sick," she said, pressing her forehead against his shoulder. "Can you believe this?"

"Not in a million years." He still sounded dazed. "We've been outclassed." His arms closed around her, shielding her from the wind.

Molly stood in the circle of his arms, inhaling the spiced flavor of his after-shave. "I'm glad you're here," she said quietly, leaning on his strength. "I'd hate to be facing this mess alone."

The thought had occurred to her more than once as they had confronted the Heart Club. Oddly, she'd been aware of Mike every single moment even though she could have sworn she was totally focused on the conversation. It was as if tiny antennae had sprouted on her body and were tuned to Mike Randall. Molly knew when he shifted in his seat or changed expression. The invisible antennae waved wildly when he leaned toward her, drooped with disappointment when he moved away. It was the craziest thing.

Mike tilted her face upward and gazed into her eyes. "I'm here, Molly McPherson. And I'm not going away."

She stared into the warmth radiating back at her and wondered if his last words referred to more than the problem with the Heart Club.

Aware that she was enjoying his embrace more than she wanted to, Molly slipped her arm through his and stepped off the porch.

"Well, will they tell us what they're plotting or not? Should we start saving our money to make bail?"

Mike grinned down at her. "Admit it, don't you feel just a tiny bit of admiration for the old girls? You and I were ranting and raving about injustice, but they're prepared to do something about it."

She glared up at him. "Mike, they're dead serious. They're planing to *steal* a lot of money. Your aunt and my grandmother are about to become criminals!"

"But you admire them, don't you?"

Afterward, they couldn't recall what started the laughter. Perhaps it began with an irrepressible twinkle in someone's blue eyes, or a twitch at the corner of someone's Irish mouth. But suddenly they were grinning, and then they were laughing. Laughing harder than either had ever laughed before.

Gasping for breath, Molly collapsed against a tree trunk and held her stomach. "Did you . . . did you hear what Jane said about going to the 'slammer'?" Tears rolled down her face and she wiped at them with a helpless gesture.

"And Alice? Asking if we were going to turn them in to the coppers?"

"Oh, God. This is so awful."

"Terrible."

"Mike, we've got to stop them." Molly tried to speak through the gales of laughter. "It isn't funny, it really isn't."

"Not funny at all." Mike rolled his head across the tree trunk and looked at her, trying to catch his breath. "They're going to . . ." but he couldn't say it.

They fell against each other, laughing hysterically.

Chapter Six

"But what else can we do?" Mike asked when Molly protested, gasping, that it was wrong to laugh. He brushed her hair back from her face, unable to resist touching her. "The situation is ludicrous. Four arthritic elderly ladies are planning a heist, for God's sake. The Heart Club Gang. What else can we do but laugh? It's crazy."

Pushing away from the tree trunk and still smiling, he stepped to the sidewalk and tucked Molly's arm through his, liking the feel of her next to him. He couldn't think of anywhere he'd rather be at this moment than here on this quiet street with Molly McPherson on his arm, her dark Irish eyes still sparkling with traces of laughter.

Enjoying her this much caused him a moment of concern. If he had the sense he thought he had, he'd pull back and keep their relationship loose and casual. Instead, he held her arm close to his body and admitted he was fascinated by her, by the study in contradictions that she presented.

If Molly genuinely was as convinced as she claimed that money was the be-all and end-all, then he doubted she would have been as worried about the Heart Club as she obviously was. She wanted the ladies to have what was rightfully theirs, yes, but she didn't want them to steal for it. Whether she admitted it or not, she was saying there were limits to what one could and should do for the sake of money.

He looked down at her, at her auburn curls flaming in the weak winter sunlight. And he wondered what had happened last night. One minute she'd been vibrant and passionate, returning his kisses with an ardor that had made him want her as he'd wanted no other woman. A few minutes later, she'd been distant and unapproachable. Fire and ice. The tug of one set of needs against another.

"Maybe we should turn them in," Molly said, looking up at him. The amusement faded from her expression as she returned her gaze to the sidewalk and sank her chin in the folds of her scarf. "For their own good."

Returning his thoughts to the current problem, Mike pretended to consider her suggestion. "Could you do it?" he asked gently. "Turn them in?"

Molly pushed her free hand deep in her coat pocket and chewed her lip. "No, I couldn't," she said finally. "Jane, Gladys and Alice have been like family to me. And Gran..." She stared into the distance. "No, that really isn't an option, is it?" Ducking her head, she kicked at a chunk of ice. "What are we going to do?"

"The only thing we can do. We'll persuade them the risk is too great to attempt anything so foolish as a theft." His mind was wandering again. Mike found himself wondering if anyone had ever kissed each of the tiny freckles dusting her nose and cheeks.

"I'm not confident we can persuade them. This isn't a whim, Mike. They didn't decide to crook Blackman on the spur of the moment. They've thought out the problem and have decided to ignore the law. They've considered the possibility of getting caught, and, incredibly, have decided the risk is acceptable." Sunlight rippled through her curls like tiny waves when she shook her head. "I feel as if I'm dreaming. This can't be real."

The situation was real all right. Mike knew his Aunt Jane too well to doubt. When Jane made up her mind to something, she was as intractable and stubborn as the proverbial mule. That's what worried him. He had an uncomfortable suspicion that the Heart Club had dug in its heels and wouldn't be dissuaded.

"The crazy thing is," Molly continued, taking two steps to match his longer stride, "you were right. I do admire them for not letting Harry Blackman get away with swindling them. Part of me wants to cheer. To say: 'Good for you! I hope you get every dime he owes you!'"

"It's time Harry Blackman got his. I admire our Heart Club for being willing to take him on."

They turned the corner and slowed as they approached Gran's front porch. "I just wish it wasn't *our* Heart Club." An anxious note thinned Molly's voice. "When they were talking about jail— Oh, Mike, they don't have the slightest notion what jail's all about."

Halting on the sidewalk, Mike turned and gently cupped her oval face between his palms. The protective instinct he'd felt on first meeting her bloomed to full chivalrous flower. She was beautiful and vulnerable, and he ached to kiss the anxiety trembling along her full parted lips.

"Molly, we're not going to let them go to jail." The rush of protectiveness extended to the women waiting inside Lucille Pratt's modest home.

"But..."

He placed his fingertip across her lips. "If we can't talk them out of this foolishness, we'll..."

"We'll what?"

"I promise you, they won't end in jail." Her small smile against his fingertip felt like a caress.

"I don't know why, Mike," she said, giving him a grateful look, "but hearing you say that makes me feel better." Then she stepped back and her smile altered to a sigh. "Even though I suspect you don't have the faintest idea how to keep that promise."

He laughed. Her faith made him feel ten feet tall. After dropping a quick kiss on her nose, he guided her up the stairs and into Lucille Pratt's living room. "If it becomes necessary, Molly, I'll find a way," he said before he turned to face the Heart Club and his smile turned a shade grim. "Well, ladies?"

Molly looked at him a moment still feeling the touch of his lips on her nose, wishing it had been her mouth. She shook her head and cleared her throat and made herself think about the immediate problem. "Gran?"

A flurry of quick glances passed between the ladies then Gladys's teeth clicked and she wiggled her fingers at Gran. "You tell them, Lucille. You're the hostess."

Lucille Pratt didn't appear enormously pleased to be appointed spokeswoman. "We've decided not to tell you." When Mike and Molly protested, she added quickly, "At least not yet. Frankly, we're divided on the issue. And we don't do anything unless we're in accord."

"The issue seems straightforward enough," Mike commented reasonably. Speaking calmly but firmly, he targeted his appeal to Aunt Jane, but he could see by the obstinate look in her gray eyes that he wasn't gaining ground. As had generations of school children before him, he began to suspect that Jane Carter wasn't open to persuasion.

"It isn't a simple issue," Jane said crisply when he'd finished his speech. "The more you know about the operation, the more deeply you're involved. Some of us wish to spare you and Molly any—'' she searched for an appropriate word ''—inconvenience.''

"Ladies, you must accept that Molly and I are already involved. And we share your outrage, your sense of justice wronged. We applaud your willingness to confront Harry Blackman.'' He spread his hands, wondering what he could say to convince them. "But we sure as hell don't want any of you to wind up in jail. All we're asking is that you share your plans with us. Maybe Molly and I will spot a flaw you might have overlooked.''

"That's what I said,'' Alice sniffed. "The more the merrier. I always say two heads are better than one.''

"That's because you live by clichés, Alice. We've talked about this before.'' Jane frowned at her.

"The reason clichés become clichés in the first place is because there's some truth to them,'' Alice said mildly.

"An interesting point.'' Gran pushed up her glasses. "I've never thought about it that way, but I believe you're right, Alice. So, there you are, Jane.'' Gran gave Jane's sleeve a pat. "Besides, you use clichés yourself.''

"Never.'' Jane blinked and looked appalled.

"Ladies, please.'' Exasperation furrowed Mike's brow. Holding them to the issue was proving nearly impossible. He closed his eyes and pinched the bridge of his nose between two fingers.

Placing a steadying hand on his arm, Molly stepped forward. "All right,'' she said, her voice resigned. "When will you decide if you'll tell us the plan?''

Gran cleared her throat. "We've decided to sleep on it. Then we'll meet in the middle of next week and take a vote.''

"I'll have the film back by then,'' Alice offered. When the Heart Club glared at her, she looked at them in confusion. "Aren't we talking about the film?''

"For pity's sake, Alice! Are you going senile on us?" Jane scowled at the ceiling. "We finished talking about the film twenty minutes ago."

"I swan, Alice, you're getting dingy." Gladys gave her a nudge. "If you weren't so vain, you'd buy a decent hearing aid. That one isn't worth a twiddle."

Alice bristled. "Don't talk to me about being vain, Gladys Price. Not when you had your colors done last fall! Now that's vain. You haven't worn anything but pink since that day!"

"That's not so. I can wear any pastel shade. If you want my advice, you'll have your colors done too. Remember that dress you wore the day Eisenhower was elected?"

"The green crepe?"

"That's the one. You never looked more beautiful in your life. But you haven't worn green since."

Mike blinked. He turned to Molly and looked at her with wide eyes. "I think I'm losing my mind."

"I know the feeling," Molly said. "Gran, ladies, excuse me a minute. Shall we agree to meet here on Wednesday?"

"After Molly and I get off work?" Mike interjected quickly before the time of the meeting could become a discussion point. "About five-thirty?"

"That's fine, dear," Gran said absently. She turned back to Alice with a thoughtful gaze. "I think it was sateen, not crepe. Wasn't it sateen, Jane?"

"It was sateen."

"Did she say sateen? No, it wasn't. It was my dress, for pity's sake, I should know what it was made of. It was green crepe. With pleats that fell to the hem."

Mike cast Molly a wild look. "If you don't get me out of here in two minutes flat, I can't be held responsible for my actions. Is it time for dinner?"

"Close enough." Molly looked at him and laughed. "Come along. There's a nice little German restaurant just around the corner. With strudel that melts in your mouth."

"How about Scotch that goes straight to your head?"

BEYOND THE RESTAURANT'S steamy windows, dusk had descended like a soft blue-gray canopy. The day had passed in a blink, Molly thought. Smiling, she gazed at Mike with affection. Halfway through his second Scotch and water, he didn't look as unsettled now as he had forty minutes ago.

"They love each other, you know," she said. "They've been friends for over forty years. They've seen each other through triumphs and joys, through heart-shattering sorrows."

Flexing his shoulders, Mike relaxed against the chair. When he smiled, it was the easy warm smile that sent tiny shivers up Molly's spine. "Do they always carry on like that?"

"Yes, I guess so," Molly answered, thinking about it. "But it's an affectionate bickering. Their friendship has progressed to honesty. They've passed beyond the need for pretense."

He studied her for a moment, his eyes intent. "How about us, Molly McPherson? Has our friendship progressed to honesty?" There was a teasing quality in his voice, but Molly recognized the serious undertone.

She didn't immediately reply, then she said, "I think our relationship is open enough that we can make this dinner dutch treat." She didn't know how much a patent officer earned, but she doubted Mike's salary approached what she called the gasp-class. In all likelihood she earned as much or more than he did. The thought depressed her.

"If that's what you want," he said, his voice carefully expressionless.

"Even us gold diggers have some scruples."

The remark was not a slip of the tongue. Deliberately Molly reminded Mike—and, more importantly, herself—that despite an undeniable attraction, they were friends. Nothing more.

She wished it didn't have to be that way. There hadn't been a single moment throughout the day when she hadn't been acutely aware of Mike Randall. How he stood, the way his hands moved, the intoxication of his mouth and eyes. Just being with him made her more aware of everything. The air had been sharper and crisper during their walk; the sky had seemed deeper and bluer. The colors in the restaurant were brighter and warmer than she remembered from her last visit. And for the first time in two years, she felt a familiar internal stirring, a yearning to paint again.

And that was a dangerous sign.

There had been other men in Molly's life, none really serious. But there were two with whom she had fleetingly thought she was falling in love. Thus she was no stranger to the warning signals. The heightened sensitivity to color and sensation and the world around her; the intense awareness of another person; the strange expectant tension. Damn. If she hadn't known better, she would have believed she was suffering all the symptoms.

And that was why she had intentionally reminded Mike—and herself—of the plan. When she was with him, the plan mysteriously and annoyingly faded from her mind. And she found herself flirting with the notion of falling for the wrong man. It would be so easy to let down her defenses. But she didn't want that. She'd guarded against a mistake for too many years.

"Tell me something," Mike said. He pushed at the ice in his drink. "What are you going to do with all those millions after you marry your millionaire?"

"I'm going to enjoy them."

"But what does that mean to you?" Curiosity arched along his eyebrow. "A step up in society? Making donations to museums? Sponsoring charity balls? Buying designer clothing? Owning a dozen houses scattered across the globe?" When Molly didn't reply, he leaned forward. "People don't usually want money for its own sake, Molly. They want money for what it will buy. What will it buy that you want so badly?"

She stared at him. He was right, of course. It wasn't the money in itself she sought.

"Money means a lot of things," she said finally, thinking about it. "It means not having to look at price tags. It means having steak in the freezer instead of hamburger. It means your heart doesn't turn over when the bank statement arrives. Most of all, it means security. Never having to worry."

"Rich people don't worry about money, but I imagine they have worries."

"You know what I mean."

"No, I don't think I do. Having money eliminates one type of worry, but it doesn't solve everything."

"It solves enough." Heat flamed in Molly's cheeks.

"Security isn't something you can buy, Molly. It comes from within. It's knowing you're where you belong, with people who love you and whom you love. That's security. It isn't having a fat bank account."

"That's where you're wrong. Look, I don't think we should discuss this any further. Okay?"

A struggle ensued behind Mike's eyes and Molly didn't relax until he gave her a short nod of acquiescence. Relieved, she eased backward and pretended to study the menu. There was no way she could make him understand. Mike had told her he was an only child, he had no experience with hand-me-downs. He didn't know about the insecurity of living among the rich without the money to compete or to be noticed.

That was part of her reason for wanting to marry a millionaire, but it wasn't all. The plan was also tangled up in the fact that she was a woman. Despite the strides made by women, a few things hadn't changed. A woman was still an extension of the man she married. She also married her husband's profession and whatever limitations that profession imposed. A mechanic's wife could expect a mechanic's life-style; a patent officer's wife would have a patent officer's life-style. There was nothing wrong with a mechanic's life-style or that of a patent officer, but Molly wanted more.

And, as she didn't believe in divorce, she was only going to have one chance at the life-style she wanted. Only one chance to reach for the stars.

Was that so wrong? To set her sights high and channel her efforts toward the life she wanted?

She gazed at Mike with a troubled expression. He was a wonderful man, sensitive, caring, bright. He would make a loving husband and, someday, a devoted father. She would have given anything if he'd only had a yacht or two tucked away somewhere.

When she realized neither of them had spoken for an uncomfortable length of time, Molly folded her hands in front of her and sighed. "Didn't you ever want something you couldn't have?" she asked quietly.

"Of course I did. Occasionally I still do." Mike returned her steady gaze, not certain he welcomed a return to the subject that lay so heavily between them. "My family didn't have any money either, not really. My father moved up in the postal service at a steady pace, but I doubt anyone ever got rich working for the postal service. I grew up in a modestly comfortable home with traditional parents who put more emphasis on values than on things."

Before she could express the defensiveness he saw in her eyes, he held up a hand. "I know. I'm sure your family was the same, it's just that your later experiences were different from mine."

Actually their family backgrounds weren't all that different. Mike's family had lived outside Omaha, Nebraska, until Mike was eleven years old. Then his father had accepted the transfer to D.C. Although Molly was correct that Mike hadn't known what it was like to receive hand-me-downs, he'd known the effect of pinching pennies. Life was lived on a different scale in Washington, D.C., than in Omaha, Nebraska. His mother had had to cut corners. He remembered wanting a radio in the worst way and the budget being too tight to provide. He had saved the money from his paper route and had bought the components to build one. Building the radio had begun his lifelong curiosity regarding how things worked.

There were other things he'd wanted that he couldn't have. His mother suffered from allergies, so pets were out. That kind of thing. But instead of looking to the future to provide what was missing, Mike had sought alternatives in the present. If he couldn't buy a radio, he built one. If he couldn't have a dog, he contented himself with the aquarium his folks had given him one Christmas.

"Sometimes the alternative worked out better than the original," he explained. "For instance, when I graduated from high school, I thought I wanted to go to Harvard. But that was financially impossible."

"So you went to M.I.T. instead?"

He nodded. "I won a scholarship there." Mike shrugged and looked at her. "Sure there were things I wanted but couldn't have, Molly. I would have liked to have a couple of brothers or a sister. I wanted to be the starting quarterback instead of a second stringer. Once there was a girl I wanted to marry."

"What happened? With the girl?"

Unless he was mistaken, Molly blushed when she asked the question. It pleased him. "Susan wanted a career before marriage. She went to New York City to conquer the fashion industry. Her life was too fast for me; mine was too slow for her. Eventually we drifted apart." He hadn't thought about Susan in a couple of years. He looked at Molly and realized Susan was genuinely out of his life. The next time someone asked who had been the important women in his life, he suspected he would remember Molly McPherson.

"The point is," he said finally, "we aren't meant to have everything we want. If we did there would be nothing to strive for, nothing to look forward to."

"Well, you have your philosophy, I have mine," Molly said. There was no point in arguing. She arranged a bright smile on her lips and changed the subject. "Did I tell you the painters have finished with my apartment? I'm moving home on Sunday."

"Are you glad?"

This was a safe topic and Molly welcomed it. "I've imposed on Gran for too long. Originally I moved in with her because a pipe broke in the apartment above me. I was only going to stay a week while they repaired the damage. Then, it seemed like a good time to have the apartment painted so I stayed longer." It would be good to get home, but she'd miss Gran. "Gran's very special, a good friend."

"Do you need help? Sunday would—"

"No," Molly interrupted. "I live in Virginia, quite a distance from you. Besides, a friend has already offered. But thanks." Greg Livingston had insisted on volunteering his chauffeur to assist Molly's move.

"I see," Mike said quietly.

Molly clasped her hands tighter. From the stiff set of Mike's jaw, she knew he was feeling the sting of another rejection. Turning, Molly stared outside at the deepening darkness. A lump of frustration lodged in her throat.

She knew she was sending Mike conflicting signals and she hated herself for it. One minute she was melting toward him; the next minute she was deliberately pushing him away. She felt as confused about what she was doing as Mike must feel.

Briefly she considered telling him about Greg, then she dismissed the idea as a bad one. If Mike assumed her friend was a love interest, and that was what his expression indicated, perhaps it was best that way. Once the business with the Heart Club was concluded she and Mike would have no reason to see each other again. They would go their separate ways.

She bit her lip and stared at the menu and tried not to think about it.

GRAN WAS STILL PUTTERING around the kitchen when Molly returned. "You're home early," she said with surprise. "Or did you bring Mike with you?" she asked, peering over Molly's shoulder. When she saw Molly was alone, she said brightly, "Mike's such a nice young man. Everyone said so."

"I suppose he's all right." The offhand remark made Molly feel ashamed of herself. But the last thing she wanted was to have Gran thinking of Mike Randall and Molly McPherson as a couple. She was having enough trouble with that one herself.

Gran glanced at Molly as she stirred two cups of hot chocolate. "He's tall, handsome and he has nice manners. He comes from a good family and he seems wild about you unless I need stronger glasses. That sounds pretty 'all right' to me."

After settling herself at the kitchen table across from Molly, Gran smoothed her housecoat and lifted an encouraging eyebrow that invited confidences. The expression reminded Molly of those long ago years when she had brought Gran her scraped knee or her bruised heart and had found sympathy and understanding.

"Mike's a terrific man," Molly agreed slowly, reluctantly. "He's so many good things. He's solid, bright, funny. He has a smile that..." Molly pushed at the tiny floating marshmallows with her fingertip. "But he doesn't have any money."

"On welfare, is he?" Gran asked, smiling.

"You know what I mean, Gran. He doesn't have any *real* money. He probably earns a decent salary. It's just that he isn't rich. Otherwise..."

Gran removed her glasses and polished them with her handkerchief. "Do you think he drinks too much?"

"What? No, of course not."

"He probably runs around with a lot of loose women."

"I don't think so, he isn't that type of man. Gran...?"

"He's violent then. Has he tried to strike you?"

Molly stared. "Gran, that's preposterous."

"Is he stingy with what money he has?"

"Not at all. We—"

"So, the only problem here is that he doesn't have wads of money." Gran replaced her glasses and folded her arms on the table. "Molly, honey, is lots of money really that important?" she inquired in a gentle voice.

"Oh, Gran." Molly pushed back her hair and closed her eyes. "I'm so tired of scrimping. I've been shopping thrift stores all my life. And I'm so worried about the gallery. Will it succeed or won't it? Will I end up losing it all? There's no safety net, Gran. There never has been. All those years I watched Mom and Dad sitting down every month to pay the bills. Pretending it wasn't a worry, pretending they didn't mind cutting corners. Pretending there was something to fall back on. But there never was. You know that, Gran."

"Your mother never complained. She loves your father. She's happy." Gran tasted the hot chocolate, looked at Molly over the edge of the cup. "What would you do differently if you had a lot of money?"

"I wouldn't cook or clean house, that's for sure," Molly said with a smile. When Gran continued to look at her, she shrugged. "I'd have a big house—paid for—and I'd travel. And I'd build a studio where I could restore old paintings. Not for the money so much, but because I love the thought of restoring something that's about to be lost."

"You've never been in love, have you, honey?"

Was there pity in Gran's soft eyes? Molly shifted uncomfortably. "I've thought I was a couple of times."

Gran patted her hand. "When you love someone, really love them, you don't care about things like big houses or travel. And it's a pleasure to do things for that person. Like cook or clean house."

"You're thinking about Grandpa, aren't you?" Her grandparent's marriage had been a honeymoon that never ended.

"I miss him, yes. But, as a matter of fact, I was thinking about Billy Summerset. Remember Billy?" When Molly smiled, Gran laughed softly. "I remember the Billy summer. You were telling me about Billy Summerset before you unpacked your bags and you were still talking about him when you went out the door to fly back to Vail.''

"You were more patient than I deserved," Molly said, remembering. But Molly had always been able to talk to Gran. When the rest of the world had been too busy or too distracted, there had always been Gran. Gran had never been too busy or too preoccupied. And she had always been just a phone call away.

"There's nothing quite like our first love, Molly. It teaches us a lot." Gran smiled. "Get ready, here comes some unasked-for advice."

"I'm ready," Molly said, returning the smile. Gran's famous unasked-for advice was a longtime joke between them.

"There's nothing as intense or as wonderful as a woman's first love, Molly. Remember Bill? You thought he was the most handsome, the most wonderful boy in the world. You didn't care that he wasn't on the football team or that he wasn't the homecoming king. As I recall, you didn't even notice the acne on his chin, prominent in his photo to those of us with clearer vision. The point is, you saw Billy's good qualities and were willing to overlook any imperfections.

"Unfortunately, we sometimes forget the lessons of childhood as we grow older. First love teaches that we can love someone who is less than perfect. The focus is on loving, not on a pebbled chin or on how well the fellow performs on a football field."

"You're saying love shouldn't depend on good looks or success," Molly said slowly.

"I'm saying the head shouldn't get in the way of the heart. It didn't with your first love. Maybe that's something to remember. If you listened to your heart about Mike Randall, what would it be saying?"

"This sounds like the advice part," Molly said, trying to keep her voice light.

"It is, honey. I'm advising you to listen to your heart. The rest really isn't important."

"I'll think about it. Thanks for listening and for caring, Gran." She swallowed hard and changed the subject, something she had been doing a lot lately. "Gran, about this afternoon—"

"Now, Molly dear, I don't think we should discuss that. I'd much rather talk about your love life."

Molly laughed. But she could be as dogged as Gran. "If for some reason Blackman was persuaded to share his profits," Molly said, phrasing the question as tactfully as she could, "how much money do you think is involved? Can you tell me that much?"

A struggle erupted behind Gran's bright eyes. Finally, she glanced past her shoulder then leaned forward over the cup of chocolate. "Well," she said in a whisper. "We hope to know more soon, but we believe Harry Blackman profited in the range of two hundred and fifty thousand dollars. A fortune. That's fifty thousand dollars for each of us! Can you imagine?"

"Wait a minute," Molly said, frowning. "There's a problem with your arithmetic. Four divided into two hundred and fifty thousand comes out to more than fifty thousand each."

"But you have to divide by five. You're forgetting Harry Blackman's share."

"*What?*"

"Well, dear, fair is fair. After all, Harry Blackman is the one who made the Croupier a success. Without him, we wouldn't have any money at all."

"*With* him, you don't have any money at all! Without him you would have had all the money! Gran, I can't believe this." Molly shook her head and stared at her grandmother. "Blackman is the one who crooked you!"

Gran's cheerful expression was imperturbable. "You're looking at this wrong, Molly dear. If it had been left to the Heart Club, the Croupier would never have been marketed. We didn't have the money for the dies and all those other things they needed to build the units. Harry Blackman must have paid the set-up costs. Therefore, he made a significant contribution. And we mustn't overlook how well he succeeded with the marketing part. So you see, dear, he deserves a fair share of the profits."

"Gran, I'm staggered. Do you realize what you're saying? You're saying Blackman is a full partner!" Molly leaned forward, speaking earnestly. "He's a thief and a blackguard. He *stole* your idea. He took out a patent without your knowledge. He made thousands and thousands of dollars that should have been yours. He doesn't deserve a share of the profits; he deserves twenty years in jail!"

Gran patted her hand. "Fair is fair," she repeated mildly.

"He didn't treat *you* fairly!"

"Two wrongs don't make a right, dear."

"You don't owe him a thing. Do the other ladies know about Blackman's share?"

"Oh my, yes. We never do anything unless we all agree."

Molly's head ached. The day had been endlessly long and numbing. Suddenly she felt exhausted by the effort to convert one shock after another into some sort of logic. A task that was proving increasingly difficult. After swallowing the last of her chocolate, she released a sigh and pushed from the table.

"Well," she said. Gran's expression of determination told her further argument would be futile. It was time to call it quits, at least for tonight. "It's bed for me." Bending, she kissed Gran's soft wrinkled cheek.

"I'm going to miss you, Molly," Gran said quietly. "It's been so nice having you here these last few weeks. I have to confess, I'm glad those pipes broke and the painters have taken so long."

Suddenly tears misted Molly's vision. "I'll miss you too. I love you, Gran," she said, giving her grandmother a fierce hug.

The moment was more emotional than Molly had anticipated and she could easily have turned weepy. But Gran's irrepressible good humor saved them both from tears.

She smoothed Molly's hair and a twinkle sparkled behind her glasses. "Good. Then I'll count on you to write me if I end up in the clink."

"ARE WE A LITTLE PREOCCUPIED today, Molly darling?"

For moving day, Greg Livingston had brought the stretch Rolls. They sat in the back seat sipping champagne while Greg's chauffeur, Tom, carried Molly's luggage and boxes up to her apartment.

"Perhaps a little. Don't you feel a wee bit guilty sitting here drinking Dom Pérignon while poor Tom totes and hauls?"

Greg looked genuinely surprised. "Why ever would I feel guilty? That's what I pay him for. To do the things I don't want to do. More champagne?" She nodded sourly. "My, we are in a testy mood today. Was it leaving Mrs. Pratt?"

"I'll miss Gran." Staring out the Roll's tinted window, Molly watched Tom skirt a patch of dark ice and start up the steps. One of the boxes shifted and knocked his cap to the ground. Molly felt an absurd urge to jump from the car and retrieve Tom's cap before the melting snow wet it through. She released a long low sigh. When she finally married her millionaire, she suspected a period of attitude adjustment would be required.

"You're sure there's nothing else bothering you?" Greg asked, tilting a shrewd eyebrow. "Have you snared a millionaire I don't know about? You have that surly glow that just screams a new romance."

"A surly glow? Do those words go together?"

"Ah, at last I've coaxed a smile from you. And yes, since you asked, those words do go together when applied to a new romance. Those delicious highs, those miserable lows and a surly glow when one isn't sure which is which."

"Thank you, Mr. Livingston, I concede the point. But you're wrong. There's no new romance. Not even an eligible candidate." Molly ducked her head and sipped her champagne.

"I'm glad to hear it, because I've located your Mr. Right. Listen and drool, Molly darling. He's thirty-two, never been married, plays polo like a pro, has a backhand that's the envy of the club, and, yes, he has hair. Ash blond. He's tall, gorgeous, and best of all, he's an only child. The sole heir to the Melton millions. And, I've saved the best for last, I've told him all about you and he's eager to meet you!"

"That's nice," Molly said. She watched Tom emerge from the building and bend to pick up his cap. He regarded the wet stains without expression, then knocked off the loose snow against his uniform pants.

"Nice? Nice, Molly darling?" Greg leaned forward to peer into her face. "You were more enthusiastic about Stavros Polopas. Winthrop Kingsbury Melton the Third is more than nice. He's sensational! If Win Melton isn't Mr. Right, there is no such animal."

"I'm sure he's everything you say, Greg, and I certainly do want to meet him..."

"But?"

"But now isn't the best moment. I'm in the middle of a project that requires a great deal of time and energy. Later would be better. Okay?"

"This doesn't sound like Molly McPherson. Are you feeling well?" He touched her cheek and stared into her eyes. "Darling, a man like Win Melton isn't going to wait and languish. Every debutante and her mother is after this man. Win Melton is a hot ticket. And right now he's hot to meet you. Can't you delay this project of yours?"

Not two minutes earlier Molly had been daydreaming about meeting her millionaire. Now Greg was dangling a very interesting possibility and her response was listless. Didn't she want to meet Winthrop Kingsbury Melton the Third? Of course she did, She wanted to dazzle him and be dazzled by him. She had been waiting all of her life for Winthrop Kingsbury Melton the Third.

"I can't manage it right now," she said. Oh, Lord, that wasn't what she had intended to say. She'd meant to say: "How soon can we get together?" Wetting her lips, Molly tried again. "Let's put him on hold for the moment."

A ghost being had control of her speech. She desperately wanted to arrange a meeting with Win Melton, but the words stuck in her throat and wouldn't emerge.

"You're sure?"

Her mind was shouting "No," but her traitorous mouth formed the words, "I'm sure."

Greg dropped back on the seat and rolled his eyes. "Sometimes, Molly darling, I suspect you aren't cut out for fortune hunting."

"What does that mean," she asked sharply.

"The pursuit of wealth requires a certain craving. A chateaubriand soul."

"And I have a cheeseburger soul? Is that what you're saying?"

He laughed and squeezed her hand. "No, but perhaps you're somewhere in the middle. Maybe an elegant little filet mignon. If we're going to be successful at finding Mr.

Right, you need to elevate your sights. Focus on what's important. And, darling, you must learn to bend a little.''

"If I'm a filet mignon, and you're chateaubriand—what is Win Melton?"

"Grade A, prime," Greg answered, laughing. "Seriously, Molly, you aren't applying yourself wholeheartedly to this pursuit. You have to be willing to devote all your energy, every waking moment. You can't let anything interfere. And it's foolhardy to be as exacting as you've been in the past. My dear, you simply must put your priorities straight."

He was right, of course. But today Greg's advice was depressing. Turning toward Tom's rap on the window, Molly noticed he was wearing the wet cap and his nose was red with cold. Somehow, that was depressing too. Greg pressed a button and the pane rolled down bringing a rush of icy damp air into the car.

"All finished, sir."

Molly leaned across Greg's lap. "Thank you, Tom." He touched the visor of his cap and rounded the car to stand beside her door. "And thank you, Greg. I appreciate your help." If he noticed any gentle sarcasm, he gave no indication.

"My pleasure." He kissed her cheek. "There's an embassy dinner Tuesday evening, I wonder if..."

"Sorry, Greg. I can't manage it."

"Good heavens. What on earth is this project anyway?"

"I'll tell you another time." She tapped on the window and Tom opened the door for her. Bending, she blew Greg a kiss, then hastened up the steps and into the foyer's warmth.

Upstairs, she pulled off her coat and slowly walked through the rooms of her apartment, studying the walls with critical approval. The lingering odor of paint filled her nostrils with a clean pleasant scent.

The deep quiet, however, was not as welcome. She missed the sounds of Gran's stories wailing from the TV, the intriguing sounds Gran made in the kitchen.

There was no noise in her apartment, just a deep quiet. And the sense of being alone.

Why that should dismay her, Molly couldn't comprehend. She enjoyed living alone. And she loved her apartment—the thick cream-colored carpet and warm wine tones of the upholstery. Turning slowly in her living room, she admired the newly painted walls and how well her paintings looked against them. She studied the splashes of greenery, the view of thick woods between the softly draped balcony curtains. Her books, the small pieces of sculpture. It was a lovely room, clean and spare, uncluttered. And somehow empty.

The sense of depression that had begun in Greg's Rolls deepened, annoying because she couldn't identify the cause.

"This is nonsense." Turning, Molly briskly entered her bedroom and brushed past the luggage Tom had placed near her vanity. But before she bent to unpack, she caught a glimpse of herself in the vanity mirror. The woman frowning back at her was the woman who had rejected a date with Winthrop Kingsbury Melton the Third, a man who was very possibly the answer to her prayers. The answer to every woman's prayers from the sound of him.

"You are an idiot, Molly Kathleen McPherson!" she said to the mirror. "You deserve a cheeseburger life."

She glared at her luggage, then on impulse she kicked the nearest bag. Immediately a hot pain shot up her leg. Gasping, she sat hard on the edge of the bed and bent over her foot. It throbbed all the way to her ankle.

"An utter idiot," she said, rocking forward. Finally, she had a good reason to cry.

Chapter Seven

Saturday passed quickly. Mike tinkered with the omelet machine until it was performing reasonably well, then he completed assembling the bicycle in his living room and took it out for a test-drive. The roads were dry and the cold air zipping past his ears blew the cobwebs from his mind. Before he went to bed, he watched David Letterman on TV while he made some adjustments to his perpetual motion machine. The perpetual motion machine amused him as it was practically standard equipment for an inventor. From the beginning of time inventors had been seeking an inexpensive energy source to generate power. In today's world the perpetual motion machine was little more than a toy.

He expected Sunday to be as productive as Saturday had been, but it didn't work out that way. Relaxing with the Sunday *Post* was something Mike ordinarily looked forward to, but today he rushed through the pages and found himself continually glancing at his watch as if he had to be somewhere at a certain time.

After giving up on the *Post*, he brewed more coffee and sipped it while standing in front of the kitchen sink. Beyond the window, a thick stand of hardwoods began at the edge of the lawn and arched around the back of the house. Thin wisps of mist drifted lazily near the tops of the trees; a shallow layer of new snow powdered the ground. It was a good day to build a fire and stay inside.

He looked at his watch and wondered if Molly had completed the move back to her apartment yet.

It shouldn't have surprised him that she had a "friend." She was beautiful, smart and vivacious. A woman like Molly McPherson hadn't lived in a vacuum until Mike met her. He imagined the only nights she spent at home were nights of her own choosing.

Raising his coffee cup to his lips, he stared out the window without really seeing the snowy scene. What puzzled him was the night she had been here. That night they had shared a warmth and intimacy; he couldn't have imagined it. He had felt as if they shared the same thoughts, the same sensations. When she'd wrapped her arms around him and had returned his kisses, he had believed they were embarking on a relationship that would be important to them both.

It had shocked the hell out of him when she had reminded him the next day that nothing had changed. She was committed to finding Mr. Rich and Mike Randall wasn't in the running. If that was true, then why had she played at making love?

She was attracted to him, he felt certain of that much. But in her eyes he lacked the essential ingredient: money. With his usual propensity to break wholes into parts, Mike refined his assessment. What he lacked was ambition, that's what Molly was picking up. And she was right.

That he had been successful with several of his inventions was merely accidental. He hadn't set out to invent an item that would make him rich. His inventions were a result of intellectual curiosity, of seeing a need and filling it.

An ambitious man would have shown more interest in the marketing side than in the inventing side of the process. An ambitious man would have treated the patent office as any other business and would have climbed far beyond examining and issuing patents.

But Mike had no interest in titles and little interest in personal riches. Growing up in a modest home had taught him that people didn't require wealth to be happy. His parents had enjoyed a strong loving marriage; he'd had a secure happy childhood. His childhood home had lacked expensive conveniences, but had been rich in books and magazines. The pursuit of curiosity and intellectual fulfillment had been the guiding factor during his impressionable years, not the pursuit of success as judged by a bank account.

Once the basics were taken care of, money had simply never been that compelling a motivation. Not for his father, not for himself. People were important, and the world around him. It was difficult if not impossible to imagine judging a man's worth based on how much he owned, instead of who and what he was.

This thought brought him back to the enigma that was Molly McPherson. Swearing softly, he rinsed out his cup and decided he wasn't going to discover any answers to the puzzle Molly presented. Not today. What he needed to do was get busy and stay busy. Concentrate on something other than the woman who had scratched his pride.

Lifting a palm-size device from the windowsill, he punched in a number code. "Where are you, Murph? Come in here and let's have a look at you."

With a squeal, speeding wheels shot out of his bedroom and down the hallway, skidded through the living room and slid across the kitchen tiles. Black button eyes looked up at him, a metallic tail wagged.

"How you doing, boy?" Bending, Mike patted the silver head. A tiny felt-cloth tongue pushed against his hand.

He no longer thought of stroking a mechanical dog as anything out of the ordinary. Murph was as real to Mike as a genuine dog. Except Murph didn't have to be fed or walked, didn't make noise and didn't make messes—which was the point of the invention. Murph was the perfect pet for people who wanted a pet but who lived in apartments or condos that didn't allow animals, or who were allergic to fur, or who traveled a lot, or worked long hours and didn't want to leave a pet alone.

At the moment Murph had a head and a tail, but his middle section was an open framework containing a tangle of wires. Eventually, he'd be covered by artificial fur.

"What we need to do is voice activate you," Mike said, absently scratching behind Murph's yarn ears. "A man's dog should come when he's called."

The problem was challenging enough to keep his mind off red-headed women.

MONDAY, MIKE HIRED the patent officer who would replace him. To his surprise he experienced a rush of nostalgia for his cluttered cubicle, a reluctance to leave the patent office now that the process had been put in motion. He'd made good friends here and had enjoyed the work.

In late afternoon he abandoned the effort to concentrate and slapped shut the file he was working on. Leaning backward from his desk, Mike clamped his pencil between his teeth and stared at a point in space. He wondered if he was a millionaire.

Such a question had never before been relevant. As long as he had enough money to pay his bills and play a little, he hadn't thought about his financial worth. But lately, he'd spent more time thinking about money than he had in the preceding ten years.

After a few minutes he reached for the telephone and dialed Roger Bradley, the genius who managed his money.

When Roger came on the line, Mike asked, "How much am I worth? Am I a millionaire?"

Rodger Bradley laughed. "Yes, I'm fine, thank you. And Marian and the kids are doing well."

Mike apologized. "How are you, Rog?"

"Like I said—fine. Want to tell me what this is about?"

"I gave notice at the office and I've hired my replacement. In three weeks I'll be unemployed. It occurs to me it might be wise to make certain I have some means of support."

"Michael, old son, you're going to drive me to an early grave. We reviewed your portfolio two months ago, just after the first of the year." A sigh crackled over the phone wires. "How many years am I going to handle your account before it sinks in that figures go in one of your ears and out the other? For all the attention you paid, we might have been discussing how to move gold bricks to the moon."

Mike chuckled. "Now there's an interesting problem."

"Thank your lucky stars the good Lord looks after fools and crazy inventors. So. What is it you want to know?"

"A belated curiosity. I'd like to know my net worth."

"Believe me, you can afford to quit the patent office. I don't know why you haven't done it before. Let's see, I can have the figures for you in—oh, about a week. Okay?"

"Rog, can you give me a number now?"

"In your bracket that isn't possible. There's accumulating interest, property appreciation—"

"I'm looking for a ball-park figure."

Roger groaned. "Do you know what it does to an accountant's soul to hear a term like 'ball park figure'?" Mike laughed as Roger put down the phone to get his file. "Okay, I've got it." He didn't sound happy.

"Bottom line?"

"As of January thirtieth, your net worth was two million, two hundred and sixty-three thousand dollars and eighty-nine cents." After a moment, he asked, "Mike? Are you there, son?"

"Where did all that money come from?"

A snort of exasperation blew over the line. "I wish to hell you'd find a nice money-mad woman and marry her. Someone who would take your affairs in hand and pay some attention to what makes the world go around."

"Did I earn that? Or have you been doing something brilliant with my account?"

"Both. Okay, here's a brief, a very brief breakdown. The royalties on Shield are earning you about two thousand dollars a day."

"A *day*?"

"Mike, old son. Shield has been on the market for over five years. It's established a firm reputation. Practically every gas station above the Mason-Dixon line uses a carton of Shield a day." Papers rustled. "Okay. The Doodle Game is earning close to three thousand a month—"

"A kid's game is earning that much?"

"You struck a nerve. My kids love it. It's one of the few games on the market where the kids don't have all the thinking and all the imagining done for them. They have to provide the thinking and their imagination can carry them as far as they want to go."

"Is that it?"

"Hell, no. You've got another thousand a month from various other novelty items that are only so-so successes. Like the tomato peeler, the bicycle signal lights and the alarm system for dollhouses. This gives you a yearly income from your inventions of roughly—let's see, about seven hundred and sixty-six thousand dollars."

Mike stared at the wall. He couldn't believe it.

"You have additional investment income from your apartment buildings and office buildings. Plus dividend income from utility stocks and—"

"Rog—Rog? Stop."

"You're glassy-eyed already? We're just getting started."

"Thanks. But you've told me what I wanted to know."

Roger was silent, then he exhaled slowly. "Okay, son. But if I ever draw up a list of my ten most frustrating clients—"

"I know," Mike laughed. "My name will top the list. Say hello to Marian and thank her again for dinner last week. Next time it's my turn."

Two million. Mike pressed backward in his chair and studied the ceiling. He was a bona fide millionaire. He had enough money to quit the patent office. He also had enough money to buy himself a beautiful little redhead with a dynamite figure and a look in her Irish eyes that drove him wild.

What the hell was he thinking? A man didn't buy a wife like he bought a pair of socks. And he for damned sure didn't want a woman on those terms. Snapping his chair forward, he pulled out the next file on the stack.

Then he laughed out loud. Someone was applying for a patent on play money.

That night when he returned home, he paused in the foyer and called. "Murph? Where are you, Murph?"

The lights clicked on, but Mike had expected that. Murph, he wasn't as sure about. But he heard the skid of wheels across the living-room carpet and smiled. Voice activation solved.

"At least you look happy to see me," he said, bending to scratch Murph's yarn ears. "Tonight, old boy, we're going to give you a fur coat." Murphy followed his voice into the kitchen. "You'll be the envy of every woman in D.C. But we aren't going to talk about women tonight. All a man needs is his dog. Right, Murph?''

Murph bumped against Mike's knee, his wheels spinning whenever Mike spoke.

THIN WINTER SUNSHINE slanted through the gallery windows and fell across the parquet flooring. Molly cupped her chin in her hand and studied the lighting with a critical eye. Odd, but she hadn't noticed before that the main room looked cold. Also, she hadn't noticed until now how her heels tapping across the parquet floor sounded like tiny muffled explosions. And finally, she was showing sugary winter scenes. It was all wrong.

The lighting should be brighter and warmer. The parquet should be replaced by carpeting. As for the paintings, the snow scenes were gorgeous, but who was going to duck into her gallery out of a blizzard and buy a snow scene? Now was the time to show portrait studies and warm tropical climes. Anything but a repeat of what lay outside the window. It was time to make some changes if she wanted the gallery to be a success.

Did she want the gallery to be a success? The answer should have been obvious, but it wasn't. Molly loved good art, and owning an art gallery was the closest she could come at the moment to surrounding herself with beautiful things. But owning and operating a business wasn't really what she wanted to do with her life.

What she wanted to do was restore beautiful paintings. The problem was the lag between assignments, the long wait as she built a reputation. And supporting herself while she waited. For that reason, the gallery needed to be a success. For the gallery to be a success, she needed a major overhaul, which required money, which meant she needed more restoration projects. Maybe it was time to quit waiting for the phone to ring and make some calls herself.

Setting her mouth in a determined line, Molly stepped behind the counter and found the number for the Smithsonian. She drew a breath and dialed the phone.

"Mr. Bostwich? This is Molly McPherson. Perhaps you remember me, I restored a Rubens for you before Christmas?"

"Of course I remember, Miss McPherson. Your work was superb."

"Well—" she straightened her spine "—I was wondering if you might have another project for me. You mentioned something about a Monet..."

"After seeing what you did with the Rubens, Miss McPherson, I doubt the Monet would provide much of a challenge."

"I'm not looking for a challenge, Mr. Bostwich, I'm looking for work. Can you tell me about the Monet?" She hoped he didn't hear the pulsebeat thudding in her ears. The chance to work on a Monet would be a dream come true.

"It requires cleaning, and there's a slight fade in the lower left corner that needs retouching. If it doesn't sound too dull, Miss McPherson, you're welcome to the project."

"Thank you. I'm grateful."

"Wonderful, I'm delighted to work with you again. I'll have the painting delivered to your gallery on Monday. Is that agreeable?"

"Monday will be fine." By that time, the business with Gran and the Heart Club would surely be finished and her mind would be free to devote to the Monet and to her future.

Would Mike Randall be as easy to put out of her mind? Probably not, Molly thought with a sigh. Glancing at her watch, she hurried into the back room and ran a comb through her hair and freshened her lipstick.

As she sprayed a mist of perfume behind her ears and on her wrists, she told herself that she was not really disappointed that Mike hadn't phoned. Why should he? And she'd been silly to think he might suggest they meet and drive to Gran's together. What was the point? She'd told him half a dozen times in half a dozen ways that she wasn't interested. The man wasn't a fool. He wasn't masochistic, for heaven's sake.

By the time she guided her car to the curb in front of Gran's house, the others had arrived. After glancing quickly at Mike's car, Molly hurried up the steps and across the porch.

Gran opened the door and enfolded her in a pillowy hug. "The house seems so empty without you," she said next to Molly's ear. "Come in, come in."

The ladies of the Heart Club were sitting along the sofa and love seat that faced the coffee table, smiling and sipping coffee from Gran's second-best cups. They called greetings to Molly and occasionally they glanced at the battered suitcase waiting on top of the coffee table.

Molly acknowledged the greetings, but she only had eyes for Mike. He was leaning in the kitchen doorway, legs crossed at the ankle, chatting with Gran and looking more handsome than a man who was not a millionaire should look. As he'd come directly from work, he was wearing a tweed jacket over dark slacks, and he still had a pencil behind his ear. His hair was tousled as if he'd just run his fingers through it. As Molly watched, he laughed at something Gran said, and the tiny lines fanning from his eyes deepened into crinkles.

Molly turned away as he laughed, noticing the ladies on the sofa smiling and nodding as they watched him. Mike

Randall might not have conquered Molly, but it was clear he'd charmed the Heart Club. She doubted any of them had noticed that Mike hadn't spoken to Molly since she came in. He'd given her a perfunctory nod and then had turned back to his conversation with Gran.

Well, Molly thought, accepting the coffee Jane offered, it was bound to happen sooner or later. She'd put that coolness in his eyes, that's what she had wanted. Only a fool would expect him to keep knocking at her door when she kept slamming it shut.

"Ladies?" Stepping forward, Mike called the meeting to order. The Heart Club beamed at him. "Now that Molly's here, we can get started. What did you decide?"

He stood behind a vacant chair and Molly was tempted to sit in it. So they could present a picture of unity. Regardless of the Heart Club's smiles and the flirtatious glances Gladys fluttered in Mike's direction, she and Mike were temporarily in an adversary position with the Heart Club. She thought it better to put forth a suggestion of solidarity. On the other hand, she could watch his expression from this vantage. While she was trying to decide whether to sit or stand, the meeting was going forward without her. Irritated at herself, Molly focused her attention.

"Tell them, Lucille," Jane said briskly. "Let's get on with it."

Gran pointed her glasses to the suitcase on the coffee table. She cleared her throat, straightened her plump shoulders and spoke in a dramatic tone. "We've decided to tell you our plan."

"Thank God," Mike said. "A wise decision, ladies."

The tension that had been drawing Molly's shoulders, eased. Now she and Mike would have a chance to halt the craziness.

"All right," Mike said smoothly. "We're in this together." His smile caused a flurry of straightened skirts and quick hair pats. He grinned at the suitcase. "You don't have a bomb in there, do you?"

They laughed and nudged each other with their elbows. "Oh my, no," Gladys said. "Those are our files."

"See? I did get the film back in time," Alice crowed.

"You did very well, dear," Gran said. Looking back at Mike and Molly, she snapped up the clasps on the suitcase. "We couldn't very well formulate a plan until we knew something about Harry Blackman. So we decided to pose as cleaning ladies. No one ever pays any attention to cleaning ladies, especially if they're our age."

"I didn't have to pose, Lucille. I clean houses to make a little extra money."

"I didn't mean you, Alice. I meant the rest of us. We took turns cleaning Harry Blackman's office. And we assembled every scrap of information that we could. It's here in our file case." She patted the suitcase. "You and Molly should look through this before we go any further. We think you'll understand why our plan is the only plan that will work."

Mike glanced at Molly then smiled. "Sounds like a good idea."

Bending, Gran flipped up the suitcase lid and stepped back. "There you are. The Blackman files."

Molly peered inside the suitcase then frowned in bewilderment. "Gran? There's nothing in the case but Christmas ornaments."

"Christmas ornaments?" Jane Carter spun the suitcase to face her and made a small sound of disgust. "Lucille, I swear you're getting as dingy as Alice!"

"It can't be the ornaments. I'm sure I—"

"Isn't that the gold angel I gave you when Milt was alive?" Gladys peered into the suitcase with interest. "If I remember right, that was the Christmas of 1975, wasn't it? I remember because—''

''Not now, Gladys.'' Gran snapped shut the suitcase. ''Just a minute, I'll be right back.''

While the Heart Club discussed the Christmas of 1975, Molly looked at Mike, silently applauding his patience. When she realized he wouldn't come to her, she decided she was being foolish and crossed the room to sit on the arm of the chair he was standing behind.

''Did you have a nice weekend?'' she asked.

''Fine, thank you. Did you get moved all right?''

''Yes.''

''You had good weather for it. Cold but not wet.''

''Yes.''

Molly dropped her eyes and bit the inside of her cheek. This is what she had wanted, she reminded herself. Nothing personal. Nothing between them but the situation with the Heart Club. She hadn't wanted intimate glances or anything to remind her that she'd almost made a mistake. But everytime she looked at him, she remembered his hands on her body and the urgency of his lips against her own.

''Here it is. This is the one.'' After placing a smaller suitcase on the coffee table, Gran dusted her hands and bobbed her head toward Molly. ''I'm sorry, they look the same.'' She shrugged. ''You and Mike have a look.''

Carefully not touching, she and Mike knelt before the coffee table and raised the lid of the case. Inside were papers and photos and a ball of pink yarn.

''Well, I swan,'' Gladys said happily. ''I wondered where that yarn had gotten to.'' While Jane rolled her eyes and grimaced, Gladys retrieved the pink yarn and laid it beside her purse. ''I'm making a sweater for my youngest grand-daughter.''

''How old is Truda now?'' Gran asked.

Mike and Molly looked at each other, then by silent assent, they carried the suitcase into the kitchen and spread its contents over the table, away from the chatter of the Heart Club.

For twenty minutes neither of them said anything, then Mike pushed a hand through his hair and said, "This is amazing."

"I wouldn't have believed it. They have photographs of every room in Blackman's house." Molly held one to the light and studied the painting over Harry Blackman's old-fashioned brass bed. "I wonder where Gran keeps her magnifying glass." Standing from the table, she rummaged through the junk drawer.

"Did you take a good look at these papers? They have copies of his bank statements, for God's sake. And the stunner—" Mike tapped his fingers on a perforated page "—they have two pages of blank checks from Blackman's account on the F.B.C. Company. Molly, this is serious."

"They're already in deep trouble, aren't they?" Returning to the table, she positioned the bedroom photo and bent over it with the magnifying glass Gran used to work the Sunday puzzle.

"Damned straight they're in trouble! Are you listening? Blackman is going to miss these checks immediately, if he hasn't already."

"What else have they got among those papers?" Slowly, Molly moved the magnifying glass over the paintings in the photograph, then she set aside the bedroom photo and took up another, carefully scanning the paintings hung over Blackman's living-room sofa.

"What else?" He stared at her bent head then lifted his hands and let them fall. "Copies of letters that don't seem to mean anything, a couple of memos to Blackman's secretary, a grocery list . . ."

Molly lifted her head and glanced at the grocery list. "That's Gran's. Efferdent and lemon polish."

Mike crumpled the grocery list. "There's nothing else that's particularly revealing or important. But the bank statement and the checks—Molly, they're important. And very, very bad."

"How much does Blackman have in his account?" The next photo she examined was, presumably, the reception area at his office. The light was poor in this photograph and she bent nearer with the magnifying glass.

"How much...? Molly, have you heard anything I've said? The Heart Club—your grandmother and my aunt— they have *stolen* four blank checks! They're on their way to a felony. They're already in big-time trouble!"

Molly tapped the magnifying glass against her chin and gave Mike a thoughtful look. "He's a collector. Blackman's got a fortune in art hanging in his house and office." A wistful note crept into her tone. "I'd give a lot to see these paintings."

"You may get the chance. For all we know, our cleaning lady crooks are going to spirit them off his walls." A slightly wild expression clouded his eyes as he touched her wrist. "Molly, will you pay attention? The Heart Club isn't fooling around. They're damned serious about this!"

"We knew that."

"Well, I can't speak for you, but it didn't occur to me that they had progressed beyond the talking stage. But this—" he waved a hand over the papers and photographs "this is step one."

"Blackman must be worth a fortune. Look at this painting in his hallway. That's a Wyeth. And this is a Singer portrait. Do you have any idea what a Singer costs today? And this one—in his den, I think—this is a Whistler."

Mike dug his fingers in his hair. "Molly! For God's sake..."

A brooding expression darkened her eyes. "This bastard didn't need to cheat four old ladies. He's richer than dirt, Mike. He could have paid them four times what the Croupier earned and he'd never have missed the money!" Her hands formed into fists on top of the table and her eyes blazed. "Blackman didn't victimize them because he needed the money. He cheated them for the sheer pleasure of it. Because it was easy. Because they're old and fragile and helpless!"

"What I'm trying to tell you, if you'd only listen, for God's sake, is that the Heart Club is *not* helpless. They've gotten inside Blackman's house and inside his office. They have rifled his papers, photographed his belongings and, Molly, they have stolen his checks." He stared at her flushed face. "Is any of this getting through to you? We've got serious, and I mean very serious, trouble here."

"Good! I hope they take Blackman to the cleaners! I hope they get every dime that's coming to them!"

Mike paused and looked at her. She was magnificent. A halo of fury crackled around her like a nimbus. If someone had told him at that moment that she could move a mountain, he would have believed it. But she was missing the point. "Look, Molly. Let's go over this again."

"Hanging is too good for Harry Blackman!"

"I agree. I'm as enraged about this as you are. And I'd like to see the Heart Club get their money." That was as true as it was true that he wanted to take Molly McPherson into his arms as badly as he'd ever wanted anything. With great difficulty he looked away from her blazing eyes and her full breasts pushed taut against a silk blouse.

"He deserves whatever happens to him!"

"I've got no problem with that, Molly. What's making me crazy with worry is what's going to happen to the Heart Club. These are nice old ladies. They've already been victimized once—can you imagine what it will do to them when they're caught? And they definitely will be caught. Newspaper photos, media ridicule and the rest of their lives in jail? They don't deserve that."

"Mike, what are you saying?"

He flattened his hand on top of the page of checks. "I'm saying we can't—we absolutely cannot—allow them to go through with this." Frustration knotted his jaw as he cut off her protests. "I'd like to see Blackman get what's coming to him as strongly as you would. But I'd rather go to jail myself than see Aunt Jane or your grandmother or Alice and Gladys end their days behind bars. And that's what's going to happen, Molly. You know what this page of checks means as well as I do. And you know they don't have a prayer of getting away with it."

Watching him, Molly's expression softened. He cared so much. She believed him when he said he'd rather face jail himself than shorten the lives of the Heart Club by letting them get caught.

Sighing she dropped her shoulders. "You're right. I hate it, but you're right." At the moment, she felt the solidarity she'd been missing. Right now, she and Mike were a unit, a strength existed between them. She certainly hoped so, because she had a sinking suspicion that she and Mike were all that stood between the Heart Club and an unthinkable future.

"We're agreed then?"

"We talk them out of it and Blackman walks. Dammit. But I guess that's better than the alternative."

Molly's anger burned like a bright hot fire, but in her heart, she held the depressing conviction that Mike was right. The Heart Club's plan was obvious and it wouldn't work. Harry Blackman was going to walk away unscathed. She could hardly bear the thought.

Standing as she did, Mike framed her shoulders between his large warm hands. "We have to be together on this. I know how you feel but we have to set aside our outrage and anger. We have to convince them to forget about Harry Blackman."

Every muscle in Molly's body went rigid with protest. She didn't want to forget about Blackman. She wanted him to pay for what he'd done.

"Molly, you know it's the only thing to do."

He was right. They couldn't in good conscience encourage the Heart Club. Sagging, she slumped forward and pressed her forehead against the rough weave of his jacket.

"I just hate this. Maybe if Blackman had needed the money, but he didn't. There was no reason for him to cheat them, Mike. He could have played fair. And the money would have meant so much to them, it would have made such a difference."

"I know." His arms closed around her. "When Alice said she cleaned houses to make a little extra money, I wanted to tear Harry Blackman into raw pieces. Alice shouldn't have to scrub floors and clean ovens at her age."

Molly closed her eyes and wished she could stay within the protection of Mike's arms. She wished she could wave a magic wand and Harry Blackman would be behind bars and the Heart Club would have their money and justice would be served. And, as long as she was wishing, she wished she'd win the Irish Sweepstakes for a trillion dollars and then it wouldn't matter if Mike Randall was a patent officer and an inventor who invented useless things like electric ladders and omelet machines.

Stepping backward, Mike tilted her chin and gazed into her eyes. Molly's heart accelerated and she thought he would kiss her and, heaven help her, she wanted him to. Whatever had happened between them the night she visited his house had stamped an indelible impression on her mind. At odd times throughout the day or evening, she found herself thinking about Mike Randall and remembering how her body had come alive in his arms. As no other man had aroused her to such sensuality she sometimes wondered if she'd embellished the memory in her thoughts. Her gaze dropped to Mike's mouth and she leaned forward, her lips parting.

He looked at her for a long moment as if struggling with himself. But he didn't kiss her. "If ever there was a time to be persuasive, this is it. Are you ready?" When she nodded, concealing her disappointment, he smiled down at her. "All right. Let's go hear the worst from the Mafia's junior league."

When they entered the living room, the Heart Club looked up expectantly, interrupting a lively discussion regarding the merits of store-bought cookies versus home baked. Molly couldn't conceive of them sitting in this same spot, politely balancing coffee cups, plotting a theft.

"Well, ladies, what's the plan?" Mike asked.

He and Molly stood together. Without being aware that she did so, Molly took his hand and gripped it.

Jane's thin eyebrows lifted in surprise. "Isn't it obvious?"

"We thought you'd see it right away," Gladys said, disappointed.

"I think they do." Gran pursed her mouth and regarded them through the glasses on the end of her nose.

"Isn't it thrilling?" Alice smiled and tapped her fingers against her hearing aid. "The first thing I'm going to do with my share is get a new aid."

Molly released a long breath. "We aren't going to believe this until we hear it from you."

"Didn't you see the blank checks?" Jane asked.

"It's simple really. We're going to write ourselves checks for fifty thousand dollars each." Gran looked to the others for affirmation and they returned pleased nods. "We have Harry Blackman's signature on a memo and Gladys has been practicing copies. Gladys can write Harry Blackman's name as well as he can."

"It's a fair likeness if I do say so." Gladys placed a hand on her ample bosom, trying to look modest.

"Now, there's something you should know," Jane said in her sternest school teacher voice. "We've discussed this and we agree that it's useless for you to try to talk us out of this. We know that's what you hope to do. But it would be a waste of your time."

Gran nodded. "We appreciate your concern, but we've made up our minds."

"We won't be budged."

"Fudge?" Alice brightened. "Are we going to have fudge?"

"Oh, Lord." Mike covered his eyes with his fingertips.

Molly leaned against him and briefly closed her eyes. Then she gazed at him with a helpless expression. "Pray for inspiration," she said. "This isn't looking good."

Chapter Eight

Nothing they said penetrated the Heart Club's stubborn optimism. First Mike spoke while Molly paced behind him, then she spoke while he paced, then Mike tried again, then Molly tried.

Gladys fished her knitting needles from the bottom of her purse and settled the pink yarn next to the sofa arm. Alice wandered toward the kitchen and returned with a fresh pot of coffee.

"Excuse me, dear," she said, interrupting Molly's appeal. "Can I warm your cup for you?"

"What?" Molly blinked then threw up her hands and cast Mike a despairing look. "I don't know what else to say."

"You did fine, dear." Gran beamed. "That was a nice speech. Wasn't it, girls?"

They agreed it was a nice speech.

"Now it's our turn to talk." Jane straightened in the chair by the window where she'd been listening with polite interest. "You've made some telling points, excellent points in fact, but you've arrived at an incorrect conclusion. Our plan will succeed." The others nodded support. As they had been for forty years, the Heart Club was in full accord. They knew the source of their strength—each other—and they weren't budging.

Mike dropped into the nearest chair, his hands dangling from the arms. An hour ago he'd removed his jacket and yanked his tie to one side, a lock of hair had fallen forward across his forehead. Molly shoved his hand out of the way and collapsed on the arm of the same chair. She suspected she looked as frazzled and defeated as Mike did.

In contrast, the ladies were as fresh and unruffled as spring flowers. They appeared relaxed, not a gray hair out of place. Gladys had happily created about three feet of pink scarf, Alice had taken it upon herself to see that the coffee didn't fall below a certain level. Gran and Jane wore the immodestly proud expressions of two aging hens whose chicks had performed well.

Reaching inside, Molly found the energy to respond to Jane. "All right, your turn. But I still can't grasp why any of you believe that forging checks will be successful. Harry Blackman is going to discover the missing checks. Maybe he already has. At any rate, he'll put a stop payment on the missing numbers."

"Exactly so. That's why we have to strike fast."

"That's a cliché, Alice." Jane disapproved.

"But we do have to act fast," Gran said. "We did agree, Jane. More cookies, anyone?"

Mike roused himself. "Either Blackman will stop payment on the checks or he'll close the account. That's a fact." He waved a limp hand. "No, no more cookies, thank you."

"Precisely the point," Jane said as if Mike had scored for their side. The others beamed at her. "We have to clean out the account before Blackman does. But the situation is not as dire as it appears, Michael. We took the checks from the last page of his checkbook." Her faded eyes sparkled. "Do *you* know the numbers on the last checks in *your* checkbook? Would you notice if a couple of checks were missing?"

"I swan, Jane," Gladys said admiringly. "Aren't you just the cleverest thing?"

"So there you are," Gran said reasonably. "The checks aren't a concern. And we know he can cover them. Blackman has two hundred and sixty thousand dollars in his money market fund."

"We know the checks won't bounce."

"We wouldn't have done it if the checks would bounce." Alice looked at Molly. "We wouldn't want Mr. Blackman to be charged a bad check fee. That wouldn't be fair."

Gladys glanced up from her knitting. "We're trying to be as fair about this as possible given the fact that Harry Blackman cheated us. And it isn't like we're doing anything wrong."

"Ladies." Mike lifted his head from the back of the chair. "The law isn't going to see it that way. The police are going to see an open and shut case of forgery. Clean and simple. I promise you this isn't going to work. All of you will go to jail."

"Don't pass Go, don't collect two hundred thousand dollars," Gran said with a chuckle. Even Jane smiled.

A pleading note thinned Molly's voice. "Gran, please listen. Mike's right. The minute Blackman hears from his bank that four checks for fifty thousand dollars have cleared his account—assuming Gladys's forgery is good enough to clear—he'll phone the police."

"No, he won't." Bright eyes twinkled above Gran's glasses. "That's the beauty of the plan. Tell them, Jane."

Jane leaned over the coffee cup on her knees, her expression eager. "You see, the checks will be drawn to cash. We wouldn't use our names, of course. But the minute he totals the amount—" she looked at the others, drawing out the dramatic suspense "—he'll know it was us!"

Gladys closed her eyes over an excited smile. "Isn't that a master stroke?" she asked happily.

"Nothing this exciting has happened in years," Alice agreed, her face lighting.

"It makes a body feel useful again." A wistful look softened Gran's eyes. "I just wish Corwin was there to share the fun and excitement."

"I can't believe it," Molly whispered, turning to stare at Mike. He looked as thunderstruck as she felt. "Say something."

"Ladies, hold on a minute. Do I understand this? You *want* Blackman to know you clipped him for the money? Don't you realize you're practically begging him to have you arrested?"

"No, no, dear. You aren't thinking this through," Jane admonished.

"They haven't had as long as we have to think about it." Gran's protective instincts flare to the surface.

"I wasn't criticizing, Lucille, I'm merely pointing out the obvious. We found an accounting sheet for the F.B.C. Company. The date was smudged by coffee grounds, but it's a fair guess it was a recent accounting. As nearly as we can determine from the figures, minus the smudges, the profit stands at about two hundred and fifty thousand dollars."

"So," Gran interrupted, "when we take the fifty thousand each that we're owed—"

"I want to tell this, Lucille. We agreed." Jane took up the story after Gran had apologized. "Harry Blackman will put two and two together and he'll know it was us by the amount."

Molly sighed. "You're figuring that he'll know you cut him in for a full share? And that's why you only took fifty thousand each?"

"Well, of course, dear. He's a businessman. And that's the beauty of the plan. Not only will he know we've been avenged, but it's our protection. That's why we don't have to worry about going to jail!"

Mike peered at them. "Am I missing something here? Suppose for a moment that you're right." The thought dazed him. "How in the hell does that protect you from arrest? If Blackman knows it's you who've crooked him, why wouldn't he have the police at your doors in five minutes flat?"

They gave him pitying looks.

"Because, dear, he knows in his heart that he owes us the money."

"He'd be too ashamed to call the police. He'd have to admit what a scoundrel he's been."

"How can he complain about us taking our own money?"

"It's not like we cheated him out of a share."

"So you see," Jane said, capping the explanations, "we're perfectly safe. You don't have to worry about a thing." Her thin chest puffed out in pride.

"Gran," Molly said after a moment, "I think you're right. Mike and I haven't had long enough to study the situation. Could you give us some time to think about this before you do anything?" Stalling wasn't much, but it was all they had.

When the Heart Club's reluctance to delay became apparent, Mike held up his hands. "Ladies, will you agree to this much? Will you agree to delay one week? We need time to assure ourselves your plan is workable." By effort of will he didn't indicate he thought their plan was as nutty as the cookies. "One week, that's all we're asking."

The Heart Club exchanged unhappy glances then Gran relented. "Well, I suppose a week won't spoil anything."

"It makes me no never-mind," Gladys finally agreed, her teeth clicking.

Weak with relief, Molly let Mike help her on with her coat and after calling goodbyes, they stepped outside onto Gran's porch. She drew a long frosty breath and held it. "We got exactly nowhere."

"You can say that again. Everything we said bounced off them like bullets off a flak jacket!"

"Oh, God, don't say that. I keep imagining them being rounded up by huge policemen with drawn guns." She gave him a worried look. "They think that crazy plan will succeed. Oh, Mike, they're really going to do this, aren't they?"

"You're damned right they're going to do it. And they're having the time of their lives. They honestly don't think they're doing anything wrong." He pushed a hand through his hair.

"As sure as we're standing here, they're going to get caught. I can hardly bear to think about it."

They glanced back at the house then looked at each other. "Look," Mike said, pushing his hands into his pockets. "I think we could stand a break from this. I have tickets to the symphony—would you like to go?"

Molly hesitated only a moment before nodding her head. "That sounds like a wonderful idea."

But the time had gotten away from them and they arrived after the doors had closed and the symphony had started. The lobby was deserted. "This just isn't our day," Molly said, her shoulders sagging.

Taking her by the elbow, Mike led her to the deep chairs near the punch bowl at the west of the lobby. In a moment he had returned with two cups of wine punch. "We'll wait for the intermission. Meanwhile, the rule for the rest of the evening is: no more talk about the Heart Club. Agreed?"

Molly looked up at him, wondering when he'd straightened his tie and how he could look so refreshed after the session with the Heart Club. She tasted the wine punch and tried to put everything out of her mind. "Do you come here often?" Curiosity lay along the brow she raised.

"I have season tickets." In the car she had done something to her hair and had freshened her lipstick. Mike gazed at her and thought she was the most beautiful woman he'd seen. "Music is like machinery, it progresses in an orderly fashion." Her smile pleased him. "I'll admit I'm not a fan of most modern music and the logic of jazz escapes me. But I never get tired of the classics."

"What period do you prefer?"

"Baroque," he said promptly. "But I admit to an occasional secret craving for Wagner and Beethoven. How about you?" It was all he could manage not to stare at her crossed legs. For a petite woman, she had exceptionally long lovely legs. It was difficult to keep his mind on the conversation.

Her smile seemed to illuminate the lobby. "I've never heard music compared to machinery or thought much about jazz in terms of logic." She admitted the Baroque period was also her favorite and they discussed music and composers for several minutes. Then a teasing look came into her eyes. "If you think music is like machinery I'm surprised you haven't written a sonata."

He laughed. "As a matter of fact, I tried it once. Randall's étude in E flat minor. It was dismal."

"You're an amazing man, Mike Randall," Molly said softly.

"What do you like to do in your spare time?" The subdued lighting made her skin look like polished ivory. About the time he believed he might possibly put this woman out of his system, she looked at him with those melting chocolate-brown eyes and his chest tightened.

"I like to read. Art books, mostly. And I play a little tennis, a little golf. That kind of thing. You look like an athlete—do you golf or play tennis?"

"Some. But I'm more interested in scuba diving and white water rafting. Once a year I take a dive trip to the Bahamas. If I can manage time for a second trip, it's Colorado for the white water."

"Do you always look at people like there was nothing else in the room?" she asked suddenly. A flare of pink colored her cheeks.

"Am I making you uncomfortable?" As far as he was concerned there really wasn't anything or anyone else in the lobby except Molly McPherson. He would have said so except the auditorium doors swung open and the lobby filled with chattering people.

Molly stood and placed her small hand on his wrist. "I'm sorry, Mike, but I'm really not in the mood for music tonight. Could we take a rain check?" For a moment her gaze lingered on his mouth then lifted to his eyes. "I keep thinking about Gran and the others. We need to talk about it."

"All right." He thought a moment. "Let's pick up your car at your grandmother's then go to my place. It's closest. I'll mix a batch of Randall Specials and we'll talk."

"Oh, Mike, I wish…" But she caught her lip between her teeth and bit off whatever she had intended to say. "Agreed. I'll meet you at your house."

Mike watched her turn on her heel and move through the crush of people crowding the lobby. She had a damned seductive walk. And he wasn't the only man to notice, he thought as he stepped forward to take her arm.

A FULL MOON HAD RISEN in the cold sky by the time they drove into Mike's driveway. Silently, Molly followed Mike inside and she turned left into the kitchen where the martini fixings were. Without bothering to remove her coat, she pulled out a chair and dropped into it with a weary sigh. A sense of depression had arisen during the drive to Mike's house, diminishing the warmth she'd felt with him at the symphony. The problems concerning the Heart Club and her anxiety about Gran had returned in full force.

"I am desperately in need of a Randall Special, a drink so icy and—" She broke off the words as several things happened at once.

First the lights clicked on. At the same moment, Mike started toward her with an alarmed expression. "Wait. Don't move that chair!" From somewhere toward the back of the house she heard a dim whirring noise that grew louder as it sped through the living room.

Before Molly could push out of the chair, a dog shot around the corner and, moving faster than she'd imagined a dog could move, careened toward her at full speed.

A sickening sound horrified Molly as the dog impacted with the chair leg. Springing up, she gasped and covered her mouth as the dog shuddered then toppled on his side and lay still.

He wasn't breathing. "Oh, my God!" she whispered, throwing out a shaking hand to steady herself. The dog just lay there like . . . "Mike . . . I've killed him. I've killed your dog!"

"Murph?" Mike looked down at the dog. "Are you dead, boy?"

"I'm sorry. Oh, Mike, I'm so sorry. I don't know what to say." Molly wrung her hands and chewed her lips. She felt sick inside. "He just . . . he just ran full blast into the chair leg and I . . ." As she spoke the little dog's feet twitched and hope flared in her eyes. But the hope faltered when she noticed nothing else moved and if he was still breathing, his breath was so shallow she couldn't see it. "Oh, God. I feel terrible about this!"

"Hey, don't worry about it. It's okay."

Her mouth dropped and she stared at Mike in disbelief. She was stunned that he was treating this horrible accident so casually. Shock had washed the color from Molly's cheeks, but Mike looked unperturbed. This was a side of Mike Randall that Molly hadn't suspected and didn't want to see. She blinked at him, trying to remember this was the same man who had composed an étude, this man who was looking at his injured dog with such indifference. Shock and a sense of numbing unreality swept her senses.

Kneeling, Mike studied the dog with about as much compassion as he'd shown when he looked at the bottom of the crazy omelet machine. Molly couldn't believe it.

Well, Mike might not care that his dog was injured or dying, but she was distraught. Twisting her hands, Molly peered anxiously over his shoulder. "Is he . . . is he dead?"

"What? Oh, no. He just can't handle a change in the furniture positions. Normally I don't use that chair." Rocking back on his heels, Mike contemplated Murph. "What we need here is a heat sensor and an adjustment to the speed levels."

His insensitivity was too much. Something snapped inside, and Molly screamed down at him. "What are you talking about? That's your dog! His neck is probably broken, he needs help, and all you can do is babble about the heat?"

Everytime she spoke the poor little animal twitched his feet. It was pathetic, heartbreaking. She couldn't comprehend why the sight didn't wring Mike Randall's heart as it did hers. Tears welled in Molly's eyes. "What kind of monster are you?" Shoving him aside, she knelt beside the dog and stretched out trembling fingers in an attempt to offer comfort in his final moments.

Immediately she snatched her hand back. Not only was the dog not breathing, he was already cold. And his fur felt strange.

"I feel queasy," she said in a shaking voice. The minute she spoke, Murph's feet moved. She would have sworn the poor thing was dead. "This is terrible! Terrible!"

Mike beamed at her. To Molly's horror, he wore a grin that was positively indecent in the circumstances. "Molly girl, I think I love you."

"It's true what they say about inventors," she whispered. "You're all crazy." Standing slowly, she started backing toward the door. If she was lucky, she'd get out of here before he flipped entirely.

"You have just paid me the supreme compliment. You think Murph is real, don't you?"

Too late. He'd gone over the edge. The thing to do was to remain calm, Molly told herself. She managed a wobbly smile and attempted to humor him. "He certainly looks real, all right. Yes siree, that dog looks mighty real." She spoke without looking at the poor little animal.

"I couldn't be happier. Come on, Murph, on your feet, boy. You have an admirer."

As Molly gasped, Mike unceremoniously picked Murph up and set him on his feet. Molly pressed against the counter top and her eyes widened into a stare.

"Just a minute." Mike reached for a black box on the edge of the table. "You'll like this." At the sound of his voice, the dog skidded forward and pushed his nose against Mike's knee.

Molly absolutely could not believe her eyes. Seconds before that dog had been nine-tenths in doggy heaven. It hadn't been breathing, she would have bet anything on it.

"First we need to switch from voice activation to remote command. Okay, now watch this."

Speechless, Molly gripped the counter top and watched with disbelief as Murph perked up his ears, tilted his head in an appealing fashion and turned toward her. Leaning back on his hind legs, he lifted furry little wheels in the air, cocked his head adorably and raised shiny black button eyes in Molly's direction.

Wheels. He had wheels instead of paws. And his eyes were black buttons. Molly leaned forward from the counter and stared at him.

"You bastard!" Molly whispered, her breath releasing in a long hiss. "He's not real."

Mike's eyebrows soared in surprise. "Of course he's not real. You didn't think—?"

"Of course I thought he was real! How was I supposed to know he wasn't?" Hot tears blurred her vision. "Why didn't you warn me or say something? How could you do this to me?" Shaking with relief and anger, she covered her face with her hands.

"Molly, I'm sorry. I didn't think...I thought Murph looked real, but I didn't know if anyone else would." Swiftly he crossed to her and gently eased her into his arms. There was nothing more devastating than a woman's tears. "Believe me, I'm sorry. I wouldn't upset you for the world. You're right, I should have warned you."

Arms limp at her sides, Molly sagged against his chest and struggled to halt the embarrassing flow of tears that seemed to spring from a bottomless source. "What kind of person has a mechanical dog, for God's sake?" How could she possibly have guessed?

"At the moment, not many. But someday I hope there'll be thousands."

"How could I know?" The tears ran down her cheeks, unstoppable. "I mean, you go to someone's house and a dog comes racing out and anyone would think...and then it just fell over and...and it kept twitching like..."

"Shh. I know, and I'm sorry." Making soothing sounds deep in his throat, Mike held her close and smoothed her hair back from her wet face.

"I don't know. I just don't know. The whole world has gone crazy." She stood within the circle of his arms, limp and emotionally drained. "My grandmother is planning a forgery, and we can't stop her, and she's going to end up in jail. And you've got crazy machines all over this place that throw things at the ceiling or seem to breathe or tick or zoom into chairs...and I..."

Mike pressed her head against his shoulder and kissed her temple. "You're just upset. It's been a long emotional day." She felt so right in his arms. She fit into the curves of his body like they were matching pieces of a jigsaw puzzle. Her soft warmth melted against him and he felt an immediate stirring. His arms tightened and he inhaled the provocative fragrance of her hair and the faint intoxication of a perfume he still couldn't identify.

"The whole day has been overwhelming. And then your dog—Murph?—he was the last straw." She scrubbed a palm over her eyes. "Damn. I can't quit crying."

"It's all right." Gently, he kissed the tears from the corners of her eyes, tasted salt at the tiny indentation beside her lips. Holding her, he kissed her tenderly, his mouth brushing her lips, his hands warm and gentle on her back. Eventually Mike became aware that her anger and dejection had altered to something else. At some point her arms had stolen around his neck and she was returning his kisses with the same heat he felt building in his thighs.

Moving slightly away from the warm curves molding against his body, Mike gazed down into her eyes, damp dark eyes that looked up at him in passionate surrender. Then her lashes dropped and she was gazing at his lips, lifting her mouth to be kissed again.

He slid his hands inside her coat and cupped her hips, moving her firmly against him before he kissed her with slow, heated deliberation, letting the fire and urgency build as he explored the sweet recesses of her mouth, felt her tongue teasing against his. Her full breasts crushed against his chest as he whispered her name against her lips, as she pressed against his rigid need.

Molly caught a ragged breath and held it as Mike's hand covered her breast with hard warmth, and she arched against his palm. When he spoke her name against her throat, she knew what he was asking and she whispered, "Yes. Oh, yes."

"Are you sure?"

"Yes, yes." When he lifted her in his arms and strode toward his bedroom at the back of the house, she pressed her face into the tanned crease at his neck and deliberately made her mind go blank. She didn't want to think about what they were doing or the consequences. She wanted him, wanted him with a fiery urgency that drove everything else from her thoughts, wanted him with an intensity that sent the blood rocketing through her veins and raised a flush of heat to her breast and cheeks.

She hadn't planned to end in his arms. But when he'd touched her, when his gentle kisses had brushed across her eyelids, the corners of her mouth, a fire had kindled inside. A fire that built to a roar as she became aware of his hands stroking her body and his mouth, his wonderful teasing mouth.

Gently Mike placed her on his bed, and in a moment dim recessed lights spread romantic golden tones through the room. Outside his bedroom window, fat raindrops pattered against wide palm fronds as a tropical storm built and a dark sea swelled beyond the sand dunes.

Palm fronds? A tropical storm?

Lifting on her elbows, Molly stared in bewilderment at the scene and the sound of rain and rising wind. Then Mike's large hands were guiding her coat off her shoulders, fumbling with the buttons on her silk blouse, and she forgot the puzzling scene outside his window, forgot everything but the mounting passion trembling along her body.

"You're so beautiful," he whispered, gazing down at her creamy skin lit by flashes of lightning zigzagging across the tropical sky.

Thunder rolled over the dunes and the spatter of raindrops increased in tempo until they matched the cadence of Molly's racing heart. Closing her eyes, she arched her head backward into the softness of the pillow and offered her trembling body to the fire of his caresses, feeling the ache of wanting him as his hands slid over her and found the secret places that made her gasp with pleasure.

"Oh, Mike," she whispered, her voice ragged with desire.

His tongue circled her nipples until they hardened beneath his teasing lips. Then his mouth explored further, dropping to taste her flat stomach and then lower to her very center. When Molly could no longer bear the tension racing over her skin like heat lightning, she placed trembling hands on his naked shoulders and drew him up to her lips, eagerly smothering his mouth beneath fiery kisses as her body arched upward to meet his thrust.

And then he was filling her and she cried out with joy as her body enclosed him and drew him deeper inside. As the storm over the dunes built toward a crescendo, they found their own unique rhythm and surrendered to a passion as furious and as demanding as the wind and rain battering the windowpanes. First they teased each other, hands touching then withdrawing, lips murmuring endearments near tendrils of damp hair. Then the pace accelerated, tracking the storm outside, until they came together with a desire neither could have halted, a passion as unrelenting and as intimate as nature itself.

A roaring sounded in Molly's ears, her body was on fire, then the universe exploded through her and her world narrowed to two shining blue eyes inches above her own, eyes as stormy and alive as the tossing seas.

After the trembling passed, she closed her arms around him and smiled as his head dropped to her shoulder. As they waited for their breathing to return to a normal level, Molly pillowed her head on Mike's shoulder and watched the storm abate. Gentle raindrops dripped from the palm fronds. The sea had ceased its stormy tossing and rolled up onto the sand, pebbled by tiny raindrops.

"Mike?" A baffled frown appeared between her eyes. "How were we transported from snowy Washington to a tropical island?"

Smiling, he roused himself from a drowsy contentment and kissed the top of her head. "Like it? I'm going to call it Moodvision." Lifting his hand from her hip, he pointed to a video projector mounted unobtrusively near the ceiling. "It uses a blank wall as a screen. I can give you a snowy day or a mountain scene or autumn leaves or rain in the city or—"

"Moodvision?" Rolling her head on the pillow to look at him, Molly said, "You know something? Coming here scares the hell out of me. This is not a normal house. Mechanical dogs, Moodvision, things that tick in the living room..."

Mike laughed then stroked her hair, watching a coppery tendril twine around his finger. "Does it bother you? Really?"

She thought about it. "I'm not sure," she said finally. She supposed one could get used to anything, even computerized dogs. But that thought led her perilously close to asking herself why she was in Mike Randall's bed, still warm and content from their lovemaking. And she wasn't ready for the guilt and self-recrimination she suspected she would feel when she examined that thought.

Pushing the uncomfortable thoughts from her mind, she snuggled back into Mike's arms, pressed her face against his naked shoulder and smiled. The sound of warm tropical raindrops was soothing and pleasant. The quiet aftermath of the storm suited her mood. Cuddled against Mike, her hand playing lightly over his smooth chest, Molly felt as if her bones had melted in the heat of passion. It was a fine lazy feeling.

Mike's hand stroked idly along the curve of her waist and hip. His breath gently stirred her hair. "You're welcome to stay the night. I'd like you to."

But the everyday world intruded. She told him about the Monet that would arrive on Monday to be retouched and how she needed to get into the gallery early and clean up all the loose ends before the Monet arrived. As she didn't know the extent of the painting's damage, she wanted to free her schedule for the next three weeks.

"I'd hoped this business with the Heart Club would be finished by next week. But it doesn't look as if it will be."

He smoothed the frown from between her eyes with his fingertip, and Molly relaxed in his arms. She didn't want to get up and dress and drive home through the snowy darkness. She wanted to remain here, lying spoon-fashioned against Mike Randall's strength and warmth, listening to the gentle patter of raindrops, her legs entwined with his.

"We're going to have to help them, you know," Molly said, smiling against the pillow as she felt his arousal.

"I know." He kissed the tip of her ear, ran his hands along the curve of her shoulders. "The only solution is to come up with a workable plan."

"I think ... that you and I have to do the swindle." Her eyes closed and her lips parted beneath his kiss.

When his mouth released hers, Mike nuzzled her throat and murmured. "An interesting challenge."

Her hands slipped beneath the quilted coverlet and found him and she smiled at his groan of pleasure. Dimly, Molly registered that they had just committed themselves to steal two hundred thousand dollars from Harry Blackman.

"Do you realize what we're saying?" she whispered against his chest, her hands moving over him. His fingers teased her nipples into an aching need.

At this moment, the idea of a swindle seemed so reasonable, so inevitable that Molly felt it had been decided long ago. All they had done was put the decision into words.

Her body melted against his, opening to the concentrated attentions of lovemaking. Then all thought of Harry Blackman and the Heart Club fled her mind. All she could think of was the man holding her and the magic he created with his mouth and body. Later, she told herself, she would sort it all out. Right now, she could think of nothing but the exquisite sensations Mike was creating with his tongue and fingertips, and she moaned softly with pleasure.

MIKE ENCLOSED HER within his arms, listening to the soft sound of her breathing against the darkness. In a moment he would wake her as he'd promised, but not yet. For a while longer he wanted to hold her and imagine what it would be like if he never had to let her go.

He had been involved with several women over the course of the last few years. Susan, Jeanne, a couple more. For a time they had filled a place in his life and he'd enjoyed the relationships. But he'd never fully shared his life with them, not even with Susan whom he'd considered marrying. The idea of Susan attempting a white-water raft trip made him smile. Susan would have worried about messing her hair or getting her designer jeans wet.

But he could easily imagine Molly strapping on a safety vest and climbing into the raft. In the end rafting might not be something she'd choose to do again, but she would try it at least once. Not just to please him, but to satisfy her own curiosity.

Softly, he ran his palm over her naked shoulder and inhaled the fragrance of her hair. After they had made love the second time, Molly had plied him with questions about Murph. What activated Murph? Why did he seem so real? What kind of fur covered his workings?

Such questions were an aphrodisiac to a man like Mike, as seductive as the soft yielding touch of her skin. He smiled into the darkness. Well, almost as seductive. The point was, he knew he could share all aspects of his life with a woman like Molly McPherson. It wouldn't be necessary to hold anything back. If he needed further proof—and he didn't— he had only to think about their lovemaking.

With Molly the lovemaking had extended beyond physical sensation and reaction. He'd experienced a strong emotional response as well. Mike had always tried to be a considerate lover, had always made a point to think of his partner's pleasure as well as his own. But with Molly he hadn't had to remind himself. He'd instinctively wanted to give as much or more than he was receiving. He'd wanted their lovemaking to be as profound for her as it was for him.

He looked at the clock then gently kissed her awake, reluctant to let her go. His bed—and his life—were beginning to seem incomplete without her.

Chapter Nine

The feelings of guilt and self-recrimination appeared as Molly had known they would.

The next few days were among the most confusing she could remember. One moment she found herself humming and smiling at nothing. The next instant she felt as if she'd eaten an anchovy pizza—wretched. Her emotions swung back and forth like a pendulum, and it wasn't difficult to identify the source of the upset.

The night spent in Mike Randall's bed had been wonderful. But she was appalled that she'd gone to bed with him.

Although Molly tried to excuse her weakness as the end result of an emotionally upsetting day, the bottom line was she could have refused. She liked Mike and she didn't want to hurt him; she should have said no.

That was the point she found so confusing—why hadn't she said no? In the past she'd experienced little difficulty identifying unsuitable men and keeping them at arm's distance. But Mike Randall had slipped past her defenses. She sighed and thought of his cobalt eyes, of the way his hair stood up when he pushed his fingers through it, of his cheerful smile. She thought of the way he looked at people, as if no one else existed. And he was marvelous in bed. She hated herself for knowing how wonderful and sexy he looked without clothing, for knowing the taste of his kisses and the touch of his skilled hands.

The guilty truth was that she, who despised injustice, was treating someone unfairly. Not just any someone, but a wonderful man who deserved better. Worse, she couldn't explain why she was behaving so contrarily and so uncharacteristically. Where and when had she lost control of the situation?

Biting her thumbnail, Molly regarded the ringing telephone with a moody frown. This wasn't like her either. To avoid phone calls as she'd been doing for the past three days. And again, it wasn't fair. At the very least she owed Mike some sort of explanation.

The problem was, she couldn't think of an acceptable explanation. Reluctantly, she reached for the ringing phone.

Greg Livingston said hello and Molly eased back on the sofa. "Well, Molly darling? It's been a week. Have you had enough time to reconsider your folly at turning down Win Melton?"

"As a matter of fact, I have." Greg was exactly the tonic she needed to refocus her priorities. "I'd love to meet him." That, she decided was an understatement. She was desperate to meet Win Melton. And she hoped to heaven he was short, blond and black-eyed—nothing like Mike Randall. If fate smiled, Win Melton would be the sort of man with whom she could fall in love at first sight.

"I'm delighted. You had me worried. I'll arrange something for this weekend. There's a dinner dance at the club."

"Greg, did you phone earlier?"

"No, darling, I've left you in dreary solitude to contemplate the dull life of a cheeseburger. Why?"

A weak smile played at the corners of her lips. "No reason." Looking at the winter-bared trees beyond the sliding doors, Molly asked herself why she didn't feel more enthusiastic about meeting Win Melton. "Well then, it's settled," she said, summoning a voice as bright as a plastic apple.

"I'll confirm the date and time as soon as I've talked to Win."

Briefly, they spoke of the latest Washington scandal, Redford's new movie and a bill Greg planned to introduce the next week. Molly mentioned the Smithsonian project and Greg congratulated her. After she'd hung up, she looked at the phone and wondered why she hadn't told him about the Heart Club and Harry Blackman.

When the phone rang again, Molly jumped, scattering pages of the Sunday newspaper off the sofa.

"Greg? That was fast. Are we set for the dinner dance?"

"It's Mike." The ensuing silence was uncomfortable. "I was beginning to worry when you didn't answer your phone."

Molly apologized, wanting to bite her tongue. "I've been busy," she lied. "I haven't been home much and I forgot to put on the answering machine."

Another silence opened during which Molly clenched her teeth and felt guilty as hell. No doubt about it, she'd made a mess of things.

"Molly, we need to talk." Mike's voice was calmer and more reasonable than Molly felt she deserved. "I don't like game playing, and I don't think you do either. So what's going on here?" He paused and she could visualize him pushing a hand through his hair. "Oh, hell, that isn't what I'd planned to say."

"You're right," she answered in a low tone. "Maybe I have been playing games. With both of us." She closed her eyes against the snowy glare slanting through the patio panes. "I'm sorry, Mike. I honestly didn't intend to mislead you."

"What are you saying, Molly? That the other night didn't mean anything? That nothing's changed?"

She heard the tightly controlled anger in his voice and she didn't blame him. She had called his name in the heat of passion, had thrilled to his caresses. With any other woman he would have been right to think there was something between them.

"The other night was wonderful." She responded slowly, searching for the least damaging words. "But it wasn't a commitment. I told you what I want, Mike, and that hasn't changed." Biting her lip, she listened to the silence. "I warned you about getting involved."

The last sounded petulant, as if she was seeking a way to emerge blameless. What he didn't know was she was as confused as he must be.

Molly pressed a hand against the sudden tightness in her chest. Thank God she'd told Greg she would meet Win Melton. Otherwise, she didn't think she could have found the strength to withstand Mike's awful silence.

"I ... I'm sorry if that hurts you." Lord, she sounded cold, and she wasn't a cold person. She tried to soften the words by adding, "Can't we just be friends?"

"Friends don't sleep together."

"I know." Avoiding his calls had been a wise decision. This was terrible. "I shouldn't have stayed, I know that. It's just that ... I ..." But there was no way to explain why her traitorous body had betrayed her when she didn't understand it herself. "Look, I apologize. It won't happen again."

"I see." Another silence stretched endlessly before he spoke again. "People don't matter. That's it, isn't it, Molly? Not you, not me. The only thing that matters is money. Everything else falls in the throwaway category."

"That's not true!" She started to explain, then gave it up and let her voice trail. If he didn't understand her position now, he never would. Trying to explain only succeeded in making her feel small and uncomfortable. "Look, Mike," she finished lamely. "I understand why you're angry. And I apologize. I didn't mean for things to go this far. It just…" She closed her eyes and pressed a hand to her forehead. "It just happened that way. I'm sorry."

If wishes were horses, then beggars would ride. That was one of Gran's favorite sayings. Even so, Molly wished she'd never met Mike Randall. Before walking into his office, her path had been as straight as string. She'd harbored no doubts, had suffered no guilty confusion. She hadn't felt like hell for rejecting a wonderful man whom half the women in American would have loved.

"Molly, there's no need to apologize." It was obvious his words came hard. "You're right. I knew going in how you felt. I'd just hoped that possibly things had changed. But you're a lady who knows her own mind, right? The future is mapped out and nothing is going to deter you from finding Mr. Rich."

Was there bitterness in his tone? Sarcasm? Before Molly could decide, he'd continued speaking.

"Well, then. To business." Now his voice was brisk and cool. "I seem to recall you and I decided we would take over the problem with Blackman. Is that how you remember it?"

She remembered a storm building toward a passionate release. Molly cleared her throat and gave herself a shake. "Yes."

"Then we're agreed that you and I will do the swindle?"

Hearing it stated so baldly gave Molly pause. In the warm aftermath of lovemaking, the idea had seemed reasonable. She had felt that, together, she and Mike were invincible; Harry Blackman was a mere piffle.

"I'm committed to helping the Heart Club and saving them from disaster," she said finally. "But, Mike, I have no idea how to work a swindle. I don't know where to begin."

"By stopping by the library and picking up whatever they have on con-games. By brainstorming. We need a plan by Wednesday, Molly, otherwise, the Heart Club is going to write those checks. Perhaps we should get together tonight and—"

"No," Molly said quickly. She ducked her head and covered her eyes. "I need more time to think about all this. Maybe tomorrow," she added vaguely.

"All right," he said quietly. "But Wednesday is the outside date."

After she hung up the telephone, tears brimmed in her eyes. She wiped them from her eyes with an irritated gesture. "Damn." She wanted to see him. And she wished she'd never met him. Figure that out, she told herself angrily.

For a long moment, she stared at the telephone. Then, with a deep sigh, she leaned over the sofa arm and dialed Greg Livingston.

"Greg? I can't see Win Melton next weekend. I'm in something of a mess right now. The timing is all wrong." The words emerged in a jumbled rush. "I wouldn't be at my best."

Today was a day for silences. It seemed a very long time before Greg said anything. "Molly, talk to me. What's going on with you?"

To her irritation, fresh tears welled in her eyes. "I don't know. I'm just—Greg, is it wrong to want money? To want to travel and live well and . . . and all the rest?"

"Lord, no! Money buys freedom, Molly darling. The freedom to do the things you want to do and the freedom to avoid the things you dislike. There's nothing wrong with wanting that freedom for yourself. Is that what this is all about? Are you feeling guilty because you want the best life can offer?''

"Something like that." Holding the phone away from her head, she wiped at the tears and blew her nose.

"Well, stop this immediately. You have nothing to apologize for. Believe me, there are few people who wouldn't marry money if they could. And you can. You're bright, beautiful and charming. You have all the tickets."

"Thank you, Greg. I needed to hear that."

"What you need is Win Melton."

"I know, he's part of the plan."

"Molly darling, Win Melton *is* the plan. Now, shall I phone him?''

Greg's support made her feel better, but she still wasn't one hundred percent. And there was the business with the Heart Club. Either Molly and Mike retrieved the money or the Heart Club would. And the Heart Club would end squarely in jail, she had no doubt about that. It was also possible that Molly McPherson would end in jail. After all, what did she know about con-games and swindling anyone?

Fair was fair. If she was caught and arrested, she would take her medicine and go to jail. Better her than Gran.

But what would all this do to a romance with Win Melton? Blow it right out of the water, that's what. If the media splashed her picture across the front pages as a swindler, Win Melton would be horrified. He'd be embarrassed by his involvement with her. Maybe he'd deny he knew her. And how would that make her feel?

"Greg, the timing is just terrible. Before I get involved with anyone, I have to find out how this ... project is going to work out."

Unreasonably, she found herself angry at Win Melton for not standing beside her in her time of trouble. How dare he deny that he knew her? Mike Randall would never do such a cowardly thing. Mike was a man she could count on. He was right in the midst of this problem, trying to help and prepared for any consequences.

Good heavens, what was she doing? She'd created a scenario out of thin air about a man she had never met.

"Look, Greg. I do want to meet Win Melton." She just didn't want to meet him in a prison uniform. "But now isn't the right time."

Greg Livingston sighed. "So we put him back on hold." His voice grew heavy with disapproval. "For how long?"

"I should know how this will turn out in about—oh, about three weeks." Surely it would be over by then. They would have the two hundred thousand and justice would have been served, or she and Mike would be talking to a group of lawyers, planning their trial. There was no middle road.

While Molly was washing her face and preparing for bed, she tried to remember any scams she had read about in the newspapers. Unfortunately, the newspapers reported only failed scams. No one ever heard about the successful ones.

Lying in bed, her arms behind her head, she considered the problem. As Mike had predicted, there was a certain challenge. How did one go about retrieving two hundred thousand dollars? There was a way to do it, of that she was certain. And the answer would come to them.

As Mike had predicted...Mike. She ran her hand over the empty side of the bed and thought about him. And tears of confusion welled in her eyes.

MIKE CROSSED HIS ARMS behind his head and stared into the darkness. He'd been too restless to work on his inventions or to watch TV, but he couldn't sleep either.

How many damned times was he going to have to be kicked before he accepted that Molly McPherson wasn't interested? He still couldn't quite believe the things she'd said on the phone. He'd been so positive their lovemaking had meant the same things to her that it had to him. He couldn't understand how he could have been so wrong.

And boy had he been wrong. She had hopped in and out of his bed and nothing whatsoever had changed. Meanwhile his own world had turned upside down. He'd thought about her every waking moment, had gone half-crazy with worry when he couldn't reach her by phone. If she hadn't answered when she did, he would have driven immediately to her apartment.

He was damned glad he hadn't; he would have made a fool of himself. Turning on his side, he stared at the digital glow of the clock, watching the numbers flip.

Who the hell was Greg? For a nightmarish moment he gave in to the blackness of jealousy and imagined Molly dancing in the arms of a handsome millionaire named Greg Somebody. It was the first time in Mike's life that he'd known the torment of jealousy and he didn't like it. It was like a knife blade slicing into his stomach.

"IT'S HERE," Ruth called.

After signing the delivery receipt, Molly carried the box from the Smithsonian into her workroom and carefully removed the packing crate. Her hands were trembling with excitement. When she had positioned the Monet on her easel, she and Ruth stepped backward in awed silence and stared.

"I'd give anything if I could create something like that," Molly breathed, her voice a whisper.

"I'd give anything to own that painting," Ruth sighed. "A Monet. And the colors would be perfect with my living room." She laughed when Molly rolled her eyes. "I'd even settle for a good copy. It's gorgeous."

The painting was a little-known work titled, *Suzanne at Midday*. A softly pretty woman wearing a Victorian suit and hat sat beneath a leafy tree at the edge of a wheat field. The canvas was washed in glorious autumn light, a collage of browns and golds and splashes of russet. Reality was suggested, but there was space for the viewer's fantasies.

Tilting her head, Ruth studied the painting. "How long do we have it?"

"Mr. Bostwich gave me three weeks," Molly answered absently. Approaching the painting, she bent to examine the left corner, running a professional glance over the faded portions. "The deterioration is minimal. Actually, I'm guessing it'll only take about three days for repair."

"I wonder..." Ruth looked at her. "Could you make me a copy? I'd pay you for it." The idea settled in her mind. "Say you will, Molly. You can copy anything. And it's been slow lately in the gallery. Please?"

The request was flattering and challenging. Stepping back, Molly narrowed her eyes and studied the painting. It was a small work. Deceptively simple. She'd copied a Monet in college and discovered the trick lay in capturing the light. She hadn't been able to reproduce Monet's concept of light, not then. She wondered if she could do it now.

"You know," she said slowly, cupping her chin in her hand, staring at the painting. "You may have a terrific idea, Ruth. This might be just what I need to take my mind off... off certain things."

Yes, she decided, this was exactly what she needed. A stimulating project to occupy her thoughts so she wasn't thinking about the Heart Club during every waking moment. Or regretting Mike Randall. Or anticipating Win Melton. Or worrying about her future.

"You've got a deal," she said, feeling a burst of excitement build. She hadn't done any painting in about six months. "I'll do it. But not for payment, as a gift for all the extra hours you've put in lately."

The more Molly thought about the project, the more eager she became to make a start. One of the best things about painting was the focused concentration. When she was straining to place herself inside the original artist's mind, there was no room for the everyday world or for extraneous worries. There was just the canvas and the paint. A scene that filled her thoughts to the exclusion of all else. It was the next best thing to a lobotomy, she thought with a smile.

To Ruth's delight, Molly cleared her schedule before noon, donned her work smock and set up her easel beside the Monet. Working in charcoal, she sketched *Suzanne at Midday* again and again, surprised when Ruth appeared in the doorway, stifling a yawn.

"It's quitting time, boss."

Molly's brow rose and she pushed back her sleeve to look at her watch. "Already?"

Ruth laughed. "You've been at this since midmorning. You didn't touch the sandwiches I brought in for lunch." She leafed through the sketchbook Molly had nearly filled. "You're good, very good." Admiration filled her eyes. "Why don't you do more painting?"

"I lack the genius," Molly said, looking at the Monet. Long ago Molly had recognized she had a magical touch for copy work, which indicated restoration as a logical career. And she was happy with the choice. Giving damaged masters back to the world was something to take pride in. Plus there was money in it. It was her contingency plan in case her millionaire didn't materialize.

"Are you ready to call it a day?" Ruth asked, tugging on her coat and wrapping her scarf around her throat.

"Not quite yet. I think I'll sketch the figure again. I don't have the tilt of her head quite right." Flipping through the pages of her sketchbook, Molly studied the copies she'd made. "I'd like to start experimenting with color tones tomorrow."

It was after midnight by the time she arrived at her apartment. Too tired even to play back the messages on her answering machine, she fell into bed exhausted but happy. She hadn't lost her touch. The sketches were good.

After setting the alarm on the table beside her satin quilt, she read a few chapters of a book she'd checked out of the library, *Famous Swindles*. But she didn't find anything applicable to the Heart Club's problem. Now that she was ready to devote her thoughts to the swindle, her mind went blank. And time was passing.

She hoped Mike was having better luck than she was.

MIKE READ through the weekend, through his lunch hours and read at his desk after work. By Tuesday morning, he felt he knew all there was to know about swindles and human greed. And none of it helped. The classic swindles were either too sophisticated and involved for him and Molly, or too simple for a sharp operator like Harry Blackman.

Tapping his pencil on his desk, Mike contemplated a point in space. Maybe he was approaching this wrong. He'd hoped to find a successful swindle he and Molly could duplicate, but that wasn't proving out. Wiping his mind clear of previous thoughts, he looked for a fresh approach.

All right, what were the talents they had to work with? Jane Carter had been a school teacher; Lucille Pratt baked wonderful cookies; Gladys Price was a whiz with her knitting needles; Alice Harper knew the ins and outs of house-cleaning.

After two minutes reflection, he dismissed the talents of the Heart Club. As far as he knew, there weren't any classic scams involving cookies or knitting. So. Would any of his inventions help? He couldn't think how. That left Molly. She owned an art gallery; Harry Blackman collected art. Was there anything in that connection?

It was the best he could come up with. After glancing at his watch, he stood and straightened his tie. They needed something terrific by this time tomorrow or Aunt Jane and her friends were headed straight toward the slammer.

It wasn't looking good. Frowning, he called out to Carla. "I'm leaving early. Give any calls to Jim. Tell him to save anything he can't handle until tomorrow." Jim Makowski was the man Mike had hired as his replacement.

Preoccupied, he crossed the river and drove to Molly's gallery without noticing the traffic. After finding a parking space, he paused before the paintings displayed in the gallery windows. Good stuff.

A minute later, Ruth poked her head into Molly's workroom. "There's a great-looking guy out here asking for you." She rolled her eyes toward heaven and grinned. "If you don't take him, I will. Boy, will I ever!"

Molly glanced up from the canvas she was priming. "A man? Asking for me?" After cleaning her hands, she cast a look toward her palette then moved reluctantly toward the main gallery.

"Mike?" She looked surprised.

"Didn't you get my message? I left a message on your answering machine that I'd stop by today about two o'clock."

Molly glanced toward Ruth. "Ah, well. Would you like the grand tour?"

"Absolutely."

As she guided him through the gallery, hesitantly explaining the changes she intended to make, Mike watched her from the corner of his eyes. She was wearing a charcoal-streaked smock that swung provocatively across the back of her stockings. At first the smock had surprised him, then he recalled the restoration project for the Smithsonian. Oddly, the shapeless smock aroused him. Perhaps because he knew what lay beneath it. To his irritation, he found himself wanting to kiss the smudge of charcoal that shadowed her cheek.

Recognizing his thoughts, Mike halted before a piece of modern art, looking up at it without seeing. What was it going to take to make him forget this woman? She'd all but told him straight out that he wasn't good enough for her. She'd bounced in and out of his bed, played with his emotions. She'd led him on then slapped him back into line. She was dating someone named Greg, probably a millionaire. Aside from the Heart Club, she had no interest in Mike Randall. None whatsoever, and she'd made that clear whenever she was pressed. So, why was he standing here wishing he could take her in his arms?

Because he loved her.

The realization struck him with the force of a thunderclap. She was a fortune hunter and made no bones about it. She had rejected him half a dozen times. But dammit, he loved her. Staring down at the top of her coppery head, his frown intensified.

He could have Molly McPherson, he knew that. All he had to do was tell her about Shield and his other inventions. Or he could arrange a dinner party with Roger and Marian Bradley and let Rog tease him about his investments. That's all it would take.

It wasn't as if she didn't like him or didn't enjoy his company. She'd made it plain that she did. And they were terrific in bed. Except for their attitudes toward money, they shared the same value system. They could have a good life together.

Except he would never know.

He'd never know if she really cared about him or if he'd bought her. When disagreements arose, he wouldn't know if she stayed with him because their relationship mattered or because he could give her fur coats and gems from Tiffanys, trips to Europe and a big house wherever she wanted to live. The not knowing would drive him crazy and eventually his own love would sour.

No, he thought grimly. His first instincts had been correct. He couldn't tell her about his finances. But keeping silent was the hardest thing he had ever done.

"Mike?" Her fingertips rested lightly on his sleeve and she looked up at him. "Are you all right? Is there something about this painting...?"

He shook his head, putting the future he wanted out of his thoughts. "It's intriguing," he commented, really looking at the painting for the first time.

"And very expensive." Gently, she led him away from the painting toward the back room where she worked.

There was no humor in Mike's laugh. He could have papered his walls with five thousand dollar paintings and would never have missed the money. And he couldn't tell her.

"If you want to see something really splendid, look at this," she said, crossing her workroom to stand beside the Monet. "Isn't it wonderful?"

Of course it was, but what captivated Mike's interest were the dozens of sketches tacked to the edges of the shelves. After glancing at the Monet and murmuring something appropriate, Mike walked slowly around the workroom, studying the charcoal sketches. "Did you do these?"

Molly's cheeks blushed a modest pink. "I'm making a copy of the Monet for Ruth." While Mike continued to examine the sketches, she went on to explain how she didn't excel at original art, but she could copy anything.

"That's hard to believe. You're really good."

"Not good enough to earn a living as an artist," she said, placing the primed canvas on her easel. "But good enough to fake a Monet that Monet himself would swear he'd painted. A strange talent, isn't it?"

"Are you serious?"

"Of course I'm—"

They stared at each other and the smiles faded from their expressions.

"My God!" Molly spun to stare at the Monet and then at her blank canvas.

"It was right there in front of us." An undertone of excitement deepened Mike's voice.

"I can copy anything!"

"You can paint a Monet even Monet would swear was his!"

"That's right." Molly stared hard at *Suzanne at Midday*. "And Blackman is a collector. He'd give his firstborn to get his hands on this painting."

"Which we have. And we'll soon have an excellent forgery."

Molly nodded, her mind racing. "We let him bring in an independent appraiser to appraise the genuine painting..."

"But he actually buys the fake. It's a bait and switch."

They stared at each other, wide grins appearing on their faces. Then Molly gave a shout and threw herself into Mike's arms, laughing as he swung her in a wide circle.

"That's it! We won't have to worry about checks and jail and..."

When Mike set her on her feet, they stood close together and the energy between them escalated to a sudden tension that snapped like heat lightning.

His eyes traveled across the planes and angles of her face; her gaze centered on his wide firm mouth and a weakness stole over her limbs.

"Molly," he said softly. "Beautiful Molly."

But Ruth stepped into the room then, carrying a tray. "Coffee?" she asked as they hastily broke apart. "Oh," Ruth said, pink washing her cheeks. She looked at Molly. "I'm sorry. I didn't realize I was interrupting."

"You're not," Molly said quickly, taking the tray. "Thank you."

When Ruth had departed, Molly chose a stool well across the room from Mike. It was too dangerous to be near him. Gradually her initial euphoria gave way to realism. "Maybe we were a little premature," she said, deliberately not looking at his mouth. "I'm afraid this won't work, Mike."

"Why not?" He studied her with an intent gaze.

"For a lot of reasons." Looking away from the intoxicating warmth in his eyes, Molly tried to focus her thoughts. "First, I can't produce an adequate copy overnight. Even if I could, oil takes weeks to dry thoroughly. I don't think the Heart Club is willing to wait several weeks. The Smithsonian certainly won't wait; they expect the return of the Monet within three weeks." She lifted her shoulders in a shrug, aware of her traitorous body beneath the shapeless smock. "Then there's the problem of the provenance. We don't have one."

"If you can fake the painting, can't you fake the provenance?"

She shook her head. "Forging a provenance would require a different discipline. The provenance traces the history of the painting. And we don't know how much Blackman might know about this painting. If he knows of one previous owner, for instance, and that owner isn't listed on the provenance, he'll spot us as frauds. Besides, there's the aging of the paper, the seals... We simply can't manage it."

"All right, let's put that problem aside for a moment," Mike said finally. "How long would it take you to copy the Monet?"

"Realistically? To the point where the fake would be difficult to spot?" She pressed her knuckles against her chin and considered. "The problem is the slow drying time. A copy artist works by layering. That won't work well unless the coat underneath is dry." She watched him, seeing that he was enjoying the challenge.

"Let's assume for a moment that the paint would dry in a day or so. Then, how long would it take?"

"That's an impossible assumption, Mike."

"Just go with it for a minute."

"Well, if I didn't do anything else... and if a miracle happened that made the paint dry... then I could probably finish in about two weeks."

"If you used the sketches you've already made and began immediately?"

"If the oil dried immediately," she corrected. "Which it won't."

"But if it did, then we'd have a workable deal."

"If—and it's a big if—it worked that way, we'd still be cutting it close, Mike. I only have the real Monet for three weeks less two days."

"But you could do it." Excitement sparkled in his blue eyes and Molly caught her breath at how handsome he was.

With a jolt of insight she realized Mike was a man who would never grow old. His enthusiasm for ideas and challenge would light a youthful glow in his eyes forever. "This will work, Molly, I can feel it."

"Maybe," she said after a hesitation. For an instant the astonishing fact of what they were discussing swept Molly's senses. Then she steadied her hands against her lap and reminded herself they had no choice. And they were acting in the name of justice for all.

"Mike, we have to face up to the fact that the oil won't dry quickly enough." She spread her hands. "Don't misunderstand, I'm not waffling. This is a terrific plan, much better than forging checks. If we had unlimited access to the Monet, we might be able to pull this off. But we're restricted to three weeks at the outside. And it can't be done." She lifted an eyebrow. "Are you paying attention?"

"It shouldn't be that difficult," he said thoughtfully. "All we need is a drying agent that interacts rapidly with oil paint. Something stable that doesn't affect the color tones. Something that applies in a spray, I think, fine enough not to leave an impression on the wet oil, but comprehensive enough to penetrate thoroughly."

Molly's eyes widened. "You're talking about inventing a quick-dry solution. Can you do it?"

"I'm sure going to try. I'll need samples of the paint you'll be using, and the same type and weight of canvas." As he leaned forward, his eyes darkened in concentration. "How long will it be before you need the spray?"

If Mike was successful they might actually have a chance. A reluctant excitement lightened Molly's expression. For the first time she began to believe they might actually save the Heart Club and retrieve the money. "Three days at the latest." But a flicker of doubt tempered her excitement. After all, none of Mike's inventions had been a smashing success.

"Not to worry, Moneypenny. We're on a roll!"

His grin was infectious and Molly smiled. "We have a few crucial details to work out, Mr. Bond."

"Leave the details to me. You just concentrate on painting a Monet for our friend Blackman."

Molly nodded. Ruth would have to wait for her copy.

When Mike had taken the samples she gave him and had departed, Molly glared at the floor tiles. Dammit. Why did he have to be so great-looking? And what was there about his intensity and enthusiasm that drew her? Before she had met Mike she'd never thought of those qualities as being particularly sexy. But she did now.

After releasing a long sigh of irritation, Molly turned her attention to the Monet. The sooner she finished the copy, the sooner the business with the Heart Club would conclude and the sooner she could put Mike Randall behind her and get on with her life. That was what she wanted.

Wasn't it?

Chapter Ten

Dark circles shadowed Mike's eyes and Molly thought he looked tired. She watched him talking to Jane and Alice as she helped Gran pour and serve coffee to the group. Gladys, she noticed, was filling a tablet page with Harry Blackman's signature. Thankfully, there would be no need for Gladys's dubious talents.

At least Molly hoped there wouldn't be. She hadn't had an opportunity for a private word with Mike as they had arrived in separate cars. From the look of the circles under his eyes, he'd stayed up most of the night experimenting with the oils and canvas she'd given him. Surely if he'd had any success, he would have given some sign.

He met her anxious eyes across the room and gave her an encouraging smile. "Well, ladies, shall we call this meeting to order?"

Molly wondered if he'd looked this cheerful on the first go-around with the electric ladder. If she remembered correctly, he'd been confident the omelet demonstration would be successful.

She smothered a sigh as the Heart Club members arranged themselves in their usual places along the sofa. Except Gran, who chose the chair by the window so she could observe Molly's expression.

Molly cleared her throat and clasped her hands in front of her. "We believe we have an alternate plan that is safer than forging checks," she began. When she finished explaining bait and switch and how it would apply to the Monet, she looked at Mike.

"There are still a few details to work out," he said, taking up the story. "Naturally we don't want the forgery traced back to Molly, so we'll arrange the sale through a private party rather than through Molly's gallery. The major problem, as I understand it, is that our success depends largely on whether or not I can develop an agent to quick-dry Molly's copy."

"And, of course, on how good the forgery is. Blackman has to believe the painting we deliver is exactly the same painting he had authenticated. We'll reframe the original in a frame identical to the copy, and that will help with the illusion. Still, I have to produce a copy good enough that Blackman won't suspect he doesn't have the original."

"As to the provenance," Mike said, "I believe we can stall Blackman until his check has cleared. After that point, the provenance won't matter. Eventually he'll realize he's been snookered, but by that time you'll have your money and we'll all be long gone."

"Well?" Molly asked. "What do you think?" When no one spoke, she exchanged a quick uneasy glance with Mike. "Gran?"

"Aunt Jane?"

Gladys was the first to break the silence. She smoothed her palm over the signatures marching down the tablet page. "I know you spent a lot of time and thought on your plan...but, well, I guess I'm a little disappointed." Her eyes were apologetic.

"Disappointed?" Mike's brow lifted in surprise. "You don't think the art switch will succeed?"

"Oh, it will probably work, all right. It's just that...I don't know, I was rather counting on..."

"I think I know what Gladys is trying to say," Gran said gently when Gladys's voice trailed. "I think what she means is that we wanted to handle Harry Blackman ourselves. We saw this as our problem and we saw each of us contributing to the solution." The others nodded soberly. "We never intended to involve anyone else. While the plan with the painting is excellent, it means we're out of the deal, and you and Molly assume all the risk. Frankly, I'm against that."

"I agree," Jane said firmly. "If anyone is going to risk arrest and jail, it should be us. Not you two."

Alice leaned forward. "We were looking forward to cashing the checks, you see. We've already planned our disguises."

"If you and Molly do everything, we won't get to wear our disguises," Gladys agreed.

"Ladies, wait a minute. I appreciate your concern for Molly and me. But that isn't the point." Mike scanned the faces on the sofa. "The objective is not to wear your disguises, the objective is to get the money. The real question is: which plan offers the best chance for success with the least amount of risk?"

Frowning through her glasses, Gran placed her hand on Jane's arm. "We can't let Mike and Molly carry the full burden of culpability."

"I agree, Lucille. On the other hand...it's their choice. They came to us. But it would be better if we share the risk."

Molly interrupted. "Gran, in your heart you must know that forging Blackman's signature is an unwise plan."

"Under our proposal, no one goes to jail." Mike hoped to heaven he was right.

"But we don't get to do anything," Gladys repeated stubbornly, holding the page of signatures to her bosom.

"You did the difficult part," Molly said quickly. "The four of you collected the photographs that told us Blackman is an art collector. Without that piece of information, we wouldn't have thought of the Monet."

"Wait a minute, ladies." Mike considered the members of the Heart Club with a thoughtful expression. "One of you could pose as the individual offering the painting for sale."

After a pointed glance around her living room, Gran smiled. "Do any of us resemble the kind of person who could afford to have a Monet hanging over our sofa? Can you really imagine inviting Harry Blackman here to inspect the painting?"

Mike swept a look around Gran's modest living room. "Regrettably, I think you're right. Any ideas?"

"Possibly," Molly said slowly, thinking it through. The swindle was getting more complicated, but she supposed these things were never simple. "Alice, do you clean houses for anyone else who has good paintings like Blackman does? Houses as large and prestigious as Blackman's?" When Alice looked blank, she repeated the question in a louder tone.

"Oh, yes. My Monday morning and my Thursday afternoon have houses like his. Big ones." She sighed.

"Are your ladies home when you clean their houses?"

"Mrs. White never is. Mrs. Spencer is there sometimes and sometimes not."

"Then, is it fair to assume you have a key to Mrs. White's house?"

Admiration dawned in Mike's eyes. "Moneypenny, you have a talent for larceny. I see where you're going. We have Blackman meet us at Mrs. White's house, where one of the Heart Club members poses as the person who wants to sell the Monet."

"Right." A talent for larceny? That was about as welcome a compliment as if he'd said she had a talent for falling over her own feet.

"Oh, I'm starting to like this," Alice crowed. She pressed her hands together and her eyes sparkled. "Everything depends on me. I'm the one who has the key."

"No, dear, everything depends on the person posing as Mrs. White. And that should be me," Gladys announced.

"Why you?" Gran asked.

"Isn't it obvious?" Gladys fluttered her eyelashes. "Harry Blackman is a man. If I do say so, I've never yet met a man I couldn't charm." Her eyelashes swept toward Mike then dropped demurely.

"This isn't a charm contest, Gladys," Jane snapped. "it's business. We're trying to get in Blackman's pocket, not in his pants."

"Jane!"

"Well, it's the truth. I should be the one who poses as Mrs. White."

A wistful expression stole over Gran's face. "I rather thought that I—"

"No, Lucille, it should be me." Jane squared her flowered shoulders. "School teachers are much like actors. We're accustomed to performing before an audience. It can't be Alice, he met Alice when she took the Croupier into his office. And Gladys would end up flirting instead of swindling. If you want to help, Lucille, then get out your sewing machine and whip me up a silk dress. And lend me your good pearls for the performance."

Gran squinted, the look magnified behind her glasses. "Something in a dusty rose, I think. With dolman sleeves. And we'll have to do something with your hair. A bluer rinse to brighten your eyes."

Mike grinned at Molly, his relief evident. "All right, then we're agreed? We go with the art scam?"

The Heart Club passed invisible signals, then Gran asked, "Will the real Mrs. White get into any trouble?"

"The police will probably question her," Mike admitted. "But she'll be exonerated when Blackman recognizes that she isn't the woman who sold him the painting."

"I still don't like you and Molly taking the bulk of the risk," Gran said.

Molly moved to press her grandmother's shoulder. "It seems to me the risk is spread pretty evenly. We're in this together."

"Except for me." Gladys looked at them and her lips formed into a pout. "Alice is providing the scene, Jane is playing the best part and Lucille is making the costume. What do I get to do?"

"Well," Mike said, "someone has to approach Blackman as the agent and inform him that Mrs. White wants to sell the painting. It can be done by phone. And I'll write a script for you."

Immediately Gladys brightened. "Actually," she said, patting her hair, "that's probably the most important part. If you'll give me the script immediately, I'll start practicing."

For the space of a heartbeat no one said anything, then the room erupted in excited voices, suggesting a detail here and a detail there, filling in the blanks.

When Mike drew Molly into the kitchen for a moment of privacy, she gazed at him with genuine admiration. "You were wonderful," she said, the compliment sincere. "I was worried for a moment, but you turned the whole thing around." They were standing too close, and she moved a step backward.

"At least we bought some time." Leaning against the counter top, Mike looked at her and pushed a hand through his hair. "But we're not home yet. I was up until three last night experimenting with various solutions. No luck so far."

"Not to pressure you," Molly said lightly, "but I'm going to need your magic solution the day after tomorrow."

"You'll have it," he said firmly.

She wondered if he would suggest they have dinner together to discuss the Heart Club's acceptance of their plan. But he didn't. When they parted on Gran's porch, he walked to his car with no more than a friendly wave.

Molly told herself that was good. It was exactly what she had wanted. Obviously they were back to a business basis. Friendly conspirators, partners in crime. Nothing more.

But for a short time it had felt like more, she thought as she drove back across the river to her gallery. When they were facing the Heart Club explaining their plan, she'd felt as if they were a unit, as if they spoke and thought with the same mind. She had anticipated his words; he had tracked her perfectly with Alice and the empty house. How many casual friends thought on parallel lines?

It was a relief to flip on her workroom lights and clear her mind of everything but the Monet and the challenge awaiting her. Concentrating, she thought about form and texture and the essence of light, feeling her shoulders relax. When she was ready, Molly spread her palette with a wheel of color then began mixing tints, holding the edge of the palette to the Monet to compare hues. Again and again, she scraped off the paint and began again in fresh oil. It was well after midnight when she released a small sound of satisfaction. She'd found exactly the tint for the sky. Hopefully, Mike was progressing as successfully.

HE WASN'T.

On the other side of town, Mike's kitchen was littered by strips of canvas smeared with paint. He'd taped the counter top into sections and had labeled the taped sections Day One, Day Two and so forth.

Pausing over the solutions he was stirring in the kitchen sink, he wiped his hands, poured another cup of coffee and touched a fingertip to the paint strips in the Day One section. "Still tacky," he told Murph who was curled near the refrigerator. "Damn."

All the batches in Day One had failed to harden quickly enough. Day Two had dried faster than Day One, but the spray was much too heavy. It left tiny depressions in the oil that Mike could easily spot beneath a magnifying glass.

"No good, Murph," he said aloud, holding the coffee on his tongue as he thought about the samples. "But we're on the right track." The telephone surprised him. He glanced at his watch then caught the phone on the third ring. "Molly?"

"How did you know it was me?" He could hear the smile in her voice.

He laughed. "Who else would call at one forty-five in the morning?"

"I've caught the right tint for the sky and the clouds. How are you doing?"

"There's reason for cautious optimism. We're not there yet, but it's coming." Hearing the weariness in her voice made him aware of his own fatigue. "Are you at home?"

"No, at the gallery. I thought I'd sleep on the cot here and get an early start tomorrow."

There were a thousand things he wanted to say to her. But none of them were appropriate. Keeping his voice detached and impersonal, he assured her. "We'll succeed."

"How's Murph?" she asked, filling the silence.

"Fine, staying out of the way."

"Mike? I just wanted to tell you that it's wonderful of you to help. I know we're doing the right thing, but it hit me tonight that if we're caught we really could go to jail."

"Having second thoughts?"

"No, what Harry Blackman did was wrong, and this is the only recourse. I don't regret my involvement; I just wanted to thank you for yours."

"There's no need to thank me, Molly." He hesitated. "I'm not doing this for you. I'm involved because of Aunt Jane and the others." It had required some soul-searching, but he'd peeled away the truth. Molly accounted for only a small part of his commitment to help the Heart Club. The larger reasons involved injustice, his Aunt Jane and the thought of four elderly women facing arrest.

"I know that. I just...I just wanted to thank you for being here." Another pause opened over the line, then she said, "Mike, did you ever imagine we'd really do something like this?"

"Not in a million years." He combed his fingers through his hair and wondered if she was wearing the smock that brushed across the back of her legs. "I keep remembering what you said about being a Girl Scout. What do you suppose our Scout masters would say if they could see us today?"

Her laugh sounded tired. "They'd be horrified."

He wanted to tell her that he loved her. For one crazy instant he didn't care if he bought her. He just wanted her. Wanted to wake up beside her, wanted to know every tiny detail about her, wanted to share with her all the details that made up his own life. He wanted to hold her close and never let go.

"Molly, I—"

In her weariness she didn't notice that she interrupted. "Well, I just wanted to touch base. Good night, Mike."

After she rang off, Mike stared at the phone and wondered why she'd really called. Outside of the Monet project there wasn't anything to talk about. She had made her position clear. As soon as they had Blackman's money, he and Molly would go their separate ways. Fini. And if he didn't accept that, he was in for a lot of hurt.

But she had phoned him.

"Women," he said to Murph, who didn't move. "Someone should invent an antidote. He'd make a fortune." A wry smile touched his mouth. "Then Molly McPherson would marry him."

He decided to try one more batch of the solution he was working on, then he'd call it a night. He was in no hurry to go to his empty bed.

MOLLY STARED at her canvas in the morning light. Last night the sky had looked perfect, maybe because she was tired. This morning it looked flat. She released a long low sigh and cupped her chin in her hand.

Technique, that was the thing. Monet had worked with wet paint, blending the oils as he worked. The meshing and blending of color, the layering of hue upon hue, succeeded on an original; that was, in fact, the genius. But a copy artist couldn't depend on the correct blend, couldn't hope that her brush strokes would be exactly as those made by the original artist. Therefore, the copy artist had to reproduce tints and colors one painstaking step at a time, seeking through deliberation what the original artist had achieved by instinct.

This morning the task appeared nearly hopeless. Each time Molly touched her sable brush to the canvas, she disturbed the underlying layer of paint and blue swirled up into the pink and gold of her clouds. Frustration pinched her mouth.

"I couldn't paint this damned thing if it was a paint by number set," she muttered, throwing down the rag she'd used to dab the blue out of her clouds.

Discouraged, she sank to a stool and glared at the real Monet. What she needed was time. Covering her eyes, she fought down a flare of panic. Maybe she'd bitten off too much. Maybe she wouldn't be able to see justice done for the Heart Club.

And then what? Assuming she and Mike could talk Gran and the others out of returning to the forged check plan, did that mean Harry Blackman would walk away scot-free? In that case, crime paid. And that wasn't fair. If there was a chance in hell of succeeding, she had to try.

Standing, Molly pressed her lips together and cleaned her palette knife then began mixing fresh colors. By God, she wasn't going to give up until the very end. Even if it meant she had to paint the wretched sky a thousand times more. Mike and the Heart Club were counting on her.

She didn't paint the sky a thousand times, but she did paint it at least a dozen times in the next two days. Each time, no matter how painstakingly careful she was, she stirred the paint beneath with the tip of her brush and had to begin again. Over and over, until her jaw was sore from grinding her teeth.

When Mike unexpectedly appeared in her workroom doorway, she looked at him from tired eyes. "You look as exhausted as I feel," she said. They both wore dark circles beneath their eyes and looked as if they hadn't slept in a week. "Would you like some coffee? I've been living on it."

"I think I've got it, Molly. Take a look at this."

Now she noticed the glow of excitement beneath his fatigue. Frowning, she took the strip of canvas he pushed into her hands and stared at it. The streaks of paint were dry.

Hardly daring to believe, she gazed up at him, a dozen questions arching along her lifted brow.

"I layered the paint on last night, fresh out of the tube. This is how it looked and felt when I got up this morning."

"This isn't possible," Molly whispered. Bending, she accepted the magnifying glass he extended and she examined the paint surface. As far as she could tell there were no marks from the spray, no damp cracks in the oil. Straightening, she stared at him. "Mike, I don't know what to say. This is a miracle. Are you sure about this? There isn't a mistake?"

"I'm sure." His grin widened.

Molly's eyes brightened and her expression curved into a smile. "Do you know what this means?"

"It means the Heart Club has their money."

"It means I only have to paint the sky one more time!"

Turning, Molly threw her arms around his neck and embraced him. God, he felt good. Until now she hadn't realized how much she had missed his strength and solidity. In Mike Randall's arms she didn't feel as tired as she had a moment ago. Closing her eyes, she rested her forehead on his broad shoulder and wished they could curl up together and talk and nap and maybe...

Mike stood very still then gently he disengaged her arms and stepped away from her. Though his indifference shouldn't have surprised Molly, it did. A flush of embarrassed color turned her cheeks pink.

What had she expected? That Mike would be waiting gratefully for whatever crumbs of affection she chose to toss? Ducking her head, she pretended to examine the strip of canvas in minute detail.

She'd rejected him; she'd told him their lovemaking had been a mistake. What right did she have to feel wounded when he didn't return her embrace? None. Drawing a breath, she waited until the heat faded from her cheeks then she glanced up at him and arranged her mouth into a smile. "Congratulations."

"Thank you." After making a point of glancing at his watch, Mike moved toward the door. "The rest is up to you. Good luck." Then he was gone.

Molly stared at the doorway.

And she'd thought she was skilled at keeping people at arm's length? Compared to Mike Randall, she was a novice. He'd breezed in, dropped off his miracle and had breezed out. They might have been strangers.

Grimly, Molly examined the spray bottle Mike had left on the table. And she made herself think about Win Melton and how wonderful her life was going to be when this whole crazy business with the Heart Club was finally resolved.

TWELVE DAYS LATER the painting was finished. And dry.

The Heart Club crowded into Molly's workroom, peeking at the two draped easels with sparkling eyes. For this special occasion, they'd each had their hair done and were dressed to the nines. Gran wore the pearls Corwin Pratt had given her for their thirty-seventh anniversary. Jane's collar was closed by the ivory cameo she'd received from the school at her retirement party. Gladys and Alice both wore lace and navy and each believed the other should have chosen something else.

"When do we get to see the painting?" Gladys asked, pointedly ignoring Alice.

"As soon as I've poured the wine," Mike answered. They would save champagne for the celebration party when the swindle had been successfully completed. "Nervous?" he asked Molly. He glanced at the emerald-colored silk suit curving over her breasts and hips then lifted his eyes to the twin dots of color brightening her cheeks.

"A little." Fresh snow had melted in his hair and he looked as if he'd just stepped from the shower. Tonight he wore a silk striped tie and charcoal wool. And his after-shave made her think of cruises and moonlight.

Against her will, Molly found her eyes following him as he served wine to the ladies. He complimented each on some detail of her dress; he laughed, he conversed easily and cheerfully. Sourly, Molly reflected that he'd said nothing about her silk suit. Suddenly she realized she'd chosen it with Mike in mind.

Knock it off, she told herself firmly. Mike Randall might be wonderfully handsome, he might have Paul Newman eyes and a laugh that drew everyone in the room, but he was a patent officer, for heaven's sake. She needed to keep that fact firmly in mind. Mike would never spend a month in Europe or bid at an art auction. His wife, when he took one, would spend her life clipping coupons and shopping sales. It would be a life uncluttered by luxury items. Brand names need not apply. The reminder made her feel better.

When she became aware that everyone was watching her expectantly, Molly cleared her throat and moved to stand between the draped easels. She rubbed the moisture from her palms. "Without further ado, ladies and gentlemen, may I present Monet's *Suzanne at Midday*. This is the genuine work," she said, removing the drape.

They examined it in admiring silence. When they'd had time to absorb the details, Molly draped the original and removed the cover from her copy. "This is the forgery."

The sudden intake of breath was gratifying.

"It's exactly the same!" Gran leaned to inspect the painting, lifting her head to peer through her glasses. "Framed the same, everything is the same." Turning, she wrapped Molly in a happy embrace.

"I wouldn't have believed it if I hadn't seen it with my own two eyes," Jane marveled.

Gladys and Alice blinked at each other. "This is going to work," Gladys said, her teeth clicking.

"We're going to get our money!"

They crowded around Molly, offering congratulations patting her hair, her shoulders, her hands, until she laughed and protested. "It wouldn't have been possible without Mike's miracle spray," she said, grinning as the Heart Club descended upon him with more pats and hugs.

"To the ladies of the Heart Club," Mike said, raising his glass high. "May justice be served and dreams come true." He looked at Molly over the group of gray heads. "May you get every dime that's coming to you."

"The next step is up to me," Gladys said happily.

"That it is. Molly?" His face was expressionless. "Are we ready to wrap this up?"

For a lengthy moment, Molly didn't answer. High color flamed in her cheeks as she stood beside her painting and looked at him, wishing things had been different. "Yes," she said finally. "I believe we're ready."

Had she shown both paintings undraped at the same time, they would easily have spotted the forgery. But viewed alone, her copy would withstand careful scrutiny. Her part was finished.

"Good." Mike smiled into the faded eyes glowing back at him. "Gladys, are you prepared?"

"Of course I am." Her shoulders squared importantly.

Mike pushed back his sleeve and glanced at his watch. "It's seven-thirty. Blackman should be home by now. Would you rather make the call privately?"

Gladys removed a well-handled paper from her purse and smoothed it open. "I don't mind if you want to listen."

As they trooped into the gallery and gathered around the counter, Jane stage whispered to Gran. "If Mike thought Gladys would have her big moment without an audience, he doesn't know Gladys Price."

"I heard that, Jane." Gladys smiled over the counter top, then composed herself and flattened the script beside the telephone. She touched her hair and straightened her collar. "I hope my teeth don't clack," she murmured.

"There's nothing to be nervous about," Gran said. The others added words of encouragement.

"Just read from the script," Mike added.

He dialed the telephone and handed the receiver to a trembling Gladys. After giving them a thumb's up sign, she gazed at the script.

"It's ringing," she said, catching a quick breath. Then her shoulders jumped. "Is this Harry Blackman?" Covering the phone with her hand, she stared up at them. "It's him!"

"The script, Gladys," Jane cautioned. "Just read the script."

"Mr. Blackman, this is—uh—Thelma Morgan. I was wondering if you'd like to buy a Monet painting?"

Mike and Molly stared at each other. Hastily, Mike leaned over Gladys's shoulder and tapped the script. "Stay with the script," he whispered urgently.

She covered the mouthpiece and cast Mike a helpless look. "I forgot my glasses. I can't see it."

"Oh, for pity's sake," Gran and Jane moaned in unison. They found Gladys's purse and dumped it on the counter, looking for the missing glasses.

Kneeling beside her, Mike covered her trembling fingers with his large hand. "It's all right. You know the story. Do the best you can."

"Uh—what?" Gladys said into the receiver. She blinked hard at the paper by the telephone. "No, sir, I'm not the seller, I'm an agent."

"Tell him the seller is a private party," Mike coached quietly.

Gladys repeated what he'd said then covered the phone. "He wants to know how I happened to call him." Her teeth clicked like castanets. After listening to Mike she spoke into the phone. "Your name was suggested by a local gallery as a possible buyer." She looked at Mike, who nodded encouragement.

"You're doing fine," he said in a low tone. Standing behind him, Molly clasped her hands and closed her eyes. "Tell him you can arrange a private showing if he's interested." When Gladys had repeated the words, he added, "Tell him you think he'll be pleasantly surprised by the asking price."

"It's a bargain at only two hundred thousand dollars," Gladys said as Mike briefly covered his eyes and Molly suppressed a groan. "And we don't take Visa, Mr. Blackman." Gladys cast a pleased glance at her audience. She was on a roll now. "It's cash on the barrel head or a certified check made out to the bearer."

"Oh, my God," Molly muttered. She dug her fingers into Mike's shoulder. "Do something."

"Gladys, ask if he'd like to make an appointment to see the Monet. And tell him he can bring an appraiser of his choice."

Gladys nodded. "You can bring an appraiser so you'll know you aren't being cheated or swindled. Do you want to make an appointment?" Her eyes lit. "Next Tuesday? That would be fine."

Groans erupted around the counter and five pairs of hands waved frantically. Alice was shaking her head so violently that hair pins rained around her shoulders.

"No, no, no," Gran gasped.

"Monday morning!" Jane whispered loudly.

"It's all right, Gladys," Mike said calmly. A trickle of perspiration leaked from his temple. "Tell him Monday morning would be more convenient for your client."

"Just a minute, Mr. Blackman." Gladys scowled. "How can I do this when you're all waving and carrying on?"

"I swan," Gran muttered. "I'm not going to live through this!"

"Monday morning," Mike repeated quietly.

Molly bit her tongue to keep from interfering. Mike's patience astonished her. In her heart she knew she couldn't have managed as well.

Mike clasped Gladys's shaking hand. "I know you're nervous, but you're doing fine. Tell him your client is available only on Monday mornings." Haltingly, Gladys repeated what he had said.

"Good," she said into the phone, her shoulders sagging with relief. "Mrs. White will see you at ten o'clock Monday morning. Good night, Mr. Blackman." The last words ran together, emerging as one long breathless unit before Gladys slammed down the phone and beamed up at them. "Well, how did I do?"

They stared at her. Finally Gran said, "There's a small problem, dear. You didn't give him the address."

"I must have." She frowned at Mike. "Didn't I?"

Turning the phone to face him, Mike dialed the number and handed her the receiver. "Tell him the address. Just be your charming self, Gladys."

"Mr. Blackman?" Gladys's teeth clicked in a series of nervous staccato noises. "Silly ol' me. I forgot to give you

Mrs. White's address.'' She spoke the address as Mike whispered it to her. ''What? Yes, that's right. A genuine Monet. For two hundred thousand dollars. Yes, you can bring your appraiser.'' She listened a minute. ''Me? No, I probably won't be there. I could be if—'' She saw the others waving their hands and making faces. ''Actually, you'll deal directly with Mrs. White.'' Gladys smiled and stifled a giggle. ''Well, it's been an experience talking to you too, Mr. Blackman.''

The instant she hung up the telephone, Gran, Jane and Alice rounded the counter and smothered her in hugs. ''You were wonderful, Gladys! A natural born actress.''

''I was good, wasn't I?'' She beamed at them. ''I guess I told him what for.''

Standing, Mike blotted his forehead and rolled his eyes at Molly. ''Do you have any Scotch?''

''Only more wine.'' She touched her glass to his. ''Step one completed.''

''Between you and me, I can't believe Blackman agreed.''

''I can,'' Molly said. ''A Monet? For two hundred thousand? Gladys was right, that's a bargain. It's worth it to Blackman to check it out.'' Now that the worst was behind them, Molly relaxed and gazed at the Heart Club with affection, a smile softening her lips. ''And he's prepared. He knows we won't take Visa.''

Mike laughed. ''Look at them. This has to be the most unlikely group of swindlers in history.''

The Heart Club was happily toasting Gladys's triumph. ''The fly is in the web,'' Gran announced.

''Thanks to me.'' Gladys tried and failed to look modest.

A dreamy look came into Jane's eyes as Mike and Molly joined them at the gallery counter. ''I have my eye on a nice little apartment near you, Lucille. It's as clean as a cat and there's a security guard at the door. I might even buy a new sofa."

"I'm going to spend a month in Florida," Gran mused. "I'll stay with Tom and Alta and I'll take them out to dinner every night. When I get home, maybe I'll hire Mr. Grosse to fix the gutters and paint my house."

"First I'll buy a new hearing aid," Alice said when it was her turn. "Then I'll give all my ladies notice. From now on, the only house I'll clean is my own!" They all cheered.

"How about you, Gladys?" Molly asked, smiling. "What will you do with your share?"

"I always wanted a rabbit coat," she said, almost shyly. "You don't think I'm too old for a rabbit coat, do you?"

"A woman is never too old for a fur," Mike answered gallantly. The others agreed, assuring Gladys as they put aside their wineglasses and moved toward their coats. "Ladies, your chauffeur awaits." Until now Molly hadn't realized Mike had driven the Heart Club to the gallery.

"Thanks, Molly." Gran wrapped her in a lemon-smelling hug. "Now that it's finally happening, I can tell you that I don't know how we would have managed without you and Mike."

"I love you, Gran."

"I love you, too." Gran winked. "Did you know Mike Randall has a coffee machine in his car? He's an interesting man, dear."

Mike called for their attention. "We'll meet at Lucille's at eight o'clock Monday morning. Agreed? We'll do a practice run, then we'll drive to Mrs. White's in two cars. Molly will drive and I'll drive. Study Alice's drawing of Mrs. White's house over the weekend." He stood beside the gallery door after the Heart Club had stepped through. For a moment he looked at Molly. "It's almost finished," he said quietly. "By this time next week, you'll be able to get on with your life."

"So will you." She cleared the tightness from her throat. "I imagine you'll be glad."

Snow swirled in the open door and coated his pant legs. "Well, see you Monday morning."

The door tinkled shut on Molly's reply and she heard the sound of laughter from the curb.

In three days it would all be over. Gran would fly off to Florida, Jane would look for a new apartment, Alice would give notice to her ladies and Gladys would shop for a rabbit coat. Mike would return to the patent office and probably work overtime to make up the days he'd missed.

And Molly? She would return the genuine Monet to the Smithsonian and then she'd set up a dinner date with Winthrop Kingsbury Melton the Third.

In a few weeks the events of this past month would begin to blur. The satisfaction of knowing Harry Blackman had gotten what was coming to him would still be there. And the good feeling of having corrected an injustice and knowing the Heart Club was secure and happy. But parts of it would fade like the center of a dream.

Sighing, Molly tipped the last of the wine into her glass and walked through the gallery, snapping off lights. As tired as she was, she felt no urgency to hurry back to her empty apartment. After a time, she settled herself behind the counter and placed her fingertips against the phone. It was early and she was dressed. Maybe she'd call a few friends and meet them for a drink. But the only person she felt like seeing or talking to was off limits.

AFTER HE HAD DELIVERED each of the Heart Club members safely to her door, Mike drove aimlessly about the city. Tonight the world seemed to be composed of couples. He could easily have convinced himself that he was the only person without someone he cared about at his side.

As it was early yet, he considered dropping in on his parents. He hadn't seen much of them during the past weeks.

But they were the closest couple he knew and right now he didn't feel up to intruding on that closeness. It would only point up the fact that he was alone.

The expressway stretched out before the car and a sign flashed past informing him that he was heading toward the Virginia suburbs. Toward Molly's apartment.

There was no humor in his grim smile. Was that how it was going to be? Was he going to turn sappy and moonstruck like a teenager? Tormenting himself by driving by her house?

Pulling on the wheel, he turned off at the next exit and circled around.

"I was wrong, Murph," he said when he'd returned to his house and flipped on the TV. Television was one of the all-time great inventions. So far no one had come up with anything better to chase away a lonely night. "We don't need an antidote for women. We need an antidote for love."

He put a bowl of fresh water on the floor in front of the refrigerator. Murph didn't drink water—it would have shorted out his insides if he had. But Mike put out the water anyway. Most of the time he forgot that Murph couldn't drink it.

Bending, he stroked Murph behind the ears. "It's going to hurt, buddy," he said, remembering how she had looked in the silk suit, remembering the sound of her voice and the laughter in her eyes. "It's going to hurt a lot."

Chapter Eleven

Following Mike's example, Molly parked down the street, well away from Mrs. White's impressive Georgian two-story.

Gran, who sat beside Molly in the front seat, pushed her glasses up her nose and twisted her fingers. "I'm as nervous as spit on a griddle." She nudged Alice. "We're here, dear. Give us the sign when the coast is clear."

"I swan, we're about to do it, Lucille. Isn't this exciting?"

Molly winced when Alice slammed the car door. The sound seemed magnified, as if it would surely bring the street's residents flying to the windows to peer out at them. She could imagine Mrs. White's neighbors picking them out of a police lineup: "Yes, officer, that's the red-headed moll who was driving one of the getaway cars."

"Alice is inside the house," Gran said, gripping Molly's sleeve. Those in the car ahead were watching as intently as Gran and Molly. "There it is, the signal. Alice is waving her dust mop."

But before they stepped out of the car and followed the others hurrying toward Mrs. White's walkway, Lucille Pratt laid her glove on her granddaughter's arm. "For one silly moment I...I almost hoped Mrs. White would be home and we couldn't go through with this." She bit off the words and shook her head. "I'm happy this is finally happening, but on the other hand..."

"I know what you mean." Molly understood perfectly. She too was having shaky second thoughts. Last night had seemed endless. She had tossed and turned and had imagined all the things that could go wrong. A hundred terrible scenarios. For two cents, she would have turned the car around and fled back across the river.

But it was too late. Mike, Gladys and Jane were already crossing Mrs. White's porch, following Alice inside. Molly squeezed Gran's glove, then they hastened after the others. Molly's heart was pounding when Alice closed the door behind them.

"Oh, boy," Molly murmured, closing her eyes. She'd never felt more uncomfortable in her life, or more like a criminal. They were trespassing, standing uninvited in a stranger's living room. Reality slipped and Molly couldn't believe she was actually here, doing this. Every small sound made her jump and she halfway expected the vice squad to burst out from behind a door and throw cuffs on them all.

Mike's expression mirrored her thoughts, and the Heart Club clumped together in a tight group at the center of the enormous living room. No one spoke above a hushed whisper.

Drawing a deep breath, Molly made herself speak in a normal tone. "This is it, friends. The last chance to reconsider. Does anyone want to call it quits?"

The Heart Club looked at each other and gathered their strength. They shook their heads. "Blackman stole our Croupier. We've come this far, we can't quit now. He owes us the money." Having drawn stubborn courage from one another, they removed their coats with an air of purpose.

"Now don't be nervous," Gran said, straightening Jane's pink sleeve and patting her stiffly upswept hair. "There's no reason to be nervous. We rehearsed this several times. Are you nervous?''

"Hush, Lucille. I wasn't nervous until you started talking." Jane turned, looking at Mrs. White's living room. "Did you ever see a room this big?''

"Like a room in one of those house magazines," Gladys commented. "It's beautiful but I don't much like it. It's too big.''

"It doesn't look lived in," Gran said. "No family pictures, nothing personal.''

Molly reluctantly agreed. She had expected to feel a pang of envy as Mrs. White lived as Molly hoped to live one day. The sunken living room was exquisitely and expensively decorated, but Gladys was right. The perfection made the room somehow cool and uninviting. The room was designed to be admired, not for comfort. As always, Molly examined the artwork and was further disappointed. Although the paintings were wildly expensive, it was obvious they had been chosen to harmonize with the color scheme rather than as a reflection of the White's personal taste.

Taking Jane aside, Molly gestured toward the artwork. "Once Blackman sees this room, he'll understand why you want to sell the Monet. Your tastes have changed. Now you prefer to collect modern art.''

"I understand," Jane answered crisply. She swept a disapproving glance over the walls. "My sixth graders painted better stuff than that." She smoothed her skirt and her voice faltered the tiniest bit. "Molly, do I look all right? As if I belonged in a place like this?''

"You look lovely. To the manor born," Molly assured her. The rose-colored silk flattered Jane's bony figure and cast a soft pink shadow over her cheeks. Her hair was swept into a stiff chignon and was a bit blue for Molly's taste, but that couldn't be helped. After adjusting the pearls Jane had borrowed from Gran, Molly gave her a quick hug. "You'll do just fine. Now then, let's pick a spot and hang the Monet."

With Mike's help she removed a Wilkerson of about the same size as the Monet. They hid the Wilkerson in the hall closet then hung the Monet and stepped backward.

"What do you think?" Molly asked.

"Don't ask. Right now I'm wishing I'd never laid eyes on you. Wishing Aunt Jane was related to someone else and wishing I'd never heard of the Heart Club."

Molly laughed, welcoming the sudden release of the tension drawing her skin. "Too late for cold feet. We're in this up to our eyebrows. Do you suppose we could convince everyone but Jane to wait in the cars?"

"Not a chance. Our Heart Club is having the time of their lives."

They watched the ladies open the door to the dining room, peep inside, then congratulate Alice on the accuracy of her map.

The layout of the first floor was simple. The kitchen, where they would wait while Jane made the sale, could be entered from the dining room or from a short hallway leading from the living room. The rest of the house, two wings opening from either side of the living room, had no importance to the scheme and they scrupulously avoided peeking into those doors.

"I've made coffee," Alice announced. "Jane, you can offer some to the johns if you like."

"Not johns, Alice dear," Gran corrected. "Marks. You call the swindlee a mark. A john is something else, I think."

Jane nodded absently and touched Mike's wrist. "What shall I do if the appraiser wants to take the painting with him, to his office or someplace?"

"Tell him you wouldn't be comfortable with that," Molly answered.

"He'll have to authenticate the painting here, Aunt Jane."

"But he'll be prepared to do that," Molly said. "Don't worry about it. Do you remember the part about the provenance?"

Before Jane could answer the doorbell sounded and they all froze. "Oh, dear, " Jane whispered. "My heart's racing like a buzz saw."

"Into the kitchen everyone," Mike said in a low tone.

They kissed Jane then scurried toward the back of the house. Molly planted a swift kiss on Jane's powdered cheek and Mike gave her a hug. "You'll do fine." They sprinted for the kitchen.

Jane waited until the whispering had died behind the kitchen door and the doorbell rang again. Then she stiffened her spine and walked briskly to the front door.

"I can't hear anything," Alice complained. She was on her knees, her eye pressed to the crack in the kitchen door.

"Shh!" came the chorus from above. There was room for Mike and Molly to see through the crack; Gran and Gladys stood on tiptoe behind them, plucking at their sleeves.

"I want to see, too," Gladys whispered.

"Shh!"

A drift of voices grew louder and in a moment, Jane appeared in their line of vision. Her hands were pressed tightly together. Two men wearing business suits followed her into the living room and, at Jane's invitation, seated themselves on a brocade sofa.

"That's him," Alice whispered excitedly. "That's Blackman in the red tie!"

"*That's* Blackman?" Molly said incredulously. She stared down at Alice. "Are you sure?"

"Well, for pity's sake, of course I'm sure."

Molly couldn't believe it. She blinked at Mike then pressed her eye firmly to the crack at the door. And she stared hard at Harry Blackman.

For weeks, months in fact, she had pictured Blackman as a Mafia thug, a swarthy man with shifty eyes and a cruel sadistic mouth, a modern day Dillinger.

But Harry Blackman looked like every child's vision of Santa Claus.

He had a white well-trimmed beard. Snowy-white hair surrounded a ruddy cheerful face that beamed goodwill toward all. Beneath thick white eyebrows, bright blue eyes twinkled with vitality and elfish good humor. He even sat like Santa Claus, with his fingers laced together over a little round belly. Harry Blackman looked like a man who carried lemon drops in his pockets for his grandchildren, like a man who laughed a lot and did kind deeds as a matter of course.

Molly nudged Mike with her elbow and they stepped away from the crack in the door. Immediately, Gran and Gladys took their places.

"Why, he's handsome!" Gladys whispered in surprise.

"It just goes to show," Gran said after a long moment. "You sure can't tell a melon by its rind."

Vindication lit Alice's expression. "There. Now do you understand why I trusted him with the Croupier?"

"Shh."

Molly drew Mike toward the back of the kitchen near the sliders that opened onto a covered porch where they could speak in low tones.

"I don't know what to make of this," she said, lifting troubled eyes. "He looks—well, nice. I wanted to sit on his lap and whisper all my secrets in his ear." She shrugged beneath an uncomfortable frown. "Mike, is there any possibility that we've made a mistake?"

"I don't see how."

Heads close together, they swiftly reviewed the facts. At the end of their whispered discussion, Mike thrust his fingers through his hair and stared out the sliders into the backyard. "There doesn't seem to be any way around it. Blackman didn't return the Croupier. He applied for and received the patent. He marketed the device and he made a lot of money on it."

"Mike! Molly!" Gran whispered urgently, waving them forward. "They've taken the painting off the wall and the appraiser is looking at it!"

They crowded along the crack in the kitchen door and watched the appraiser smile at Jane. "Mrs. White, may I take this into the kitchen where the light is usually stronger?"

Jane nodded graciously and returned to Harry Blackman.

Mike and Molly stared at each other. "Oh, Lord, he's coming in here!"

Frantically, they pushed away from the door. Alice toppled backward and sat hard on the kitchen floor with her legs sprawled out in front of her. Gran wrung her hands and panic spread behind her glasses.

"Quickly," Mike whispered. "Into the dining room!" Pushing open the door with his shoulder, he urgently waved them forward.

Molly caught Alice under the arms and she and Gladys hauled Alice to her feet. Trying to move quietly, they rushed into the dining room.

Hearts pounding, they held their breath, stared at each other and made small shushing sounds in the backs of their throats. From the living room, Jane's voice rose sharply.

"Oh, wait a minute, Mr. Whitney. I just remembered. Not the kitchen, if you please. There's good light in the dining room and a table large enough to spread out your tools and things. I think you'll find the dining room more suitable."

"Oh, my God," Molly murmured, pressing her hand to her lips. "Now he's coming in here."

Mike spread his arms like wings and herded them toward the door. "Quickly." They rushed back into the kitchen and crowded against the counter top seconds before they heard the dining room door push open.

Gran placed a heavy hand on her bosom and covered her eyes. Alice dropped into a chair and stared at the ceiling. Gladys fanned a crimson face with a dish towel and tried to stop her teeth from clicking.

Molly sagged against Mike's shoulder. He blotted a trickle of perspiration from his temples with his handkerchief. "Not a word," he mouthed silently, pointing to the dining-room door.

They waited, watching the dial on the kitchen clock, listening to the murmur of Jane's conversation with Harry Blackman. Occasionally a rustle emanated from the dining room, the sound of something being moved, items picked up or set down.

Finally, after what seemed an eon, the appraiser, Mr. Whitney, called from the dining-room door. "Harry? May I speak to you for a moment?"

In the kitchen, everyone straightened and leaned toward the dining-room door, straining to hear. The voices came through clearly.

"Harry, it's a genuine Monet."

"You're absolutely certain?"

Molly looked at Mike then dropped her eyes. Blackman even sounded like she wanted Santa Claus to sound. His voice was deep and cheerful, a voice that inspired trust and friendship.

"Certain enough that if you don't buy it, I will."

"If it's genuine..." Blackman paused. "Then it's worth at least twice what Mrs. White is asking. Maybe I'll..."

"Are you crazy?" Whitney's voice sank. "You only have to talk to Mrs. White for five mintues to know she's nobody's fool. And she knows art—you saw the work she's collected. I'll bet my license she knows what this painting is worth. If she's only asking two hundred thousand, she has her reasons."

To the astonishment of those blinking at each other in the kitchen, Harry Blackman still hesitated.

"I don't know, Bill. I'd hate to take unfair advantage."

In the kitchen eyes widened and mouths dropped.

"You're not cheating her, Harry. She set the asking price. Pay what she's asking and count yourself lucky."

When Whitney and Blackman returned to the sofa where Jane was waiting, she stood and her mouth clamped in a thin starchy smile.

"Mrs. White," Harry Blackman said, "I'd like to buy your Monet. But are you asking enough money?"

"Is this some kind of trick?" Jane's eyes narrowed.

In the kitchen, everyone was jostling for a spot along the crack in the door.

"Frankly," Blackman said, "the painting is probably worth at least twice what you're asking." Mr. Whitney sighed and leaned back against the sofa cushions. "I don't want you to think about this later and feel as if you've been cheated in any way."

For the first time Jane appeared flustered. Her hands fluttered over her lap. "I know my price, Mr. Blackman. Two hundred thousand. I won't take a penny less."

Blackman took her hand. "My dear Mrs. White. I'm offering you more money, not less."

"No sir," Jane said, her voice stubborn. "Fair is fair. Two hundred thousand is what you owe. It wouldn't be right to take a penny more. Our price is firm, Mr. Blackman."

Molly straightened suddenly and spun away from the crack in the door. "My God," she breathed. "What am I doing standing here? I have to switch the paintings!" Spinning on her heel, she cast a frantic glance around the kitchen. "Gran, did you bring in the copy?" Her voice was a hoarse whisper.

"I thought you did."

Mike stared at her. "We don't have the copy?"

Biting her lips savagely, Molly wrung her hands. "I must have left it in the car. I was nervous and—"

"All right." Running his hand over his chin, Mike stared at nothing. "Okay. Here's what we'll do. Give me your car keys and I'll get the painting. Signal Jane and tell her there's been a slight delay."

After Molly fumbled in her purse and found her keys, Mike slid open the patio doors and sprinted across the back yard. Molly watched him vault the fence, his jacket flying behind him, then he cut across the backyard of the neighboring house.

Oh, Lord. In about two minutes, Jane was going to hand over a genuine Monet worth more than half a million dollars. Molly chewed her lips. The Smithsonian would clap her in jail quicker than she could say Heart Club.

"Gran, come here." Snatching a towel from the basket near the refrigerator, Molly hastily wound it around Gran's head, then she pushed an apron into her hands. "Go out there," she whispered, frantically, "and say 'Mrs. White, lunch will be delayed.'" She stared into Gran's widening eyes. "Exit through the dining room and close the dining-room door behind you."

Gran's hands trembled over the apron strings. "Mrs. White, lunch will be delayed," she muttered, nodding. "Mrs. White, lunch will be delayed."

"Go." Molly pushed her out the kitchen door and leaned to the crack. "What are they talking about out there?" she whispered to Gladys.

"Jane's telling Blackman that the provenance is in the family vault in San Francisco. She's telling him it will take about a week for her attorneys to mail the provenance."

"Good, good." Molly pressed her eye to the crack at the door and watched as Gran threw back her shoulders and walked forward.

"Mrs. Lunch," Gran said solemnly, "white will be delayed." Turning, she started toward the kitchen door, then veered toward the dining room. The towel began to unwind from her head.

Jane stared. "Lucille, what on earth are you talking about?"

Clamping a hand to the unwinding towel, Gran summoned a reservoir of dignity. She gave Jane a meaningful look. "*Delayed*, Jane. Lunch."

"I see." Immediately Jane stood. "Gentlemen, would you care for coffee?"

Mr. Whitney glanced at his watch and rose to his feet. "I don't think so, Mrs. White. I have another appointment."

Jane hadn't been a school teacher for forty years for nothing. Her steely gaze planted Mr. Whitney firmly back on the sofa. "That's better," she said crisply, scowling at him. "I'll just be a moment, gentlemen. If you'll excuse me."

When Jane entered the kitchen, she leaned against the door for a moment, then whispered in annoyance. "It sounds like a hive of bees behind this door. And a herd of cows would make less noise! What's going on?"

"Do you have the money yet?" Alice asked, looking up from the coffee service she was preparing.

Gladys gazed at Jane with a mixture of admiration and envy. "You're handling your role wonderfully well!"

"Why are we delayed?"

"It's the copy," Molly explained in a whisper. Embarrassed color flooded her face. "I left the damned thing in the car. Mike went to get it." She thought quickly. "When Gran comes in to collect the coffee tray, that will be your signal that the switch has been made."

Gran looked startled. "I wasn't supposed to have a role." A pleased smile touched her mouth. "If I'm going to be the maid, I need to do something about this towel on my head. Gladys, do you have any pins in your purse?"

"This is it, girls." Jane made a circle with her thumb and forefinger and winked as she picked up the coffee tray. "The next time we meet, I'll have our money!"

Gladys opened the kitchen door for her. "Is Harry wearing after-shave?" she whispered as Jane passed.

Jane sniffed and rolled her eyes. "Bay Rum," she said out of the corner of her mouth.

"I knew it!" Gladys murmured happily.

Pacing, Molly stalked back and forth in front of the sliding doors. Her shoulders dropped in relief as she saw Mike crawl over the fence, straddle it a moment and shake his leg violently. Then he limped across Mrs. White's backyard and appeared at the sliding door.

Molly pushed the doors open and stared down at his shredded pantleg. "What happened?"

"A toy poodle," he said, gasping for breath. "Vicious animals, toy poodles." He thrust the copy into her hands. "Go."

Whirling, Molly ran across the kitchen then slowed and peeked through the dining-room door. The door to the living room was shut. On tiptoe, she entered the dining room and approached the table where Mr. Whitney had left the genuine Monet and his bag of small tools. First she studied the position of the Monet, then she lifted it soundlessly and placed the copy. It was an excellent copy, she told herself proudly. Then, heart thudding in her chest, she tucked the Monet under her arm and eased back into the kitchen.

"It's done," she said, her whisper weak with relief.

"Now it's my turn," Gran murmured.

"Wait!" But Gran was out the kitchen door. Molly peered through the creak then glanced at Mike and gave him a helpless shrug. "If we get through this..."

Jane had just finished pouring and serving when Gran marched up to the sofa and took the tray from the table in front of the men. Without a word, she took Jane's cup and saucer from Jane's hand, then stood before the men, holding the tray. The men looked at each other, hesitated, then surrendered their full coffee cups. Turning smartly, Gran carried the tray back into the kitchen.

"Oh, this is such fun!" Alice whispered.

"It is," Gran said, placing the tray on the counter top. "I wish we could do it again."

"And take turns playing Mrs. White," Gladys agreed.

Molly looked horrified. Kneeling, she pushed up Mike's pantleg. The neighbor's poodle had ruined his pants, but there were only a few harmless scratches on his leg.

"I'll live," he said, pulling her to her feet.

"I'm not sure I will. My nerves are riding a roller coaster."

In short order, they heard Jane walking Mr. Whitney and Harry Blackman to the front door. Indistinct murmurs

came from the front of the house. Then silence. They stared
at the kitchen door and waited.

When Jane entered, she placed her hands on her silk hips
and frowned. "I swan. You might at least have let us finish
our coffee." No one spoke. Then Jane grinned, a broad
smile that folded her cheeks into accordion pleats. "I've got
it!" Bringing her hand from behind her back, she bran-
dished the check in the air. "Certified funds, made out to
the bearer. For two hundred thousand dollars!"

A cheer broke over the kitchen. Gran's head towel
zoomed past the light fixture. Then everyone was hugging
everyone. Laughing, Molly threw herself into Mike's arms
and he swung her in an exuberant circle.

"We did it! We..." But suddenly she was conscious of his
hard body against her breasts and hips, acutely aware of
warm breath flowing over her parted lips. "We..." Her
voice strangled as she looked at his mouth, inches above her
own, as she felt the strength of his thighs, the enfolding
warmth of his arms. Her heart skipped and accelerated and
her lips trembled. When his arms tightened, Molly closed
her lashes and lifted her mouth for his kiss, a kiss she knew
she had been waiting for.

When Mike's lips touched hers, electricity raced through
her body leaving a tingling urgency in its wake. And a be-
wildering array of emotions spun through Molly's mind.
First and foremost she experienced a strong sexual response that left her feeling weak-kneed and shaky inside.
None of the chemistry between them had diminished.

But there was something else. She felt a...bonding, for
lack of a better description, a feeling of unity and oneness.
She told herself the oneness had arisen from all they'd been
through together, but the explanation left her feeling uneasy as if she was fooling herself.

Gladys and Alice were tugging at them, laughing and shouting congratulations. But before Mike released her, he gazed deeply into her eyes and Molly's feeling of oneness expanded. She looked into his gaze and felt connected to Mike Randall, truly connected in all ways. She knew this man physically, emotionally and spiritually.

She didn't understand what she was feeling but she knew she didn't want to feel it. This was the last thing she wanted. Confused by the strange tug-of-war going on in her thoughts, Molly allowed herself to be whirled out of Mike's embrace and into a fierce pillowy hug from first one member of the Heart Club and then another.

And then it was over.

They straightened the rooms they had used, rehung the Wilkerson painting, closed the door behind them, and rushed to the cars. In a squeal of tires, Mike made a U-turn and wheeled past Molly, laughing and waving as if he'd been untouched by their kiss. Gladys and Jane lifted coffee cups in a toast made from Mike's car brewer. Suddenly feeling better, feeling as euphoric as the others, Molly laughed out loud and turned the wheel to follow.

They left Georgetown and drove directly to Harry Blackman's bank. While the others waited, Mike accompanied Jane from the underground parking lot upstairs to the tellers' cages.

"You were wonderful," he said to Jane, still not quite believing what they had done. He and Molly and four elderly women had actually pulled off a successful swindle. Concentrating, he tried to focus his thoughts on the astonishment of it instead of remembering Molly's soft pliant body pressed against him.

But his effort failed. She had felt so good in his arms, so right. And when he'd looked into her eyes, he'd been loving her so hard that he felt certain she must feel the force of his emotion.

But nothing had changed, he knew that, too. Molly still had her plan and he still had his pride. After the celebration with the Heart Club, there would be no reason for him to see her again. Except that he loved her.

Upstairs, he leaned against a marble column and tried to look inconspicuous while Jane slapped a battered suitcase on the counter and pleasantly requested two hundred thousand dollars in cash. The teller's eyes widened and she cast an uneasy glance toward an official wearing a carnation in his lapel.

Mike's attention sharpened as the cage teller and now the head teller tried earnestly to convince Jane that taking two hundred thousand dollars in cash was a desperately unwise venture. He needn't have worried.

"Piffle," Jane said. Her eyes narrowed into a flinty stare that had dried the mouths of generations of school children. "Band it in fifty thousand dollar batches if you please."

The tellers looked at Jane Carter, then looked at each other, then they sighed and began to count out the money.

When the suitcase had been filled, Jane snapped down the lid and eased it over the counter. The suitcase dropped like a stone, taking Jane's arm with it. "Well, I never! I had no idea money weighed that much."

"I'll call the security guard," the head teller said, reaching for a buzzer beneath her cash drawer.

"That man in the uniform?" Jane sniffed and shook her head. "He has shifty eyes and tiny earlobes. Never trust a man with tiny earlobes." She beckoned to Mike. "Young man? Young man, come here at once. I require assistance."

The tellers cast horrified stares at Mike's disheveled hair, at his shredded pant leg. Their faces turned the color of curdled milk. Mike gave them a weak smile, trying his damnedest to look wholesome and honest. He hoped they wouldn't remember his face, hoped there were no cameras trained on Jane and him. He knew there were.

"Move it, Michael. Let's get out of here," Jane said from the corner of her lips. She sailed through the bank ahead of him, her stiffly upswept chignon bobbing like a blue beacon.

Molly and the others were waiting beside the elevator doors opening onto the underground parking lot. When Jane and Mike stepped out, she grabbed Mike's arm, feeling his muscles tighten under his jacket sleeve.

"I'm so glad you're here," she said, her breath emerging in a rush. "It seemed like you two were gone forever." The heady scent of his after-shave enveloped her. There was nothing sensual in the scent now; it smelled like strength and safety to Molly. Nothing could have pried her fingers from his arm as she led the way back to the cars. They locked the suitcase in the trunk, then drove to the First National where the Heart Club banked. Forming a tight group around Mike, they rode the elevator upstairs into the lobby.

As planned, Molly took the suitcase, her hand trembling slightly. She'd never imagined so much cash in one spot before. Mike pressed her shoulder before she and the Heart Club disappeared into the ladies' room. "We're on the home stretch now, Molly."

"I couldn't be happier. My nerves are shot."

After Alice peered under the stalls and gave the all-clear signal, Molly placed the suitcase on the ladies' room floor and flipped the latches.

"Even with Mike standing guard, someone could come in at any time," Molly cautioned, "so put the money in your purses immediately." Then she saw the stacks of money. "Good heavens." Gran was the only one of the Heart Club who had a purse large enough to hold fifty thousand dollars. A German shepherd would have fit into Gran's purse, but the others were carrying small bags that were already bulging.

"Isn't this lovely?" Gladys said, lifting one of the money bands. "I don't mind carrying it. We're just taking it across the lobby. This is a bank, after all. With guards."

Alice agreed. "Who would rob four old ladies? In a bank?" She held her band of money with both hands as if the bills might suddenly shatter into confetti.

"Indescribably tacky," Jane muttered, her nose wrinkling. "But apparently unavoidable. We'll have to carry it."

"I wonder if we should count it," Gladys asked. She made a small cry as the band broke on her share and hundred dollar bills fluttered over the floor. Gladys stuffed them into her coat pockets.

Instantly Jane's gaze chilled. "Are you suggesting the shares aren't equal? Or perhaps you're inferring Mike and I helped ourselves while the money was in my safekeeping?"

"Oh, for pity's sake." Gran pushed her portion into her purse. "The tellers will count it. Let's not waste time with nonsense. Come along." Without waiting to see if they followed, she pushed through the ladies' room door and marched across the lobby tiles.

Mike's mouth dropped when they emerged and he turned to stare at Molly as she collapsed against the wall beside him.

"You let them walk out of there carrying the money in plain sight?"

The Heart Club was causing something of a stir as they lined up behind each other in front of a busy teller's window. Nothing in their expressions indicated there was anything unusual afoot. Watching them, Molly decided one could almost believe people appeared all the time with wads of money sticking out of their pockets and clutched to their breasts.

"I'm too tired to argue about it," she said, leaning against his shoulder. Mike brushed an auburn curl away from her forehead and she closed her eyes above a soft smile, enjoying the feathery warmth of his fingertips.

"Glad it's over?" he asked gently.

"Honestly?" She opened her eyes and met his gaze. "I'm not sure. In some ways, yes. But in others..."

They were standing close, shoulders pressed together, the back of their hands brushing.

"In case I don't have a chance to say this later, Molly, I want to tell you that I'm glad we did this. It was the right thing to do, to help them. I'm especially glad I met you." His blue eyes touched her mouth. "You're a very special lady. I hope you find that millionaire, a man who appreciates you and gives you a lavishly happy life."

She frowned up at him, wanting to melt into his arms, wanting to cry like an idiot. He was saying goodbye. "Thank you, Mike. I'm glad I met you, too. You're going to make some lucky girl a—"

But the Heart Club descended upon them before she could finish. They flourished deposit slips and happy smiles.

"Oh, Mike, Molly, take us home," Gran said. "We're about to collapse from all this excitement." The others nodded above tired but excited smiles. "We'll have our celebration party tomorrow night. At my house. Mike, will you bring the champagne?"

So it wasn't goodbye after all. Molly summoned a bright smile and looked up at him. "Would you like to share a ride to Gran's for the celebration?" She kept her voice light, but her eyes betrayed her. Suddenly it seemed very important that they say their goodbye in private.

Mike hesitated, then briefly he placed his palm against her cheek, his touch gentle, almost reluctant. "I don't think so, Molly. I'll meet you at your grandmother's. At seven o'clock."

Enough of the sense of oneness remained that she'd been sure he would agree. But she'd been wrong. She watched Mike place his arms around Jane and Gran and turn toward the door. And with a tiny shock she realized that it really and truly was over. All of it.

Suddenly she felt like crying.

Chapter Twelve

Being late didn't improve his day, Mike thought, as he glanced at his watch then strode up Lucille Pratt's porch steps. Buttery light spilled from the front window and splashed across the winter lawn. Through the curtains he could see the Heart Club sitting around a card table. Alice and Gladys wore brightly colored paper hats but they weren't smiling; Lucille and Jane appeared to be scowling. The scene in the window was about as festive as a gathering of insurance underwriters, not at all what he'd expected.

Molly opened the door and Mike shot her a questioning glance as she took the bottles of champagne from his hands. "Is something wrong?" All day he'd steeled himself for this moment. He'd promised himself that he'd enjoy the evening and he wouldn't think about not seeing her again. But he looked at her and couldn't imagine a life without Molly as part of it. Even frowning, she was beautiful.

"I'm glad you're here. Maybe you can do something." Their hands brushed as she took his coat. Unless he imagined it, she drew a quick breath and her eyes closed briefly before she gave him an uncertain smile. "They were like this when I arrived. Hardly speaking to each other. I have an idea they've been arguing, except I've never known them to argue."

He placed his hand at the center of her back to guide her forward, remembering her velvety skin beneath the sweater she wore. It was inconceivable that another man would stroke that skin or touch her. Jealousy stiffened his shoulders and his mouth tightened. Only by great effort did he manage to push the thought away and concentrate on the Heart Club's glum expressions.

Hostile was more the word. And even to Mike that was startling. It appeared the Heart Club had split into two opposing camps. Lucille and Jane glowered at Alice and Gladys. Alice and Gladys frowned heavily at Jane and Lucille.

"Good evening, ladies." As the Heart Club returned his greeting, he gave Molly a puzzled glance and wondered what had happened since yesterday.

Even though he hated paper hats, Mike snapped one over his head in response to Molly's nudge, then he grinned. They looked like Ken and Barbie dolls in a party mode. "Well, then, if you'll pour the champagne, Molly, we can get this celebration underway." It was more like a wake. Cheering them was going to be an uphill battle.

"Yes, indeed," Jane snapped. She spoke to Mike but her eyes remained fixed on Alice and Gladys. "Bring out the champagne. That *you* bought and paid for. Just like you paid for the solvents you used in your hundreds of experiments to make the quick-drying agent. And like you paid for the gas to drive us around, and—"

Mike exchanged a quick look with Molly. "It wasn't hundreds of experiments, Aunt Jane," he interrupted quickly. "More like a dozen or so."

"Taking up time you might have spent more profitably," Lucille Pratt observed coolly. Like Jane, she spoke to Mike and Molly without removing her gaze from Alice and Gladys. "Just like all the hours Molly might have spent more profitably instead of painting us that Monet. Not to mention the cost of the paint and the canvas. And the risk she took borrowing the Smithsonian's painting."

"Everything worked out fine, Gran. I returned the painting this morning."

Jane's voice cut her off. "Of course cost and inconvenience doesn't matter to some people. Some people are so selfish and greedy they don't care about being fair. They don't care who they accuse of being a thief."

"I never said you were a thief, Jane," Gladys said, her teeth clicking in short furious bursts.

Gran's mouth pursed into a circle. "Some people forget who made it possible for them to get their money. If they weren't so small-minded, they'd agree to share equally. They'd agree the pot should be split six ways."

"Wait just a minute, Lucille Pratt." Alice cupped her hand behind her ear and leaned forward. "Who are you calling small-minded?" Crimson burned in her cheeks. "Gladys and I love Mike and Molly just as much as you and Jane. And we've admitted they made a contribution."

"But we didn't ask them to," Gladys said. "We had a good plan without them! If you ask me, it's you two who are being unfair. You're changing the rules to suit yourself."

"Ladies—"

They ignored Mike's interruption.

"They didn't have anything to do with inventing the Croupier and that's where all this started." Alice gave Mike and Molly a glance that was partly apologetic, partly defensive. "We invented the Croupier all by ourselves. Just the four of us."

"We know that," Molly said hastily. "We don't—"

"I thought I knew you, Alice Harper. And you, Gladys Price." Jane's expression was hurt and angry. "I wouldn't have believed either of you could be so petty and selfish. Just plain mean-spirited, that's what you are."

Alice puffed out her cheeks and Gladys stiffened. "Mean-spirited? You're the one who's always telling everyone else what to do, passing judgment like you were Queen for a Day! Well, all you are is a bully, Jane Carter. No wonder you never married. Well, it's not going to work this time. It's my money, and you're not going to tell me what to do with it!"

Molly gripped Mike's arm. "Mike, this is serious. It's getting out of hand. They're saying things that can't be forgiven." Her hand on his arm was electrifying and for a moment all he could think about was Molly.

Gran's eyes snapped and she shoved at her glasses. "All right, Gladys. You keep every dime of your share! You go buy your silly fur coat and I hope you remember that Molly can't afford a fur. You can be as vain and foolish as you want to. And while you're doing it, you just think about how you cheated the people who helped you get that money!"

"Gran, no one cheated us," Molly said.

"Lucille Pratt, are you accusing us of being cheats?" Gladys asked.

"It was *you* who suggested we should count the money because you didn't trust me!" Jane said angrily.

Alice's shoulders jerked back. "I never cheated anyone in my life!"

"How do you think you got your share in the first place?"

"Who are you to pass judgment on Gladys and me, Lucille? Just because you were president of the PTA for two terms back in the forties, you think you can—"

"That's enough!" Gran stood and pressed her shaking hands flat on the card table. "You two had better leave.

Right now. And I don't ever want to see or speak to either of you again!"

Alice and Gladys jumped to their feet, their paper hats trembling with indignation. "That suits us just fine!"

"We don't have to stay here and be insulted," Alice said, glaring at Gran and Jane.

"What Lucille said goes for me too," Jane said. "Don't ever speak to me again."

"Oh, shut up, Jane." Gran glared at her.

"You can count on that! Just don't try calling us!" Gladys and Alice pulled through the coats stacked over the arm of the sofa. "We have nothing more to say to you two."

Mike and Molly looked at each other with astonishment.

Jane drew herself up and squinted at Gran. "Who do you think you're telling to shut up?"

"You. Gladys was right, Jane. You always have to have the last word."

"Well, at least we agree on that," Gladys muttered, pushing her arms in her coat sleeves.

Alice glared. "Are you siding with them?" she demanded.

"Oh, Alice, don't be stupid."

"Now you're calling me stupid?"

Mike stared at them. This wasn't affectionate bickering, as Molly had called it, this was the ending of friendships that had endured for forty years.

"Stop this!" Molly's voice rang through the room.

The Heart Club paused as if frozen and looked at Molly as if only now remembering they had an audience.

"Listen to yourselves," Molly said, her voice incredulous. "Listen to the hateful things you're saying." She spread her hands. "You can't mean these things."

"Yes we do!" they said in a single chorus, glaring at each other.

Mike moved up beside Molly, his expression as concerned as hers. "Jane, Lucille, Alice and Gladys. Please sit down. I'm sure we can straighten this out."

"There's nothing to talk about," Gran said. But after a pause, she and Jane sat down. Alice and Gladys hesitated, then responded to Mike's request with obvious reluctance. Their expressions were angry and shuttered.

Molly pushed the ridiculous paper hat back on her head and scanned the angry scarlet faces. She couldn't believe what she'd just witnessed. "The four of you have been friends for *forty* years! What on earth happened tonight that is so important that you would jeopardize forty years of caring? Gran, you love Alice and Gladys like sisters. Why in the world are you ordering them out of your home?"

Gladys's teeth clacked in the silence. "I'm not ashamed to tell you why. Lucille and Jane insist that we give up part of our shares to create equal shares for you and Mike." She dropped her glance. "But we've already planned how to spend our shares."

"So this whole argument is about money? About how to spend your shares?" Molly stared at them with disbelief. "Are you actually willing to let a few thousand dollars destroy forty years of love and friendship?"

They looked at her in tight silence.

Molly leaned against the card table, her face pale with anxiety. "Please don't do this. All the money in Fort Knox can't buy forty years of friendship. The money isn't worth destroying what you have together." She looked at Alice and Glady's. "If you walk out of here tonight, what will you have left? Gran? Jane? If you let them go what will you have?"

They looked at each other from the corners of their eyes.

"Gran, please listen. How many times have you told me how you couldn't have gotten through Grandpa's death if it

hadn't been for the love and support you received from Jane
and Alice and Gladys?'' She looked at Jane. "These women
are your family, Jane. Who else cares about you like they
do? And you, Gladys. Who do you call when you feel under the weather? Your children in California or these
women? Who do you play bingo with and talk to about your
shows?'' Alice dropped her eyes when Molly looked at her.
"When you were too sick to clean your ladies' houses, Alice,
who did it for you?'' She looked at all of them. "That's
what's important. The love you have for each other. Not the
money or how you spend it.''

Molly's words hung in the ensuing silence. "Oh, Lord,''
she whispered. Everything she'd said to them was true. Her
spine stiffened, and she straightened, and slowly she repeated her words, but this time she wasn't looking at the
Heart Club, she was looking into an inner space. And she
was speaking to herself.

Mike released a long low breath as she turned to look at
him. "It isn't the money, it's the loving. That's the only
thing that's important. Oh, Mike, I was so wrong. I've been
such a damned fool.'' She hoped to God it wasn't too late,
prayed that he'd give her another chance.

A smile of elation wreathed his face and he stepped forward and clasped her hands. He was loving her so hard that
his chest ached with it. "Molly...''

She gazed up into his eyes. "I've been so stupid. All those
things I said...''

"You'll have a chance to unsay them,'' he said softly,
touching her face. "I'm not going anywhere, Molly Mc-
Pherson. I'm right here, waiting for you.''

Before she turned back to the Heart Club, she gripped his
hands and the radiant look he had believed he would never
see illuminated her face. Her eyes shone, and more than
anything he wanted to be alone with her.

She was still holding Mike's hand when she again faced the card table. "Are you truly willing to throw each other away?" she asked them. "Because of an argument over money? Is the money more important than your shared history and forty years of loving?" She looked at each of them, thinking before she spoke then speaking as much to herself as to them. "Money can only buy things. A fur coat, a hearing aid, a trip, a better apartment. Bigger, better, more. That's all money can buy. It can't buy affection or trust or security. It can't buy someone to love or someone to love you."

Mike's hand slipped around her shoulder and she covered his fingers with her own, feeling her heart expand as she did so. Looking up at him, she continued speaking, the words emerging slowly. "It's all right to want money," she said. "But only if it doesn't become an obsession." His hand lifted from her shoulder to stroke her cheek and he was smiling. "And not at the expense of loving. If you love and are loved in return, then you're rich in spirit. That's the only thing that's important. To love and to be loved." Mike's arms slipped around her waist and she looked deeply into his smiling eyes before she turned back to the Heart Club.

"Were you happier yesterday?" she asked quietly. "When you had no money but you had each other? Or are you happier now?"

In the following silence, shame filled their eyes. Alice stared at her lap. "I want to give part of my share to Mike and Molly," she said in a low voice.

"So do I," Gladys said.

Mike closed his arms around Molly's waist and addressed the Heart Club over her head. "No one asked Molly and me if we wanted a share," he said, his breath stirring tendrils near Molly's temple. "I think I'm speaking for both

of us when I tell you we don't. We never did. We just wanted
to help the people we love.''

Molly's eyes moistened as she nodded. In the last few
moments, something profound and wonderful had happened. Suddenly her heart was free and she felt as if she
would float away if Mike's arms hadn't anchored her. If
they hadn't been standing in front of the Heart Club, she
would have turned in his arms and covered his dear face with
kisses. She wanted to tell him she'd been an idiot, a fool,
that she'd almost made a disastrous mistake.

Gran was watching her with knowing eyes. ''I think,'' she
said quietly, ''that everyone here has a little patch work to
do. Molly, I wonder if you'd take Mike into the kitchen and
give us a few minutes of privacy.''

The kitchen was dark and warm and smelled of yeast and
cinnamon. Lacy frost patterns spread across the windowpanes. But Molly didn't notice. She ran into Mike's
arms and pressed her face against the crease at his neck,
breathing deeply and hungrily of the scent that was Mike
Randall. He held her so tightly that she laughed softly.

''Did you mean what you said in there?'' he asked, his
voice husky against her ear.

''I love you, Mike Randall.'' She clung to him, feeling his
solidity and the hard length of his body. ''I'd rather be flat
broke with you than filthy rich with someone like Winthrop Kingsbury Melton the Third.''

''Who is Winthrop Kingsbury Melton the Third? I
thought you were seeing someone named Greg.''

''Oh, Mike, tell me you love me.'' She covered his neck
and face with kisses. ''You do love me, don't you? It
wouldn't be fair to love someone this much without them
loving back.''

He held her hard against his body, letting her feel his
arousal, his love for her. Then he cupped her face between

his hands. "I love you, Molly McPherson. I want to spend the rest of my life loving you." He buried his face in her silky hair and held her so tightly he was afraid she might shatter in his arms. Gently, he eased her back so he could kiss her mouth, her eyelids, the freckles powdering her cheeks. "Are you sure, darling?"

"I love you. I've never been as sure of anything in my life!" All the world's riches couldn't have made her happier than she felt at this moment. "I don't care if we never have any money. I really don't." The wonder of it glowed in her eyes. "Money was never important, I just didn't know it."

"Then you'll marry me?" He couldn't stop touching her, her hair, her face, her throat.

"I promise to love, honor and cherish you and your mechanical dog." She smiled when he chuckled, his hands warm and strong on the curve of her hips. "And I promise never to complain about machines that throw eggs at the ceiling—"

"I've about got that worked out."

"Or compost machines in the kitchen or strange things that go tick in the night."

"And you're not marrying me for my money?"

Molly laughed, looking up at him through shining eyes. "No, my darling inventor, my beloved patent officer. I am definitely not marrying you for your money. I'm marrying you because I love you and all the wonderful things you are."

"In that case," he murmured against her lips, "there's something I need to tell you."

But Gran snapped on the lights and Mike and Molly opened their eyes to find the Heart Club gathered in the doorway.

"We came to apologize," Jane said quietly. "And to thank you, Molly, for saving us from a terrible, terrible mistake."

Gladys pressed Gran's hand and winked at Jane before she directed a sigh toward Mike and Molly. "Aren't they a handsome couple?"

"I think we'll have a lot to celebrate tonight," Gran noted shrewdly. She embraced Molly and looked deeply into her granddaughter's eyes. "Am I right?" she asked, smiling.

Molly blushed and clasped Mike's hand.

After receiving the glad news, the Heart Club took turns hugging them both, then Alice insisted it was finally time for the champagne. They gathered around Gran's card table and began the celebration with thick slices of iced carrot cake. Everything was all right now. There was love and friendship and victory to celebrate. And an upcoming marriage.

But the celebration party fell flat.

Gran didn't touch her carrot cake; Gladys pushed hers around her plate. Alice fiddled with her hearing aid and Jane stirred her champagne with a listless fingertip.

"Something's still not right," Molly observed gently, leaning her head on Mike's shoulder.

"No," Jane said finally. "It's just that ... Well, I know this is going to sound awful, but I liked Harry Blackman." She sighed.

"He was worried that he was going to cheat Mrs. White," Alice mentioned. "Even I heard every word he said and that's the truth."

Molly laced her fingers through Mike's. There were so many things she wanted to tell him, so many plans to be made. But tonight was the Heart Club's night. She and Mike would have the rest of their lives. She squeezed his hand and felt his lips brush the top of her hair.

Alice moved her spoon in circles across the tablecloth. "Still, Harry Blackman took advantage of us. He cheated us first." She looked up. "Then we cheated him."

"I keep thinking about that," Gran said unhappily. "Blackman stole our device, that's true. But we stole his money. That makes us as black as he is. We're just as bad."

Gladys nodded. "I wasn't going to say this, but I feel...well, funny about the money. Like they say on the TV, it's tainted. Blood money. It wasn't honestly earned."

Jane bit her lip and shrugged. "Now that I've had time to think about it I wish we hadn't done this. I agree we had justification, but I don't feel very good about it."

"I taught my children that stealing is wrong. That's what I've believed all my life," Alice said. "I guess I forgot that stealing is stealing no matter what the justification is."

"And look what the money almost did to us," Gran said. She reached across the card table to pat Gladys's hand and squeeze Alice's fingers. she smiled fondly at Jane. "I almost lost my dearest friends."

Jane nodded then spoke in a low voice. "Now that I can afford a new apartment, I don't think I want it. Not badly enough to steal for."

"If I bought a rabbit coat with tainted money," Gladys said, "I'd never be able to wear it anywhere. I'd think everyone knew how I got it."

A silence stretched, as brittle as the frosty night outside the window.

Lifting his chin from the top of Molly's hair, Mike examined their faces. "Ladies," he said gently, "am I hearing you correctly? You regret having clipped Harry Blackman?" He read the answer in four pairs of miserable eyes. After a moment he sighed and pressed Molly's hand. "There's a solution to this. Alice, what did you do when you caught your children stealing something?"

"I made them give it back," Alice said promptly.

The Heart Club straightened and stared at each other.

"That's it," Jane said. "We have to give the money back. It's the only way we can live with ourselves."

"I won't sleep a wink until I've given up this life of crime," Gladys agreed.

"We know where he lives," Lucille reminded them.

"That's it, then," Gladys pronounced. "We take back the ill-gotten goods."

Gladys turned toward Mike and Molly, her voice suddenly shy and uncertain. "Will you go with us?"

Mike touched Molly's face. "How do you feel about this?"

She didn't have to think about it. "I hate what Blackman did to the Heart Club. But I understand what they're saying. What we did was wrong."

He dropped a kiss on her nose. "All right. But there's something we should talk about. By returning the money, we're admitting to a criminal act. Blackman could prosecute."

"That would be a double travesty," Molly protested.

"I agree. But it could happen. Confessing and returning the money will help if the worst happens. But it could still get nasty."

The Heart Club exchanged glances; the invisible network was operating again. Without having spoken a word, they bent for their purses, withdrew their checkbooks and began writing out checks for fifty thousand dollars. When they finished, they pushed the checks toward Molly.

"Will you be our spokeswoman, Molly?" Jane requested. "You have a way with words."

Molly nodded slowly as they all stood. "Do you think Blackman will prosecute? Are we going to start our new life behind bars?" she asked Mike as he helped her on with her coat. She gazed at him with love in her eyes, thinking how close she'd come to losing him. The thought made her tremble and she leaned against him for a moment, her thoughts jumping ahead to the time when they could finally be alone.

"Don't worry, darling," he said, smiling. "No jail can hold the Heart Club Gang."

HARRY BLACKMAN'S HOUSEKEEPER let them in, her eyebrows soaring as they trooped into his large living room. Blackman lowered the newspaper he was reading before the fire and peered at them through half-glasses, Hastily, he stood and swept them with a puzzled glance. "Mrs. White?" He peered at Jane and then at Gran and Alice. "I think I know you," he said to Alice. "Just a minute, don't tell me. I'll remember."

Molly drew a breath and stepped forward. She wasn't certain what she would say until she started to speak.

"I'm Molly McPherson, Mr. Blackman. I painted that picture." She pointed to the forgery he'd hung over the fireplace mantel. "It's not genuine. It's a copy."

"A forgery?" Blackman blinked at her then looked up at the painting. "Young lady, I had that painting authenticated by—"

"By William Whitney. Mr. Whitney authenticated a genuine Monet, but we switched the paintings while you were making the purchase. What you bought is a forgery."

Molly pushed her hand into her coat pocket and withdrew the four checks. She laid them on the table beside his newspaper. "We swindled you, Mr. Blackman. Just like you swindled my grandmother and her friends." She had to remind herself that this was Harry Blackman the swindler, not Harry Blackman, a man as benign as a Christmas elf. "Unlike you, we couldn't live with ourselves knowing we'd cheated someone. So we're returning your money."

"I swindled...?"

"I hate it that you cheated the Heart Club out of their share of the Croupier profits. I despise it that you're going to get away with what you did to them. But you can keep your profits, Mr. Blackman. Unlike you, the Heart Club doesn't want money at the price of honor. Apparently you can live with yourself knowing you victimized four decent women. But we can't and won't live as cheats. We're better than that."

"Bravo!" Gran said softly.

"We know you can prosecute us for selling you a forged painting. And knowing you, you probably will. But we don't care. We have each other." Pausing, Molly looked up at Mike. "Did I forget anything?"

"You forgot to mention anything about slime or son of a bitch or hanging's too good for you," Mike said, staring over her shoulder at Harry Blackman. "Otherwise, I think we've covered it."

"Good night, Mr. Blackman. You have your money and you have the Croupier. I hope you sleep well."

They were halfway to the door before they heard Harry Blackman's burst of delighted laughter. "Young lady! Ladies! Come back. You, too," he said, pointing to Mike. Looking up at the Monet, he clasped his stomach in a fresh shout of laughter. Looking more than ever like Santa Claus, he laughed until tears streamed from his eyes. "Sit down, sit down," he said, gesturing them forward. He took off his glasses and wiped his eyes.

"There's nothing to discuss," Mike said curtly.

"That's where you're wrong, young man. I've been looking everywhere for these brilliant ladies." He took Alice Harper's arm and gazed at her. "Mrs. Harper, isn't it? Why did you disappear? Your phone is unlisted, I couldn't find a trace of you."

Alice looked over her shoulder at the Heart Club. "I got tired of salesmen calling. I had it unlisted a couple of years ago."

"I tried writing to the address on your stationery, but my letters were returned."

"I moved a few years ago." Alice looked confused. "I thought I'd used all that stationery, but—"

Mike stepped between Blackman and Alice. Alice gripped his sleeve and peeked under his arm. "What are you trying to prove, Blackman? That you aren't to blame?"

"To blame?"

"For cheating the Heart Club out of their share of the profits on the Croupier. Which you stole from them."

"Is that what you think? Of course that's what you think. Yes, I see. Now it makes sense." He glanced at the Monet then at the stony faces watching him. "You swindled me because you think I swindled you."

Mike's fists opened and closed at his sides. "I'm going to resist the very strong urge to lay you out on the carpet, Blackman. Instead, I'm going to drive these ladies home."

Harry Blackman stepped backward and raised his hands. "But you have it all wrong. Wait a minute." They hesitated, turning to stare at him. "You can't leave, ladies, not when I've finally found you." He hurried toward them. "Ladies, you own the Croupier. When I couldn't locate Mrs. Harper, I made the decision to go ahead and manufacture and market the Croupier in the hope you would see it in the stores and, when you did, that you would contact me immediately. I couldn't understand it when you didn't."

They looked at each other, exchanging puzzled glances.

"Hold on here," Mike said. "The Heart Club specifically instructed you not to manufacture the Croupier as the costs were beyond their means."

Harry Blackman frowned and now he looked puzzled. "If so, young man, this is the first I've heard of it. Mrs. Harper requested a breakdown on production costs and promised to let me know if the group intended to go ahead or not. But I never heard from her again."

Gran, Gladys and Jane fixed collective stares on Alice. "You said you would write Harry Blackman and tell him we couldn't afford to manufacture the Croupier," Jane said.

"I did write him," Alice protested stoutly. "Exactly as you said. And I can prove it. I have the letter right here." She rummaged in her purse and produced a tattered envelope. "See?"

"You still have it?" Gladys gasped. "You didn't mail it?"

"No one ever said to mail it. You just said to write it. We were still talking about how we wished we had the money and how we wished we could find a way to do it. The question was never really settled, was it?"

"Of course it was," Jane said. "Lord, Alice, if you don't buy a new hearing aid, we'll all chip in and buy one for you."

"I swan, Alice," Gran marveled. "If you'd just listen."

"Well, all of you got mad when I left the sample at Mr. Blackman's office. So I decided I wouldn't do anything unless you said it exactly step-by-step. For pity's sake, what's a body to do? It's not my fault that you all talk in whispers!"

Molly bit her lip. "I think maybe a terrible mistake has been made here. Mr. Blackman, are we to understand that you believed the group would authorize you to produce the Croupier?"

"That was my hope, young lady. When I didn't hear from Mrs. Harper, I decided to back the project and put the Croupier into production. I did so in the belief that Mrs. Harper understood how strongly I believed the Croupier would be a success and that she would convince her group to manufacture the item. I couldn't imagine that they wouldn't. If they had to beg, borrow, or steal the money." He glanced at the Monet and smiled. "They stood to profit a hundred times over."

"But you acted without their approval. And patented the Croupier in your company name."

"Not exactly. When I couldn't locate Mrs. Harper I decided to go ahead with the patent application. I know it wasn't proper to proceed without you ladies," he said apologetically, "but I was so certain the Croupier would be a success and in novelty items the market timing is crucial. So, I took it upon myself to patent the item and prepare production before Christmas. Throughout that time I was searching for you and your friends."

"I told you all about them, didn't I?" Alice said.

"You didn't say much. All I could remember was that you and your friends met every Friday to play bridge. So I formed a company called—"

"Called the F.B.C. Company," Mike interrupted. "The Friday Bridge Club."

Harry Blackman smiled. "That's correct. The Friday Bridge Club owns the patent on the Croupier. And you ladies are the Friday Bridge Club. You own the Croupier."

"I think I will sit down now," Gran said. She looked a little stunned.

"Please do, all of you. Mrs. Kinski?" Blackman beckoned to his housekeeper. "Champagne for my friends." His eyes twinkled. "I have an idea when these ladies hear about their profit sheets, they'll agree we have a lot to celebrate. But first—ladies, may I know your names?''

When introductions had been made and champagne had been served, Molly smiled at Mike and moved into the circle of his arms. "It looks like this story has a happy ending."

Blackman confirmed it. "I've been operating the F.B.C. Company on your behalf. Now that I've found you, you'll each receive a full accounting by this time next week. I've reimbursed myself for production costs and your company has a full-time secretary. But I think you'll be pleased by your profits." His Santa eyes twinkled. "Two hundred thousand was far short of the mark. I'd say you're worth about—oh, somewhere in the neighborhood of half a million dollars each."

"How much?" Alice gasped, knocking her fingers against her hearing aid.

"A half a million?" Gladys pushed her teeth back into her mouth.

"Each of us?" Jane's eyes widened to the size of half-dollars.

"I swan," Gran breathed. She gulped her champagne then laughed out loud. "Girls, I'm not going to visit Florida. I'm going to buy Florida!"

After a while Mike placed his mouth near Molly's ear. "I know a place not far from here where they serve Randall Specials and Moodvision. Could I interest you in a storm?"

She wrapped her arms around his neck and laughed. "Everything about you interests me. Especially your storms. Do you think anyone will miss us?"

When they looked across the room, they smiled. Alice was happily pouring more champagne into everyone's glass. Gladys was batting her eyelashes at Harry Blackman who appeared to be loving the attention. Gran and Jane had their heads together, adding up columns of figures.

Leaning back in Mike's arms, Molly murmured. "Do you think we'll ever have an invention that successful?" She laughed and lifted her mouth to kiss his lips. "Forget I asked that. I don't care." It was the truth. She didn't.

"Possibly," Mike said, his blue eyes dancing as he swung her into his arms and carried her out of Blackman's living room. "Have you ever heard of a product called Shield?"

"Shield?" Molly covered his neck with kisses. It was going to be an interesting life living with an inventor. It would be a bit crazy and a struggle to make ends meet, but her life with Mike Randall would never be dull. "Doesn't Shield have something to do with cars?" she made little circles on his neck with her tongue as he carried her out the door and toward his car.

During the drive, Mike told her about Shield and something called the Doodle Game. Molly murmured "Hmm" and kissed his ear, his neck, the corner of his mouth. She'd never been happier. For herself, for the Heart Club, for lovers everywhere. She looked at him adoringly and touched him and loved him even when it penetrated her mind that he'd just told her he'd quit the patent office and would be inventing full time.

He carried her inside his house and straight to the bedroom, the lights flipping on behind them. And he made love to her, slow passionate love.

Later, cradled in his arms, Molly smiled drowsily. "I love you, Mike Randall. More than anything."

He pulled her into the curve of his body and was almost asleep when Molly bolted upright in bed, holding the sheet to her naked breasts as she stared down at him.

"In the car—did you say something about two million dollars? What two million dollars?"

Grinning, he reached for her. "Who the hell is Winthrop Kingsbury Melton the Third?"

They tumbled across the bed, laughing. Neither question was important.

Epilogue

Humming softly, Molly tied a checkered apron over her Levi's jeans and sweater and bent to brush melted butter over the turkey before she closed the oven door. The kitchen was warm with the smells of Thanksgiving dinner, chestnut dressing, candied yams, cranberry sauce, fresh bread—all the wonderful holiday scents.

After checking the tables set up in the dining room and the den, she poured a cup of coffee from the coffee spigot on the sink and smiled out the window toward her studio. It was connected to Mike's workshop by a covered walkway.

Five years ago, Mike had built the studio for her restoration projects and, a year later, had built the connecting workshop to contain his inventions and his clutter.

Life hadn't unfolded quite as she'd expected, Molly thought. She'd always believed that if she had more money than she knew what to do with she'd build a mansion and wear nothing but designer clothing. She'd travel constantly and surround herself with servants.

Smiling, she looked down at her clothes beneath her apron hem. They weren't even designer jeans. And they lived in Mike's house instead of a mansion. In spring the daffodils and tulips she'd planted along the driveway waved at her as she returned from the grocery store, and in fall the hardwoods sweeping around her studio windows flamed into brilliant color. They had spent a month in Europe on their honeymoon but they hadn't traveled much since. Home was where she and Mike both wanted to be.

All those years, she thought, smiling, she had imagined having money would make such a difference in her life. In reality, very little had changed.

"Ms. Moneypenny?"

"Yes, Mrs. Z-II?" Molly wasn't certain she'd ever be comfortable talking to machines. When she turned to look at the robot, she grinned. In honor of Thanksgiving, Mike had dressed Mrs. Z-II in a pilgrim collar and a black pilgrim's hat.

"The living room is dusted and vacuumed," Mrs. Z-II said in a low pleasant hum. "The children have been gone for thirty-six minutes and forty-two seconds. Your guests will arrive in fifty-two minutes and eighteen seconds."

"Thank you, Mrs. Z-II. I see the children now. Will you prepare their baths, please?"

As Mrs. Z-II wheeled toward the children's rooms, Molly watched Lucy and Harry, aged five and three, emerge from Mike's workshop and skip toward the kitchen door. Murph and Son of Murph rolled behind, their tails wagging.

"Did you remind Daddy that it's November?" she asked, as they clattered inside. When she kneeled to remove their coats and scarfs, they smiled at her with Mike's blue eyes beneath a tumble of her own coppery curls. "Harry, don't—"

But Harry had already poked his finger in one of the pumpkin pies. He leaned against Molly, happily licking his finger, as Lucy climbed on her lap.

"Are the Granny Hearts coming, Mommy?"

"And Granny Gran, and Grandma and Grandpa Randall, and Mr. Blackman, and Mommy's friend, Greg, and

Ruth and Tom." She brushed an auburn curl behind Lucy's ear as the child leaned up to whisper in her ear.

"I know a secret," Lucy said, her bright eyes sparkling.

Molly wiped the pumpkin pie from Harry's chubby fingers. Harry crossed his arms on her knee. "Daddy has a 'chine that shoots eggs."

"Oh, Harry, I wanted to tell. It's a nifty machine, Mama. If fires eggs at the ceiling! Can we have one in here?"

"Throws eggs at the ceiling, does it?" Molly repeated with a grin as Mike came into the kitchen and tossed his coat toward the peg by the door.

"So you guys ratted on me, huh?" He gave them a mock frown and they giggled. He winked at Molly. "I've about got it worked out. The omelet machine is going to make us a fortune."

She laughed and sent Lucy and Harry to find Mrs. Z-II and their bath, then she wrapped her arms around Mike's neck. "We don't need a fortune. Forget the omelet machine."

"What? And abandon my life's work?" Sitting down, he pulled her onto his lap and nuzzled her neck. "You smell like fresh-baked bread. If I could invent a perfume that smelled like fresh-baked bread, no woman would be safe. Men would chase them up trees."

Molly dropped a kiss on his nose. "You need to shave and stir up a batch of Randall Specials. Everyone will be here in an hour."

"Which reminds me. We need a bigger house. Where are we going to put all these people?"

"Where we put them every year. Two tables in the dining room; two tables in the den."

"I want to eat Thanksgiving dinner in the same room with my wife, dammit. Leering at you through the doorway isn't the same. We need a bigger house."

"This house is perfect. You have your workshop; I have my studio. If we move you'll have to reprogram Mrs. Z-II and Murph and Son of Murph. You'll have to plumb in a new coffee spigot and redo the Moodvision and all the rest."

"Molly..."

"Can't we just remodel? Maybe add a second story?"

The suggestion interested him as she'd known it would. "A second story." He looked at her. "Mrs. Z-II can't do stairs. We'd have to have a Mrs. Z-III."

"I can handle it," Molly said, smiling. "Think about it." The buzzer sounded on the oven and she reluctantly stood up from his lap. Wrapping her arms around his neck, she looked into his eyes and said, "I love you, Mike Randall."

"I love you, Mrs. Randall. Are you going to change out of those jeans into something fabulous?"

"Lemon silk, cut down to here," she said, touching her breast. Then she laughed as he gave her a kiss that started at her lips and ended near her breasts.

Two hours later the house was filled with noisy laughter and animated conversation. Mrs. Z-II served drinks and the children darted from one lap to another. The Granny Hearts fussed over Harry Blackman, and Greg, who was an ambassador now, regaled everyone with stories about the Far East. Ruth and her husband, Tom, had bought the gallery two years ago and they chatted with Mike's parents about the new trends in art.

When Molly led everyone in to dinner, tears of happiness sparkled in her eyes. Long ago, Mike had told her security lay in being where one belonged, among people one loved and who loved in return.

She looked at the people sitting down to Thanksgiving dinner: Gran, Jane, Gladys, Alice. Greg and Harry Blackman. Mike's parents. Ruth and her husband. Her children, Lucy and Harry. And Mike.

For a long moment Molly's soft eyes met Mike's through the doorway. Then he blew her a kiss and mouthed the words, "I love you."

And Molly knew she was the richest woman on earth.

Keeping the Faith

by
Judith Arnold

It renewed old friendships, kindled new relationships, but the fifteen-year reunion of *The Dream*'s college staff affected all six of the Columbia-Barnard graduates: Laura, Seth, Kimberly, Andrew, Julianne and Troy.

Follow the continuing story of these courageous, vital men and women who find themselves at a crossroads—as their idealism of the sixties clashes with the reality of life in the eighties.

You may laugh, you may cry, but you will find a piece of yourself in *Keeping the Faith*.

Don't miss American Romance #201 *Promises* in June, #205 *Commitments* in July and #209 *Dreams* in August.

KFaith-gen

Harlequin American Romance

COMING NEXT MONTH

#205 COMMITMENTS by Judith Arnold

In the seventies they'd have called it "bad karma." Andrew Collins, self-avowed cynic of *The Dream*, and Kimberly Belmont, its resident optimist, seemed destined to remain antagonists forever. But shortly after the magazine's anniversary bash, something extraordinary happened. They'd become lovers. Was it an accident? Or a mistake? Catch the second book in the *Keeping the Faith* trilogy.

#206 FAIR GAME by Susan Andrews

Being a winner on *Love Life*, TV's popular dating game, meant that Julie Turner had to spend a week in Atlantic City with Marcus Allen, TV's heartthrob. To publicity-shy Julie it seemed more like a chore than fun, but how could she resist a man who whisked her away from the prying eyes of the media to a seaside hideaway?

#207 CHRISTMAS IN JULY by Julie Kistler

Kit Wentworth was furious. How dared Riley Cooper call her a lily-livered coward! The time had come for her to go home. But that meant seeing her family, and confronting the man who had prompted her exodus four years earlier.

#208 A QUESTION OF HONOR by Jacqueline Ashley

Helping people was a matter of honor to Frances McPhee. But traveling with her cantankerous old uncle Fergus and his companion to his Oklahoma cabin was pure torture. With Ash Blair's penchant for gourmet foods and pricey hotels—and his devastating charm—would Frances bring Fergus home safely without first falling in the poorhouse—or in love?

Harlequin Signature Edition

Carole Mortimer

Merlyn's Magic

She came to him from out of the storm and was drawn into
his yearning arms—the tempestuous night held a magic
all its own.

You've enjoyed Carole Mortimer's Harlequin Presents
stories, and her previous bestseller, *Gypsy*.

Now, don't miss her latest, most exciting bestseller,
Merlyn's Magic!

IN JULY

MERMG